I0731432

For *Love* of THUNDER

By the author

Up the Garden Path

Isabel and Friends

Isabel's Healing (Book One)

A Girl on the Plane (Book Two)

Into the Rough (Book Three)

Love Under Lockdown (Book Four)

Behind the Camera

Heatwave (Book One)

Wildfire (Book Two)

Love and Money (Book Three)

For *Love* of THUNDER

Ryeland Press
Books by Women For Women

By Maggie McIntyre
2022

For Love of Thunder © 2022 by Maggie McIntyre.
All rights reserved.

This trade paperback is published by Ryeland Press

This is a work of fiction: names, characters, and incidents are
the product of the author's imagination or are used fictitiously.
Any resemblance to actual persons, living or dead, business
establishments, events, or locales is entirely coincidental.

This book, or parts thereof, may not be reproduced in any form
without express permission.

Cataloging information
ISBN: 9781739637019
CREDITS
Editor: Nicci Robinson
Cover Design: Nicci Robinson
Production Design: Global Wordsmiths

Acknowledgements

Warm thanks and appreciation go to my editor, formatter, book designer, and marketing guru, Nicci Robinson of Global Wordsmiths, without whose attention to detail and sheer hard work, this book could not have happened.
I would also like to thank the loyal band of beta readers, advisers, proofers, and good friends who have given up their valuable time to read early and later drafts, and tried to keep me on the straight and narrow. You know who you are! Any remaining faults are, as always, entirely my own.

In fond memory

of the horses who meant most to me through my life, Buttons, Darling, (who kicked), Ziggy, and Pippa. I loved you all and will never forget you.

Dedication

This book is dedicated to the many volunteers and workers within Riding for the Disabled (RDA), a charity based in the United Kingdom, who focus on providing therapeutic horse-riding, equestrian vaulting, and carriage-driving to people with developmental and physical disabilities, as well seeking to improve the lives of those with mental health difficulties.
They do great work.

PROLOGUE

Saturday, June 2, 2012

Ricky Gates sat on the retired thoroughbred racehorse, Tacoma Thundercloud, about to show a group of her twelve-year-old admirers how to do half-passes. She had practiced long and hard on other horses in Tara Morris's equestrian center, but none was as responsive and as easy to ride as Thunder, the star of the stables. He was the most expensive horse and the only stallion on the yard, and Ricky worshipped him. Previously trained to race, he had taken to dressage like a pro and seemed to enjoy every session in the manège.

Since he'd arrived on the yard six months before, Ricky had adored him with only a little less passion than she did his owner. But whereas her crush on Mrs. Tara Morris, her riding teacher, was a tightly guarded secret, her love for Thunder could be openly expressed, and was one she shared with anyone who would listen.

Ricky freely admitted she was horse crazy. The pictures of horses in the margins of her schoolbooks and the collage of horse images around her bedroom walls were evidence enough. She even wore her wavy brown hair in a long ponytail, so it bounced behind her, like a horse's tail.

Ricky treated each horse in Meadowlands, like her own and spent hours grooming and talking to them all. When she wasn't in school, she lived every waking moment there and now, with the long summer vacation about to begin, she saw no reason to be anywhere else for the next eight weeks.

After her parents, Tara Morris had been the most dominant influence in Ricky's life. It started the first day she had turned up at the stable door, clutching payment for a series of ten horseback-riding lessons, an eleventh birthday present from her grandma. Nothing had changed in the last five years either, apart from her natural progression and growing confidence. These days, everyone knew Ricky was Mrs. Morris's unofficial head girl at the stables. Tara relied on her to come early and stay late, to lock up at night, check hay nets were filled, water troughs were clean, and to make sure the younger riders always wore their proper safety gear and hard hats.

In the sunlight of Tara's occasional words of praise, knowing Mrs. Morris trusted her and that she was useful, Ricky was a happy girl. Her clothes permanently smelled of hay, leather, and saddle soap, and she slept with her riding boots next to her bed. She wanted nothing more than to be a horse trainer like Tara one day, to own her own stables, and to teach others to ride.

She hadn't noticed anything different when she'd first arrived. Thunder was standing quietly in his stall, not yet tacked up, so she assumed Tara hadn't yet taken him out, which she often did, trail-riding with one of her women friends. They were probably in the house having a quick coffee before the ten o'clock group lesson.

Ricky's enthusiastic little group of disciples had gathered around her, and one girl said, "Show us some dressage moves, Ric, please. You're so good at it."

Buoyed by this little piece of fandom, Ricky had agreed. She'd saddled Thunder and led him into the manège, tightened his girth, put her foot up into the stirrup and jumped into the air. If slim Mrs. Morris, who was shorter than her, could manage to mount without a leg-up, Ricky was determined to do the same.

She set off around the perimeter of the school in a steady walk and then in response to a light squeeze from her legs, Thunder broke into a slow canter. As they circled, Ricky heard the sound of an argument unexpectedly emerging from within the main house, angry raised voices, a slammed door, and then Mrs. Morris came running across the stable yard. She vaulted over the corral fence and pounded across the sandy manège, aiming straight for Ricky and Thunder.

"Ric!" Mrs. Morris shouted. "Dismount at once! Get off the

horse immediately. Can't you see he's lame? You're far too heavy for him. Off, now! Get down! Here, hand him to me, you stupid girl!"

The words made Ricky slide to a halt. For a moment she was too stunned to move and sat there, six feet high, in full view of all the other young riders. Then she began to tremble uncontrollably with fear, shock, and horror that she might be injuring this beautiful horse. The humiliation and the emotional devastation of the verbal attack was bad enough, but then Mrs. Morris grabbed Thunder's stirrup leather, reached up, and began to haul Ricky from the saddle.

Ricky kicked both feet out of the stirrups and slithered to the ground in a panic, almost as if the saddle was on fire. She banged her mouth against the pommel as she almost fell and tasted blood. She threw the reins toward Tara, turned, and ran as fast as she could toward the corral gates. She struggled with the latch on the big gates, pulled them open, and then bolted toward the tack room. Half-blinded by tears, she still sensed the shockwave going around the group of girls watching.

What had just happened? She'd ridden Thunder dozens of times before, and Mrs. Morris had always encouraged her; she'd never implied Ricky was overweight. It made no sense. Ricky wasn't skinny, but she wasn't that chunky either. But Mrs. Morris made her feel as fat as an elephant, a big lump who shouldn't have even mounted the one quality horse in the stables, let alone tried to ride him.

Ricky couldn't stop her tears falling. She gathered all her gear from the tack room, pulled her bike from the rack, and cycled home. She needed her mom, and she needed her now.

By the time she'd reached home, Mrs. Morris had already called Ricky's mom and apologized. She claimed she'd panicked when the horse went lame, that she hadn't meant to be so mean, and that Ricky should come back to the stables and Mrs. Morris would let her ride for free.

Ricky didn't care what Mrs. Morris had said or what she had to say in her texts. Ricky could never just forget how humiliated she felt, and she couldn't face all those younger girls again.

They'd be whispering behind her back and laughing at her. No. She wouldn't go back. She wouldn't forget. And she wouldn't forgive.

She ran up to her room and tore down all the posters of horses. Tomorrow, she'd ask her mom to cut off her ponytail too. Maybe short hair would make her look older, not like some stupid, horse-addicted teenager. Because there was more to what had happened than she would ever tell her parents. Ricky had been besotted, completely in love, and Tara had carelessly crushed that love under her boot and stamped on it. She didn't think she would ever feel so bad again, nor would she ever be so stupid as to fall in love with a woman.

chapter one

Ten years later, June 2022

Ricky's mom handed her a steaming cup of coffee. Topped with a large dash of half and half, just like Ricky liked it, her mom's small act of love didn't go unnoticed.

"Have you heard?" her mom asked. "Tara Morris is selling her horse ranch."

That little thunderbolt almost made Ricky drop the mug. Her mom must know that any mention of Tara Morris was off limits even now, ten years later. The miserable feeling of remembered shame flushed Ricky's cheeks. "Really?" She tried hard to control her voice and keep it steady, "No. I haven't heard anything, but why would I?"

"Oh, I don't know. Smalltown grapevine gossip spreads far and wide, even up to New Jersey. I thought maybe some of your old horse pals might've told you. Aren't you still Twittering with some of them?"

"It's tweeting, Mom, and no, not really." Ricky turned away so her ever-observant mom wouldn't see any hint of her reaction, which was ridiculous after so many years. "It's been a long time since I last rode at Meadowlands. Everyone's dispersed. We were just kids. People drift apart."

Her mom poured herself coffee. "Yes, but for five years, Mrs. Morris saw more of you than I did. I was quite jealous at times. Such a shame you stopped riding completely because you were always so good with the horses." Her mom stirred her spoon idly in her cup. "I'm sorry we were never in a position to be able to afford to buy you your own horse. But after your dad's accident, we couldn't have afforded to keep it, so maybe it was for the best you moved on to other sports when you did."

Her mom gazed at Ricky's various cups, ribbons, and trophies for track and field and swimming displayed above the sideboard in their small dining room. The tender display of parental pride made Ricky squirm. Yes, she'd moved on in the last decade, grown tougher, more confident, harder to humiliate, and she'd become a successful athlete. Tara's vicious attack had motivated Ricky in more ways than she knew at the time, and she'd wanted to prove she didn't care what Tara had said and that she could do anything she damn well wanted…without horses.

For years, she'd thought the plan had worked and the pain had gone but now, coming back into the family home and revisiting her childhood, she wasn't so sure. The painted horse frieze had been removed, but she could still see it and unwelcome memories came so easily back into her head. She stirred her coffee with more vigor than necessary and took a deep breath. "Mom, please drop it, okay? We both know why I gave up horseback riding and why Tara Morris's business decisions don't interest me, so let's chat about something else, okay?" It was embarrassing having to spell it out and even worse still to feel the pain she thought she'd forgotten.

"Okay, I won't mention her again, not if it upsets you so much even to hear her name. She tried to apologize many times though, don't forget. But yeah, let's change the subject. It's so great to have you back in Florida for the summer. You're still my baby girl and always will be. We've missed you so much in the last year or more."

Ricky loved her mom for always trying her best to keep everything as sunny as the weather. It helped lift the guilt she carried for not coming home more often. Difficult times had started with her dad's fall from a construction site scaffold back in Ricky's high school senior year. The accident fractured his spine, rendering him incapable of work and causing her parents' income to plummet, taking them immediately from modest middle-class comfort to a more meager existence.

Now her mom worked shifts as a cashier in the local grocery store, while her dad mainly sat about the house in chronic pain, coupled with depression from feeling so useless. It could've been worse though. At least her mom had been able to stay at work when COVID-19 had hit.

Today was her first chance to share a Sunday dinner with her parents in more than a year. COVID had ruined her plans for summer 2021, and a Christmas visit had also been cancelled because of similar restrictions, but now she was home and planned to stay there for the rest of the summer. She hoped to unwind in the gentle company of her parents and maybe do some light coaching for the little league soccer and softball teams in which several of her nephews and nieces played.

"How's Dad really doing?" Ricky asked. "I saw he managed to sit up at the dining table for most of the meal."

Her mom closed her eyes briefly and shook her head. "He did that for you, honey. He usually eats off a tray on his lap. But don't say anything. You know how he hates a fuss."

"I'm sorry to see he's still in so much pain," she whispered. "He's looking older than he used to."

"Of course he is, Ricky. We both are. Your dad only copes by wearing a morphine-type pain patch. It's the one thing which works, but the medical insurance barely covers it. And with all this talk about opiate addiction, the doctors are trying to take him off the patches. I don't know what we'll do if that happens."

"Mom, I'm so sorry. Look if it's the cost, I can help out. I only have myself to keep." Offering money was easy. Time and her presence weren't on the table.

"Thank you, honey, but he's a stubborn man. You take after him like that. We don't want your money. Just having you home is gift enough."

Ricky heard what her mom was saying and not saying. Her elder three brothers and her sister all lived within twenty miles of their parents in and around the Tampa Bay area and so, were always on hand. Ricky was the only one to have left the state to go to college. She'd majored in sports science and physical education and was now head of girls' sports at a large high school in urban New Jersey. To her siblings, it seemed an exotic thing to do, even though inner city Trenton wasn't exactly Honolulu. She sensed they viewed her not exactly as a prodigal sister but the one who had flown the nest. And as her daddy's darling, they must assume she was too sensitive to stay home to watch him suffer through months and years of frustrating rehabilitation that barely helped at all.

Only Ricky knew there was more to it than that. Ricky left Florida at eighteen and hadn't returned often enough since, not because her dad had been injured but to seek recovery from a stupid teenage crush, one which had ended in emotional meltdown and humiliation.

Maybe being shouted at and pulled off a horse wouldn't have bothered most people, but the brutal Thunder incident had nearly broken sensitive, soft-hearted Ricky. Her mom must remember how many tears she'd shed. So why had she mentioned Tara Morris, of all people, within six hours of her arriving home? She should know better.

Ricky finished drying the cutlery, took her coffee mug, and went through the back door to sit with her dad on the back porch. He had one favorite chair, which tipped back into a recliner, and he sat in it now, the local free newspaper on his knee.

"It's so good to have you with us," he said. "Is all your work done for the year?"

"Yeah." She dropped into an Adirondack chair beside him. "I'm not teaching summer school this year. I've sub-let my apartment for the next three months, so I won't be going back north before Labor Day. I've missed you both so much, and I haven't seen you in so long."

Her dad squeezed Ricky's hand. "We missed you at Christmas especially but knew you couldn't travel. It's been a tough two years."

"I know. It's been rough on everyone, especially hospitals and businesses."

"Yep. Speaking of which, did your mom tell you your old riding teacher, Mrs. Morris, has been forced to close her horse business? Look, the property's listed here."

He tapped the ad, but Ricky didn't look. Why was everyone so eager to tell her about what Tara Morris was doing?

"The land will be snapped up and developed, I reckon. She

must have more than five acres over there, and that whole section will be popular with folk moving out of central Tampa."

"I guess so." Ricky didn't care who'd be interested in the damn land.

Her father sighed. "I wish I was still in the house-building business. There's a fortune to be made right now from small tracts of land like that. I'd enjoy putting up some new family homes. There are some grants available for building in rural areas too. I'm just out of the game and wouldn't know where to start."

Ricky controlled her expression. Her dad was barely sixty, and she felt sorry for him, effectively turned out to pasture like an old, injured horse. He'd been a top-quality house builder in his prime, a master craftsman who built substantial and pretty homes, designed to withstand hurricanes. Those days were well beyond him now, but she didn't have the heart to stop him talking and dreaming about it.

Being forced to think about Meadowlands Horse Ranch for the first time in years made her wonder how her favorite horse, Thunder, was doing these days, or if he was even still alive. She hoped so, given he'd only be fourteen, not so old for a horse. She came back into the present with a jolt.

"Yeah, Mom did mention something. I suppose COVID finished her business off. But she'll get a hefty sum of money for the land and will do fine. Her husband was wealthy too."

It wasn't like they'd ever have to know anything about the kind of problems her parents had.

"Oh, that marriage ended years ago, didn't you know?"

That *was* news, though she shouldn't be interested. "No, I didn't."

"They divorced back in 2019. I heard Geoff Morris remarried, moved south toward Fort Myers, and now has a kid. Tara's been on her own ever since. With looks like hers, everyone thought she would remarry quickly but it ain't happened yet. You've been out of touch, hon."

Ricky let her dad chatter on. His knowledge of their small town was pretty comprehensive. She let the two major pieces of information about the woman who had been her first great love, and her worst nightmare, filter into her brain. So Tara was alone and her business had been killed off. Neither thing should matter to Ricky, and yet…

She responded on cue to her dad's continued gossip about other local characters, some she knew well and some she couldn't even remember. But her brain was focused only on Tara Morris, a name almost branded onto her heart and one which still made her flinch to think of. Even saying it gave her intense flashbacks. She could taste the iron on her tongue where she'd bitten it so hard as she stumbled off, hear that sharp voice shouting at her, and the shocked murmurings from the group of twelve-year-olds she'd been about to coach. And she felt again those tears which had half-blinded her, sticking painfully to her eyelashes as she struggled to cycle the two painful miles home.

The whole incident remained glued into her memory like some nightmarish commercial. It played over and over again, its colors bright scarlet and black, refusing to fade. Strange as the comparison might seem, it was the mental equivalent of her father's thirty-foot fall from a faulty scaffolding platform, one devastating incident which altered the course of her life. Part of her wanted to rejoice that Tara was divorced, that her business had failed, and that she was forced to sell off all her beloved horses. But despite everything, she still held a passion for her and remembered all her physical attractions in glorious technicolor.

But one thing she wouldn't be doing was going over to Meadowlands Equestrian Center to revisit the scene of the crime. Tara Morris could sell and move to Alaska for all she cared. She swiveled her attention back to her dad, who was attempting to finish the crossword on the back page of the newspaper. He looked so sweetly serious, with his glasses propped up on his head as he licked his pencil, that she was filled with love for him. "Give me a clue, Dad. Let's get it done together."

"Okay. Fifteen down. Caught out, beginning with B. Six letters."

"Busted?" Oops. That was a quick little kick in the ribs for her lie to herself. Did the crossword compilers have second sight?

Her dad smiled. "Hey, you're good. That fits right in. Here's a real long one. Fourteen letters. T is the eleventh letter. When enemies forgive and make up.”

Ricky mentally counted the letters. “Reconciliation?” Maybe the universe, in the shape of the *Tampa Bay Herald,* was trying to tell her something?

“Honey, you’re sharp,” her dad said. “No wonder you were the only one in the family who went to college. The puzzle’s done. Do you want to watch TV with us? Your mom and I like to watch the Sunday evening show from Montpellier. It’s our favorite channel. Katherine Konrad is something else. She runs the whole station but still does her own weekly news and discussion slot on Sundays. Right now it’s all about the campaign against the decision to reverse Roe v. Wade. Join us if you like.”

“No, thanks, Dad. I’ve spent so long campaigning with my colleagues up north against it over the last few weeks, it’s given me a headache. I think I might take a run outside for a while before it gets too dark. The air’s cooled off now. I won’t be long.”

Ricky helped her father back into the family room as he struggled with his walking sticks. She left her parents to watch the show, one she’d never watched, because Sunday nights were training nights. But like most people, she knew about the West Coast’s best-known opponent of Fox News, Montpellier Media. Its founder, Katherine Konrad, took few prisoners in her interviews and was a living legend among younger viewers and, since coming out as gay, the LGBTQ community.

Ricky went up to her old bedroom, changed into running gear, and headed outdoors. After such a long day of travel, it would be good to pound the streets for a while. She turned away from the direction of the main road, having no desire to inhale gasoline fumes as she ran, and decided to take the old back lanes where she’d used to cycle every day as a kid, which coincidentally led to Meadowlands Horse Ranch. She thought she might just take a last quick look at the old place for old times’ sake as she ran past it. Past it being the operative phrase. She certainly wouldn’t be going inside its gates.

CHAPTER TWO

It was only early June, but it felt like late August. The heat had been rising all weekend, and little swirls of dust lifted off the yard and blew around like mini tornados in the wind. The faded *Meadowlands Horse Riding School and Livery Stables* sign swung back and forth in the breeze. It clanged on its hinges, squeaking as it moved. The gates were propped wide open to let out the last of the livery clients' horse trailers to leave. The people had just gone.

After she waved them away, Tara Morris turned wearily back toward the empty horse barns and the house without bothering to shut the gates behind her. There was no need to keep them locked now. There were no animals to keep from getting loose, and no small children who might run out into traffic. Hers was the last property along the road, and her school had finally closed down in May, after fifteen years of teaching hundreds of young riders.

The quiet desolation mirrored the rest of her life. She was tired, thirsty, and if she was honest, as depressed as she'd ever been. And there was still the problem of Thunder to solve. She walked back into her house and poured herself a long glass of water from the faucet. Every penny counted, so she'd cancelled her subscription to the bottled water company, along with Netflix, HBO, the NYT, and all the other monthly additions to her expenses.

Now she was forced to scrimp together every dollar to cover the costs of closing down the business and paying the property taxes. Even her old house looked worn out. With no one but her around, it was quiet as a grave and the opposite of celebratory for her fortieth birthday, though today she felt nearer to ninety.

No one but her even knew about the birthday. Her parents were dead, and she had no children to bring her cards and flowers.

That was her own fault and her choice. The horses had been her children. But she couldn't help thinking of all the billing and cooing there would be in her ex-husband's house right now in a big fat celebration of young fertile motherhood.

Charmaine, Geoff's new wife, barely twenty-three, had made him a new father at fifty, and they were naming the baby girl today with a big party. They'd even invited Tara, in a magnanimous, patronizing sort of way. She supposed Geoff wanted to show her how settled and happy he was, which wasn't unnatural after all the years of misery they'd shared. She'd sent back an email, politely refusing, and tried not to show how insulted she was by the perky little invitation card.

Well, good luck to him. After years of seeming not to care, in his forties Geoff had declared he wanted children and even cited it as one of the reasons he was asking for a divorce. She didn't blame him. Their marriage had ended years before he moved out. They'd had separate bedrooms for more than the final five years, from the time when—Tara shook the thought away; she didn't want to wander down that particular memory lane right now.

She had never admired people who whined and felt sorry for themselves. But after drinking a glass of the metallic-tasting tap water while thinking about the state of her life, she allowed herself to collapse onto the sofa and shed a few tears in a little misery session now. She felt lonely, washed up, and regretful of chances she'd missed and the bad choices she'd made. If there was any liquor in the house, she might have hit the bottle to drown her sorrows, so maybe it was good she could no longer afford the Johnny Walker whiskey she'd once enjoyed.

A hopeful whinny came from the looseboxes in her yard and Tara pulled herself together. She couldn't let Thunder see her upset. Horses were so empathetic. He might take on her anxiety and begin to gnaw at his stable door, and she needed him to exhibit his best behavior for his new owners when she finally managed to deliver him.

She wiped her eyes roughly with a piece of paper towel and went outside to check that her darling boy had sufficient water for the night and his hay net was full enough to sustain him until the following morning.

"Hey, how ya doing, my best boy?" she asked in the special voice she used. Thunder had been born on a Washington state stud farm, which had given him his official name, but moved southeast down to race in Florida as a colt. He was her pride and joy, still worth twenty thousand dollars of anybody's money. He'd never been gelded and had sired some nice foals, so she was able to sell him as a proven stud.

It broke her heart to do it, but she had no choice. The IRS had valued her land and property as capable of bringing in twice the income she'd received through COVID, and they'd re-zoned it into an impossibly high bracket, similar to the millionaires' houses on the next block. She had to find the money to pay them or go bankrupt. The property was already listed with a realtor and would no doubt go to one of the new moneyed people wanting to move out of Tampa. Then she would find a job away from horses. How was she supposed to start again at forty? What was she supposed to do that would make her happy? But then, she hadn't really been happy for years.

Tara's immediate problem was supposed to be good news. The people who wanted to buy Thunder owned the stud ranch adjacent to the one in Tacoma where he'd been born. They knew his breeding, and it fitted in well with their own mares. But they'd only sent her a thousand-dollar deposit so far, which she'd already spent on settling her horse-feed account, and they'd agreed to pay her the rest on delivery. But it was a three-thousand-mile trip. Shipping a horse that far would cost a fortune. Worse than that, Tara hated the idea of consigning Thunder to one of those great horse transporters which kept moving for fifty hours at a stretch. To make the trip in her own elderly horse truck would take six to eight days, possibly longer, and cost hundreds in gas. But it would still be cheaper than using one of the professional companies and right now, every dollar counted.

She gave Thunder a great big hug and nuzzled her face into the soft, short hair of his summer coat. He was a shining chestnut with large kind eyes. He looked good, even at fourteen, and his skin felt reassuringly warm, not too hot or too chilled. She loved the smell of a contented horse and breathed it in. He was her best friend and now, her only significant other. If he'd known what day it was, Thunder would surely have wished her a happy birthday.

Tara registered quiet footsteps slowly walking along the concrete approach to the stables. The pathway in front faced west, causing her to squint straight into the setting sun, and she didn't immediately recognize the tall figure approaching her.

"You don't remember me?" the person asked softly. "I didn't expect you to, of course. It was a long time ago."

Tara put up her hand to shield her eyes from the low sun and gasped. She placed the voice at once, a little deeper perhaps but unmistakable. "Ric? Richenda Gates. Of course, I remember you!" Something profound stirred inside her, mostly guilt mixed with a large measure of joy. A tall young woman with short, wavy brown hair came into focus.

"What brings you back to Florida? I heard you went away to New York to train to be a teacher."

"I did," Ricky said. "I'm settled in New Jersey now. I've come home to visit because school's out for the summer, and I haven't seen my mom in more than a year." She looked up at Thunder and half-smiled. "But I won't stay to bother you. I can see this is a bad time. I heard you were selling and wanted to see the old place before…"

Ricky seemed to falter, as though she'd lost her nerve and was about to bolt. This was no casual meeting. It meant a lot to Tara. Perhaps it did to Ricky too. She gently held Ricky's wrist to keep her from running, hardly knowing what she was doing. Her skin was warm and damp. She'd obviously run here, judging from her outfit. That's why there'd been no sound of a vehicle turning into the yard.

Tara's mood lifted, sharpened. She came alive. To have Ricky Gates here in front of her after all these years, the unwitting casualty of what had been one of the worst days of her life, was a surprise birthday gift which Tara intended to make the most of. She'd always wanted to apologize in person and now she had the chance. Probably Ricky had recovered long ago and had forgotten the stupid, bitchy comments Tara had made and had immediately regretted. But if she hadn't forgotten, then here was the chance to make things right. It was unfinished business, business of the heart somehow, and she didn't want it hanging over her any longer.

"Ric, please don't go. It's so good to see you. Come into the house for a drink. I have a couple of beers in the refrigerator." She became acutely aware she hadn't released Ricky's arm and abruptly dropped her hand.

Ricky looked at her with those great big soulful eyes of hers. They reminded her, not in any derogatory way, of Thunder's, kind and honest. Once, she remembered, they had always been so happy to see her. Now they held a maturity and a caution which hadn't been there before. The girl she remembered had become a grown woman. Handsome, athletic, and a good three inches taller than Tara, but in essence, she could still see her favorite young rider in there. The slight sheen of perspiration across that familiar face didn't spoil her look either. "You've been running fast, I see. You seem very well."

"Thunder looks well too," Ricky said, moving her arms behind her back as though she feared she would be scolded if she tried to touch him.

"You remember him?" Tara asked. "I think he remembers you too. Look how he's trying to nuzzle your shoulder."

Ricky started to slowly relax, and then she gently reached her palm out to let Thunder smell her hand and nuzzle her fingers. He snickered, almost as though he was saying hi. Tara wanted to keep Ric talking. She still looked as though she might dart away at any moment. If she was a horse, Tara would have thrown a rope over her shoulder to keep her close, but she had only words.

"Yes, he's very well. But he's the only horse I have left now." A sweep of melancholy stole across her and settled uncomfortably in her gut. "I've sold him and need to deliver him to his new home by the end of this month."

Ricky bit her lip as she continued to stroke Thunder. "I'm sorry I made him lame."

Ricky was clearly more mature, but her voice had the same

tentative nervousness about it, something Tara had always found pleasant in the past. So many of the kids hanging around her stables had been loud and insensitive in the way they shouted at each other. They made the horses nervous. But Ricky never had. "Oh, Ric, you didn't make him lame. On the day before I shouted at you, a careless farrier had put a nail into his shoe too deep, and it caused an abscess. I found it that morning but didn't have time to tell you. You weren't to blame at all. Come inside with me and let me apologize properly. I was in a foul mood that day, and I took it out on you. I'm so sorry. It's really good to see you, you know, even in these circumstances."

Tara gave Thunder a last pat and pulled his ears, before leading the way from her stables, trusting Ricky would follow her to the house. She had no idea why her old riding pupil had come to visit her after a decade of frozen silence, but she badly needed to know why.

CHAPTER THREE

Ricky's legs wanted to follow Tara, so she decided to let them, even though she still wasn't sure why she was there at all. The two-mile run had started in a fury, with angry adrenaline pumping through her body. She had wasted far too many hours pining for this woman, and she wanted to be free of her for good. But as she'd neared the stables, she'd decided that seeing her again might help kill off the old attraction and cure her stupid obsession. So far that hadn't happened. Her riding teacher was as lethally lovely as ever. Maybe she should just give it more time. A beer and a confrontation combined might do the trick, though Tara's immediate apology and her obvious sincerity took the sting out of Ricky's anger.

Tara opened her back door and ushered her inside. The house, which Ricky had always remembered as being beautifully decorated with the kind of furniture and fittings her parents could never have afforded, now seemed smaller and shabbier than it had been before. It didn't seem to have been updated much in the last decade, and several of the old paintings and nicer pieces of horse statues had disappeared. Her display of riding trophies and the many cups she'd won no longer ran along the shelving through the hallway.

As a girl, it had been a rare privilege for Ricky to be invited in the house for a lemonade on a hot day, or in the winter months, occasionally being treated to a mug of chocolate and a cookie after cleaning out the stables.

Ricky had by no means been the only one to have a teenage crush. There had been no shortage of young, unpaid acolytes, the teens and pre-teens who would do any job, however dirty, in return for the privilege of being allowed to hang around the stables and groom the horses. Tara had seemed to tolerate them kindly in a brusque, off-hand manner, which further fascinated and attracted the girls.

Coming into the house brought it all back. And as an adult, the why of it all was even more obvious. At thirty, Tara had been stunningly good-looking, with a lean elegance and the style of a true horsewoman. The past decade had been kind, and she still had plenty of that special something, that pizzazz.

What was the attraction? Hard to define. Her jet black, almost navy-blue hair shone like a crow's wings. Her intense brown eyes and angular face wouldn't have been out of place on the cover of Vogue, if Tara had been six inches taller. Even in her uniform of worn blue jeans or jodhpurs and faded denim shirts she looked glamorous.

Tara had never seemed to care much for fancy clothes or makeup, but she vibrated with an inner fire. It was a passion stoked by her devotion to horses, the only thing Tara really seemed to care about. This evening, that fire looked to be barely flickering, but it wasn't entirely extinguished. Even depressed, Tara could exude more vitality than anyone else Ricky had ever known.

It almost made her angry to see how little Tara had changed in ten years, how good she still looked, damn it. Talking to her still raised Ricky's heartbeat. It thumped away right now, beating faster than when she'd been running to get here.

Tara's best gift had always been the ability to teach and to inspire young riders. In her early twenties she had been an internationally successful show jumper and eventer, trained in Germany on the large Hanoverian horses, and Ricky believed there was nothing she didn't know about riding in the European manner, especially dressage, the art of making a horse almost dance on command, with balance and subtle control.

Western riding, with huge heavy saddles and painfully severe bits wasn't for Tara, though that was how many of the local adults wanted to learn these days. Ricky wondered if that was one reason Tara's business had fallen on hard times, and why she had lost too many clients and customers to be able to survive the many months of lockdown.

They went into the kitchen, and Tara took a couple of cans of Bud Light from the fridge. She handed one to Ricky, along with a glass.

"It's not much. But it's cold."

Ricky popped the can and poured her beer. In the old days it would have been Mountain Dew or Coke, but the simple action sent her back to those magical days when she could pretend that Tara cared especially for her, before the day when it became obvious that she didn't, and everything turned to mud. "It's fine. It just feels strange to be drinking beer with you. I feel almost as though I'm in high school again. It's been a long time. I'm sorry it's taken me so long to visit, to come back to see you." Was that even true? Ricky really didn't know, or why she'd said it at all.

Tara led her over to an old leather sofa where they sat down.

"For God's sake, don't apologize. I'm the one who needs to do that. I treated you horribly. You were always one of my best girls—the best, actually, the one who had a special gift with horses—and I took advantage of your kind nature, always asking you to stay late, to lock up, or come early to do morning feeds while I went out riding with my friends."

"I remember. I loved all of the work though. It was never a chore." Ricky wondered if she could summon up the courage to do what she had come here for, to confront Tara and get to know the truth. She decided she could. Her mouth was as dry as a bale of hay, and the palms of her hands were clammy, but she ignored them. "I never understood why you turned on me that day when I was riding Thunder. What was it all about, truthfully? I never saw you behave like that to anyone else, ever, and I thought you liked me and trusted me with your horses."

Ricky realized that asking the question which had burned at the back of her brain all these years marked a new beginning. She had finally grown up. She had the confidence not only to drink beer with Tara, but also to challenge her as an adult and face whatever pain the answer might entail.

Tara stared fixedly at the opposite wall. "Yes, of course you deserve to know. The first thing to make clear is that none of what happened was your fault. I can tell you things today that would have been impossible back then. There was far more going on with me than you could possibly have understood and things about me you were far too young to be burdened by. This isn't easy, but…"

"But you can tell me now." Ricky really had no idea where Tara was going, but she was desperate to hear it.

"Do you truly want the truth? It's not pretty."

Ricky didn't care for pretty. She just wanted to know why Tara had treated her so badly. She wanted closure. She was so close, she could feel it. "Of course I do."

Tara took a deep breath and a mouthful of beer. She finally looked Ricky in the eye. "I bought Thunder when he was four, straight off the track with money my mother had left me. Having him on the yard brought me in several new clients, including a woman named Marcia, who only wanted to ride him. She came early every morning, and we started trail-riding together. She was older than me, married to some rich guy, and we became close." She glanced up at Ricky briefly. "Marcia grew obsessed with me and became jealous, not of Geoff but of the older girls I had working at the stable. And for some reason, she fixated most of that on you." She shook her head. "You won't remember any of this."

Tara stared at Ricky, curling up one side of her mouth in the quirky way Ricky remembered so well. Ricky's breathing quickened, and she said, "Actually I do. Her name was Marcia Cunningham," Ricky said. "I remember her well. She had ash blonde hair and drove a convertible Porsche. I would saddle Thunder up for her and then cool him down afterward, but she rarely thanked me. You went on long morning rides together. I remember it very clearly now." Ricky had been so envious of Marcia, spending all that time with Tara, side by side. "But I just thought she was one of your regular clients."

"Yes, that's her." Tara still seemed hesitant, and Ricky guessed there was a lot she still wasn't saying.

"But I still don't get it. Are you saying that you hauled me off Thunder and sent me packing purely to show her I didn't matter to you?"

"Yes, partly, but there was more to it than that. I have no excuse, but you were a casualty in our battles. It was a particularly bad day. Marcia and I had fought, and she threatened to tell my husband and the whole town that I was playing about with underage stable girls and having an affair with you. She accused me of all sorts of behavior, and then when I saw you out in the manège, riding Thunder on his abscess, I just freaked out. I took my anger out on you when I should have been angry with Marcia and thrown her out."

Ricky didn't need any help remembering the five minutes in the manège, but now she could take in more details of the wider scene. Hadn't she glimpsed Marcia lurking in the shadows by the house? "She was there, wasn't she? She was standing on the back porch, watching."

"Yes, she was. It turned into some nasty little show for her benefit." Tara held her glass of beer to her forehead as if the chill might fend off a tension headache. "You didn't know anything about Thunder's hoof injury, and I was frightened he might throw you off in his pain, and you'd get hurt. I ran over to you to make you dismount for your own safety, but the words came out all wrong. By the time I'd taken him back to his stable and calmed down, you were long gone."

Ricky snorted. "Were you surprised?"

"No, of course not, but I was sad," Tara said. "Seeing you run away in tears excited Marcia, and I could tell she had somehow orchestrated the whole incident. For a while, dealing with her distracted me from chasing after you." She placed her glass on a side table and rubbed at her temples. "I'm so, so sorry, Ric. I tried to make it right, and I kept trying to reach you, but you never came back. I realized that by trying to placate Marcia and losing my temper with you, I'd lost my best stable girl and also a special friend."

Special friend? Ricky had wanted so much more than that at sixteen. "Not so little. You said that I was far too heavy to ride him." Ricky swirled the beer in her glass. "I've never sat on a horse since." There was no point in pretending that Tara's words and behavior hadn't hurt or had lasting effects. Ricky had spent a long time in pain, and the memory of that wouldn't dissolve away after one apology and a not especially convincing explanation.

"Ric, try to forgive me even if you can't forget. I said stupid things I didn't mean. I'm so sorry they hurt you." She looked into her glass and emptied it. "Look, why don't you come back tomorrow and ride Thunder again? Please. Let me give you back the joy of riding. I used to see it on your face so often, and I loved that. I'll lose him in a week or two. But for now, he and I would be honored to see you again, really. Come back to us."

This was Tara in a different light from any version of her that Ricky remembered or had created in the past decade. Open, generous, and charming, and maybe genuinely remorseful. Ricky thought through what Tara had said. There was enough space between the lines of her account of her friendship with Marcia to read a heck of a lot more into it than friendship. Tara and Marcia must have been lovers. Did that make Tara bisexual or gay? Had her relationship with Marcia been the end of Tara's marriage? Ricky knew from personal experience just how difficult it was to come out. She hadn't even managed to do it with her parents, loving and liberal as they were.

If Tara had been in the middle of sexual turmoil over Marcia Cunningham, without anyone else being aware of what was going on, then that would easily explain her behavior. But Ricky still couldn't totally excuse or forgive Tara for the way she had treated her. The scars remained red and sore in her mind.

She managed a smile. "Thanks. I'd be as stiff as a board and probably couldn't even mount him without a leg-up. But it's a tempting offer." What was she doing though? This was supposed to be about closure, not opening the door to spend more time with Tara again. "You're not really serious about selling Thunder though, are you? I can't believe you would ever do that."

Tara looked at her living room wall as if it held some deep fascination for her. Ricky didn't miss Tara's hand tremble.

"I wouldn't if I had any choice. But I have big debts and a property tax bill to pay. I've been offered a good price for him from a guy up near Tacoma in Washington State. I just have to get him there, but it's too far to risk driving alone." She shrugged.

"But I can't afford to hire someone as a co-driver, so I don't have much choice."

Ricky could only guess how painful it must be for the proud and formerly successful Tara Morris to sell her favorite horse. She had suffered such losses. But Ricky's attention turned back to her fascination with Tara's romantic dealings. "Tara, tell me what happened with Marcia Cunningham in the end. Is she still on the scene? Was she the reason you and your husband ended the marriage? My dad told me you divorced years ago."

"Yes, we did. Marcia did her best to help things along. Punishing me became her favorite leisure activity. Making me cry seemed to stimulate her somehow. She loved provoking conflict and making people unhappy, especially me."

Ricky couldn't even imagine what it would take to make the powerful Tara cry or how she could be bullied by another woman. It revealed a vulnerability Ricky would never have expected, and she could hardly believe that Tara had confided these things to her now. But she was hungry to know more. She wanted to strip the truth from Tara to get the full picture.

"Tell me what happened next," she said gently and was rewarded by Tara turning back and giving her the full benefit of an intense, focused gaze from her beautiful, though war-weary face.

"Marcia and I continued our…friendship for years after that day when you left. After my divorce, she was never away but then, out of the blue, two years ago, she and her husband abruptly moved to Southern California. I should've been happy. It hadn't been a healthy relationship, but I walked around like a zombie for months afterward. Finally though, I actually felt better for not having to work my entire life around her."

She rolled the glass in her hand thoughtfully, as if she were off somewhere in her mind with Marcia. "For a few weeks after they moved, we exchanged emails but then she suddenly stopped replying. Like a fool, I kept calling and writing but got no response. Finally she sent a short text to say she had someone new in her life and she wanted me to stop bothering her. End of story."

"I'm sorry that she hurt you." Ricky had broken up enough times to know it was rarely painless. But as the prime mover in ending her three previous relationships, she'd always tried hard to ease out gently.

Tara sighed. "Marcia had always hurt me but finally breaking up was tough. Like quitting smoking. You know it's really bad for you, but you still crave the nicotine. But she wasn't done. She'd loaned me a sizeable amount of money to expand the business. It was done legally. We had a signed agreement, and the interest rate for repayment was affordable. But soon after she left, I received a letter from her lawyer saying that Marcia wanted all the money repaid within six months, or I'd face a much higher rate of interest. I was so angry that I decided to pay everything I owed her, and it cleaned me out. I could've fought her on it, but I just wanted to be done, and that left me penniless."

Tara ran her hand through her hair in that characteristic way Ricky had always loved.

"And after that, well, everything went bad. When my husband had asked me for a clean break, I'd had no reason to refuse him a divorce. The horse business we co-owned still seemed viable. I kept it and this property, and he'd claimed the rest of our joint assets. Then COVID struck and shut me down; now I'm close to bankruptcy."

Ricky moved closer to Tara and leaned toward her. She resisted the insane desire to take Tara's hand and squeeze it. What the heck was she thinking?

And now that Tara had started off-loading, she couldn't seem to be able to stop. She talked about selling off her riding school horses and ponies, one by one, and then losing her livery clients as the price of feed and vet bills had rocketed, and they'd mostly given up their horses, or found even cheaper stabling for them.

"And what about you?" Ricky asked, emboldened by how the conversation was going. For the first time since she'd known Tara, she was her equal. And she felt empowered. "I guess you and Marcia were having sex. Was she your lover?"

Tara jumped, no doubt shocked by Ricky calling her relationship out for what it was. They looked at each other in an intense silence, and Tara's face turned quite red under her tan.

"Yes, she was, and it wasn't easy. She was demanding. She took what she wanted when she wanted it, even when…"

An indefinable expression passed across Tara's face, and alarm bells rang for Ricky. Tara didn't have to say the words. Perhaps she couldn't even if she wanted to. Ricky's heart ached to see such the strong woman she remembered reduced to the almost broken person sitting in front of her now. "Have you even gotten over her yet?"

Tara paused for far too long a time before answering and then focused her gaze at the one remaining picture above her fireplace, a beautiful oil painting of Thunder galloping to victory.

"I suppose so, just about. It was pretty bad for a while though. I had this obsession about her, you know, what she did to me, the feelings she could still evoke. It was my first serious relationship with a woman, and it blew my mind. I'd been in denial for too long, so when it finally happened, I guess I went over the top. I gave in to her demands all the time."

Ricky swallowed down the last of her beer. Tara was acknowledging the parameters of what had clearly been a destructive relationship and talking about it with Ricky gave her the impression Tara finally saw her as the adult she was.

She'd done what she came here to do, *and* they'd crossed some bridge into a new beginning, into a far more equal relationship. But she still had a fierce, painful stab of jealousy toward Marcia. Ricky wasn't convinced Tara was over her, and if she walked onto the ranch right now, Ricky wouldn't be surprised if Tara fell into her arms.

"You probably don't understand," Tara said. "The power one woman can have over another… I'm sorry to blurt all this out. I've never told anyone else. But it's strange how easy it is to talk about it with you, of all people. I suppose it's partly the need to confess, and to explain. The memory of how I hurt you has gnawed away at me all these years."

"I do understand because I'm gay too. I split up with my last girlfriend six months ago, and there were others." Ricky calmed her racing heart. She may as well join in the confession time.

"And back when I was much younger, there was this woman I had a huge crush on for five years. She's still in there, messing with my head. It's hard to stop loving some people, no matter how wrong they are for you."

"Then you do understand."

Ricky sighed. Was she relieved or disappointed that Tara didn't understand she was talking about her?

"I'm truly sorry to hear that, Ric. It must have been so hard. But here we are, both able to talk about these things. We've somehow survived, and you've obviously flourished." She stood up and started to pace restlessly around the room. "I've missed having you around. You were always such a ray of sunshine in my world. Will you come and ride Thunder with me for old times' sake and show me I'm on the way to being forgiven?"

Ricky put down her empty glass on the coffee table. She couldn't say she'd completely forgiven Tara. Nor did she trust her not to hurt her again. Tara's confession explained her motives and her behavior, but she'd still taken her emotions out on a vulnerable sixteen-year-old kid, one who'd shown her nothing but kindness and reverence. Forgiveness would take a little while longer to be earned, but how could Tara do that if Ricky didn't put herself out there and risk her heart one more time. "Sure, thanks. I'll come tomorrow if that works for you. Can you provide a hat and the gear though? And don't expect anything much in the way of riding skills. Ten years is a long time out of the saddle."

Tara stood and picked up Ricky's glass. "You'll be fine. It's like riding a bicycle. How about nine a.m.? I'll get Thunder ready and warm him up beforehand."

"Sure. Oh, and Tara…"

Tara looked at her, her expression full of hope. "Yes?"

"I may never totally forget what happened, but I promise I'll work on it. So don't worry any more, okay? I'm going to be around for a few months, and I'd like to be friends with you."

Tara's expression brightened like the sun bursting out from behind thick clouds, and its warmth penetrated the insufficient layers of protective padding around Ricky's heart. Damn it. If Tara smiled at her like that, she'd be slipping back into a tarpit of obsessive attraction and crushing on her just as much as she had at sixteen.

"Let me drive you home," said Tara as they stepped out of the house and into the night. "It's dark already, and I don't like the idea of you running down the highway against the traffic."

Ricky shook her head. "Thanks, but there's no need. I won't be running down the highway. I'm a backroads kind of gal. See you tomorrow." She turned and ran away before she said or did anything else, like saying she'd missed Tara, or reaching for Tara's face and stroking away her forlorn expression. Ricky didn't look back, but she could sense she was being watched all the way through the gates and down the graveled road.

Everything would be fine, Ricky told herself. She was home for nearly three months, and she had no idea what Tara's plans were after she sold Thunder and her business. She'd probably move away because there'd be nothing here for her anymore. There was no harm in spending some time with her and getting to know her as an equal.

No harm at all.

CHAPTER FOUR

"Where are you off to, so bright and early?" asked her mom as Ricky breezed through the kitchen the following morning, pulling on a light summer jacket, about to leave the house.

"I'm going over to Tara Morris's stables. She invited me to ride there one last time. You and Dad had gone up to bed by the time I came home, but I dropped by to see her last night. Despite what she did to me, I kind of feel sorry for her. The whole place is empty apart from Thunder. Do you remember him, her best horse? He's the only one she has left, and she's selling him to some ranch in Washington."

The smell of fresh coffee tempted her, and Ricky poured herself a cup from the fresh pot. "But don't worry, I won't be out more than a couple of hours. I can sit with Dad this afternoon, and maybe help you clean up the backyard."

Her mom, dressed in the cashier's uniform of the Happy Buy grocery store chain, also seemed about to leave. She smiled. "I'm really pleased that you've made up with Tara at last. She's a good person despite her rather abrupt manner and sometimes appearing not to care. She asks about you every time she comes into the store."

"Maybe we can get to be friends, on a more equal footing this time. I'm no longer quite so terrified of her anyway."

Those words echoed in her head as she went through the Meadowlands open gates, and Ricky knew she was deluding herself. She could've easily been eleven again, her knees knocking at the thought of mounting up in front of Mrs. Morris and being put through her paces. Today though, she parked her car instead of stowing her bike by the looseboxes and headed straight around the house to the manège.

Tara was already exercising Thunder, cantering slowly around the perimeter of the sand rectangle and changing legs across the center in a figure of eight pattern on every other circuit. Horse and rider moved as one, with Tara's legs molded around Thunder's body, and her butt never leaving the low saddle. Her aids were so gentle and subtle, it appeared Thunder moved of his own accord and changed legs under his own volition.

Ricky stepped up onto the bars of the fence and watched them work. Within a minute, Tara changed direction at the end of the manège and came toward her. Thunder stopped in a perfect four-square stand, almost as though they were finishing a dressage demonstration, and nodded his head as if in salute. Ricky smiled, and Tara jumped off his back.

"Climb over the fence and hop on," she said, moving as if to hand the reins to Ricky.

But Ricky was attacked by an acute fit of nerves and temporarily became paralyzed.

Tara seemed to understand. "Come on. I'll help you. Drop your jacket outside the fence. Good. Now come around to his right-hand side. I would lift the stirrups up a notch for you, but I think they need to be lengthened instead. I'm sure you've grown at least three inches since you last rode him. You're so much taller than me now."

Tara removed her riding helmet and passed it over. Ricky drew on the hat and pushed her hair behind her ears. But then she froze again and just stood there, not moving.

"Mount up, Ricky," Tara said firmly. "Thunder's waiting. I'll give you a leg-up."

Ricky, who had always automatically obeyed Tara when she was in teaching mode, did as she was instructed. Thunder was a tall horse, so when Tara bent down and linked her hands as an aid for Ricky to step on, she didn't argue. She placed her boot in Tara's grasp and jumped as she was helped from below. Within seconds, she was aloft and eased herself gently down onto Thunder's back. She pushed her boots into the stirrups, settled into the saddle, and gently made a connection with his mouth through the reins. She couldn't help but remember the last time Tara had grasped her boot, but she shook it off and tried to be positive. Maybe today would go some way toward making up for last time.

It felt so good to sit on a horse again. She'd made herself forget just how good it felt. All those years running, playing various sports, and even learning to waterski, nothing had come close to the joy of horseback riding. A flare of anger rose for denying herself this pleasure for so long, and tears threatened to blur her eyesight. She would have been happy to sit astride the broad back of any old cart horse, but this chance to ride Thunder again, such a superbly trained, well-bred, responsive animal, was a real privilege.

Tara stepped away. "Take him around for a few circuits. He'll do the work. Just relax and let your muscles remember their job."

"Not too heavy for him then?" Ricky couldn't resist the jibe.

Tara had the grace to look embarrassed.

She shook her head. "No, of course not. You're absolutely fine, looking lovely in fact. Go on and give me something good to look at. I'll grab my phone while you're warming up and take a video to send to his new owner. I haven't had anyone to ride him well enough to do it before, and there's been no one around to video me."

Tara headed toward the house, and Ricky realized it was now or never. She had to ask Thunder to move off and start riding for real. She nudged him and gave him the aid for moving away from the fence back onto the main track of the manège. Then she urged him into an extended walk.

"A horse which walks well, gallops well," she remembered Tara saying. Thunder had a long rhythmical gait, and he covered the ground smoothly and evenly. Ricky began to ask for a slow rising trot, and she barely had to think of the movement before it somehow transmitted from her brain to his, and he quickened his pace.

All was going well. Tara had been right; it *was* like riding a bike. The aids came back into her fingers and calf muscles instinctively. She moved from a trot into a lope and asked him to change his leading leg every few circuits. He seemed happy and showed no resistance, and she kept the pressure on his gentle snaffle bit as light as possible, just enough to feel a constant connection with him. Tara could ride him without a bridle at all, they were in such fine sync with each other. Once again, the catch of sadness that Tara had to sell him hit home.

If Ricky had had sufficient funds, she might've bought him herself and given him straight back to her old teacher in appreciation for all the training she'd received as a child. But she had no savings. Paying off student loans swallowed most of her spare cash.

Tara returned to the fence and beckoned her over. "See. Not so hard, was it? But at the end, you were starting to daydream, and Thunder was beginning to do his own thing. Don't let him get faster without listening to you first. You have to be in charge at all times when he's under the saddle."

Ricky smiled to hear the teacher in Tara coming out again, and as usual, knew she was dead right. The fact that she'd been thinking about ways to save Thunder for Tara wasn't the point. "You still notice everything."

"Yep. Start up again and give me a demonstration of all the paces, so I can shoot a video for the new owner. Maybe a minute or so at each speed. Then finish with three minutes of level one dressage, some half-passes, and a little bit of a passage. I'm sure you remember how."

"Tara, I haven't ridden in ten years! Wouldn't it be better if you rode him, and I filmed you?"

Tara shook her head. "I'm a weather-beaten old thing. Let's send them the sight of someone beautiful on top to go with the beautiful horse under the saddle."

Buoyed by the unexpected compliment, Ricky didn't let her mind wander. She kept her back straight and her hips glued to the saddle and rode to the best of her ability for ten minutes, finishing with an extended gallop around the circuit, before slowing right down and putting on a little dressage show, one Tara had taught her so long ago. It worked, thank God, but when she finally gave a little mock salute and finished, she was absolutely exhausted. As she dismounted her legs turned to jelly, and her knees nearly buckled.

Tara laughed gently and reached out to support Ricky's elbow as she found her feet again.

"I don't envy me tomorrow," Ricky said. "I'll be aching from head to foot." She handed Thunder's reins over to Tara and bent over to stretch out her back. "Thank you. That was totally wonderful. It's actually made me a bit emotional." Her tears began to threaten again, and she fought them off. It would be just too revealing and immature to cry in front of Tara, but now that Ricky had dismounted, the enormity of what she'd just done hit her.

She'd ridden Thunder for almost half an hour, something she had convinced herself would never happen again. But it had.

"No, thank *you*," Tara said. "You were great. Let's go inside and perhaps you'll help me transfer the film onto my desktop. Then I'll send it off to Washington."

Ricky walked with Tara and Thunder back to the stable and watched Tara untack him and gently rub him down to remove the small streaks of sweat marks on his otherwise shining coat. He marched straight into his stall, took a long drink, and then pulled a mouthful of hay from his net.

"I'll turn him out later when the midday heat has dropped. He can't understand where the other horses have gone. I wish I could explain to him why I'm having to do this."

"Tara…"

"Yes?"

"I've just realized I'm now calling you Tara instead of Mrs. Morris."

Tara rolled her eyes. "Not exactly a life-altering event, surely?"

"Yes, it is, actually." But Tara had no idea why it would mean so much to her. "But that's not what I was going to say. Is there really no alternative to selling Thunder? I have a full-time job. I could maybe take out a bank loan or something to help you."

The offer was out of Ricky's mouth before she'd fully thought through the consequences and what such an offer would tell Tara. She looked into Tara's face and was astonished to see her eyes fill with tears. "Oh my God, I didn't mean… Not like the loan from monstrous Marcia. I didn't mean to upset you."

Tara shook her head and gently touched Ricky's arm. "It has nothing to do with Marcia. Your generosity just took my breath away. I could never take a loan from you. And you could never remind me of Marcia. You're so completely different from her, the exact opposite, thankfully."

They went inside, and Ricky watched Tara struggle to transfer the video from her phone to her desktop computer. Ricky thought about what Tara had said and couldn't figure out whether it what was a good or bad thing that she was the exact opposite of Marcia. Tara had loved Marcia, found her physically irresistible, and probably was even now still at risk of falling at her feet if they were ever to meet again. This was cast-iron proof that there was zero chance of Tara falling in love with her.

Which was for the best. Three months would zip by in a blur, and Ricky would return to her teaching job. Knowing there was no chance of even a vacation romance should veer her away from a dangerous cliff edge. She would settle for friendship, and her heart would be safe. But Tara had said she looked beautiful on a horse. She remembered Tara well enough to know that any compliment from her was a rare event and was never given lightly. Ricky supposed Tara could acknowledge someone was attractive without *being* attracted to them.

"Damn it, Ric, I'm hopeless with technology. Can you help me here?" Tara handed her phone to Ricky who did the transfer in no time. "Thanks. Now sit with me and watch yourself on camera. I'll give you a few pointers where you can improve, even though your dressage was a creditable effort, especially since you haven't been on a horse for ten years."

Ricky pulled up a chair, still eager enough to receive instruction. Even with no horses or pupils, Tara would always be a riding teacher through to her bones, so Ricky might as well learn from her. They watched the short video, with Tara's perceptive commentary, and then Tara asked Ricky to stay for an early lunch, which turned out to be a cheese and tomato sandwich with an Advil for dessert to ease her already aching muscles.

Nothing much more was said, but Ricky caught Tara staring at her now and then, almost as if she couldn't believe she was truly there. That made two of them. Seeing the time on the kitchen clock, Ricky remembered her promise to fix lunch for her father. She jumped up and said she needed to get home.

"Same time tomorrow?" Tara asked her as she went to the front door to see her out.

Ricky nodded. She drove home and fixed lunch for her dad. She ate a second sandwich with him on the back porch, all the time thinking about what an amazing morning she'd had, but how hopeless it would be to spend any more time lusting after Tara. Craving her was about as pointless as Tara secretly pining for her own lost love, failed business, and the soon to be loss of her wonderful horse. They had more in common than she thought.

CHAPTER FIVE

As soon as Ricky drove away in a cloud of dust, Tara retreated to her desk and reran the video of her old student putting Thunder through his paces. It was a simple pleasure to watch them. Ricky had such good balance and a gentleness about her that made the equestrian art look effortless, and it was clear from Thunder's responses that he appreciated being ridden by such a natural, empathetic rider.

It was hard to believe Ricky hadn't sat on a horse once in the last ten years. When she'd told Tara that, she effectively told her that being insulted and pulled from Thunder all those years ago had effectively destroyed her enjoyment of riding. The guilt was all Tara's, and she had to live with it. She believed people should take responsibility for the damage they did to others.

She wondered whether Marcia would ever take responsibility for all those years of physical and emotional abuse she'd inflicted, when she claimed to love Tara so much. She was still bewildered by their relationship, even years after it had ended. It had been far more violent and coercive than she'd told Ricky. Tara hadn't told her the half of it.

For ten years, Tara's life had essentially been on a downward slope. After Geoff left, Marcia had become even more controlling until Tara was frightened of her own shadow. Losing her so abruptly had been equally painful. The bitter epilogue of being forced to pay off her loan early was the final straw, like being kicked in the ribs, and Tara knew what that felt like.

But now, bleak though the landscape still was, Tara could see a faint light ahead. She'd reconnected with Ricky Gates, had been given the chance to apologize and ask for redemption, and sweet as she was, Ricky had given it to her. She'd always thought Ricky was a good kid, but she'd turned into quite a woman.

Losing Thunder was probably her punishment for all her past mistakes but as far as she could tell, he was going to a good home, and his memories of her wouldn't be anything other than happy. Then she would sell the ranch, clear her debts, and begin the rest of her life.

She wrote an email to the guys in Washington who were buying Thunder, attached the video footage of him, and said that she would deliver her horse as promised by the end of June, even if she had to make the trip alone. Then she went back to talk to Thunder and let him out into the pasture to enjoy some hours of relaxation and a good roll in the grass. She leaned on the fence for a long time, simply enjoying watching him graze.

Thunder was clearly puzzled as to where all the other horses had gone. As the only "intact" horse in the herd, he'd been the leader. All the other male riding school horses had been geldings. Now he would sometimes stand with his head high and his ears pricked, listening for other horses and sniffing the breeze, in hope of finding another equine in the area.

The five-acre field attached to the school was probably worth more than her house, and she could see a new buyer quickly turning the whole place into a building site for new luxury housing. Their small community was already creeping north toward Tampa, and developers were hovering around any available building plots. The old strict zoning planning regulations had been dramatically slackened in recent years, and to have a horse ranch so close to an urban sprawl was an isolated relic of quieter, calmer days.

Tara decided to count her blessings though. She'd survived COVID where at least half a million other Americans hadn't. She still had a property to sell, and she had her health. Her heart was battered, but the affair with Marcia had freed her to be honest about being a lesbian. Florida wasn't a good place to be gay right now, despite all the thousands of people in the state who shared her sexuality, so maybe she would move away to somewhere more liberal and accepting. The idea of finding a new partner was completely off her radar; Marcia had made her feel totally unlovable. But she wanted to live somewhere where she could be herself, where who she chose to love wasn't an issue.

Ricky had understood. Tara still didn't know why she had talked so openly about her private life. It had all somehow emerged in a kind of blind trust that it would be received kindly. As it had been. Finding out Ricky had been in lesbian relationships too was a nice bonus.

There were fourteen years between them, but maybe her suggestion that they might become friends wasn't so strange after all. She might even be able to help Ricky get over her own sad history of loving a woman who clearly didn't deserve her. Maybe she could help her find a new girlfriend. It was a nice idea, to be of use to someone she had injured so badly in the past.

But now, she had things to do. She picked up the keys from the kitchen counter and went to her elderly horse truck to assess its roadworthiness. It had covered thousands of miles over the last thirty years, and when she was in her late teens and early twenties touring the circuits of the horse shows and competitions, she and her mother had slept in it on many occasions. It was an all-in-one horse truck, not a trailer like more modern versions. It had a front compartment with a bench seat behind which folded out into a small double bed, and a tiny kitchen. They'd had great fun traveling around and cooking supper on a campfire or the tiny gas barbecue.

Her mom had been her greatest supporter and losing her so young, when she was barely fifty and Tara was only twenty-one, had been a great shock. She lost her motivation for top-level competitions and left the show-jumping circuit for more than a year. She lost her place on the US team for the 2004 Athens Olympics as a result. When she returned to serious competitions, she turned from show-jumping to dressage and met Geoff, twelve years her senior, who liked horses, was really attracted to her and was initially happy to act as a co-driver when needed.

The old blue horse truck reminded her of those happier years, and she supposed that once it had performed its final act of delivering Thunder to his new home, then she should sell it too. She wouldn't get much for it, and it would probably be best to trade it in for a cheap car she could drive back to Florida. She looked at the tires and as expected, two of them would need replacing before the trip. She wasn't going to risk injuring Thunder with a blow-out on the freeway.

She decided to take it to the local mechanic where they knew her and would do an honest job servicing it in preparation for the journey. She'd reconciled herself to making the trip alone, so she needed to make sure her vehicle was at least safe on the road.

After she called and arranged to take the horse truck first thing in the morning, she walked Thunder back to his stable and opened a can of soup for dinner. She had little appetite these days, but the thought of Ricky returning the following morning cheered her up.

Maybe Ricky would give her a ride back from the car repair shop, and they could catch breakfast together in one of the budget diners downtown. Then Ricky could ride Thunder, and she would enjoy watching them work out together. She just hoped Ricky wouldn't be in too much pain after a decade of not exercising the unusual muscle combinations needed for horseback riding.

She never wanted Ricky to be hurt again and certainly not by anything she did. She felt a great tenderness for her, and just meeting her again had brought back the five years she had watched her grow from a shy little earnest thing of eleven to a blossoming sixteen-year-old. She was proud to have been Ricky's riding teacher and regretted the lost years since. If she was honest, teaching her to ride had been one of the best achievements of her life.

Tara settled down with the soup then headed to bed for an early night. There was nothing to stay up for.

So much for not caring about sex. Tara woke sweating in the middle of the night. Ricky's voice echoed in her misty mind; "I haven't had sex with anyone in ten years because of you. You've ruined me for life, and I hate you."

What the hell did that mean? She eventually drifted again, but Ricky's sweet lips, soulful eyes, and soft, luscious hair haunted Tara in her next dream. When she woke, it was almost as though she really had had sex with Ricky. Tara had always dismissed therapy as a waste of time, but maybe she should make an appointment to see someone, when she could afford it, of course, which wouldn't be any time soon.

CHAPTER SIX

When Ricky arrived bright and early, Tara could hardly bear to look at her, but she could tell she was pumped up about something. There was an energy about her Tara hadn't seen before, and she was virtually bouncing from foot to foot.

"Before you ride, will you please do me a favor and follow me to the car repair shop?" Tara asked. "I'm taking my horse truck in for some new tires and a service. I'll treat you to breakfast at the Cheerful Chicken as a thank-you."

"Oh yeah, I remember that place," Ricky said. "Downtown, isn't it? Those red plastic seats won't do my saddle sores much good. Is that place still open? It used to be the original greasy spoon."

"Sure is. It still has the best homemade hash browns in the county."

"Of course I'll give you a ride back, but you don't have to buy me breakfast," Ricky said. "I know times are hard."

Tara laughed. "Oh, I think I can afford ten dollars."

"Well, okay, because I want to butter you up. I have something I want to suggest once we've eaten."

Despite all her troubles, Tara felt optimistic and knowing Ricky was gay had fired up her responses. Seeing her, she realized she did find Ricky attractive in real life, not just in a dream, and her insides clenched with desire. She was sure her body language would give her away. "What do you want to ask me?"

Ricky shook her head. "Later, while we're sitting down."

"Okay, follow me." While Ricky tailed her the three miles to the repair shop, Tara turned over the possibilities in her mind. What on earth could Ricky want to ask her? And why would she need buttering up? Not wanting to get carried away, Tara turned on the radio loud to drown out the wild possibilities.

Moments later, she pulled into the shop, dropped off the keys, and approached Ricky's car. She settled into the Camry's passenger seat and reached for the seat belt. "I have to pick up the truck tomorrow. Would you be able to spare the time to drive me?"

Tara guessed that Ricky must think it incredible that she, who had once been popular, now had no friends to call on for help. But that's how it was. As a single divorcee, she'd found she mysteriously was dropped from invitations at the country club, where Geoff still retained many friends. And Marcia hadn't wanted her to have any other friends; she'd stopped her from accepting any social invitations. "Let's go and eat breakfast. I'm starving," she said, shivering at the memory. "I haven't eaten much since I saw you yesterday."

Ricky frowned. "That's not good for you."

Tara smiled at the show of tenderness. "No, it's fine. I was just involved in something and couldn't be bothered. Come on, I'm looking forward to hearing all about your big suggestion."

The eatery was packed with rather noisy groups of people holding breakfast meetings over large plates of eggs, steak, grits, and other calorie-loaded specialties. It had once been featured on Food Network's *Diners, Drive-Ins, and Dives* and had obviously kept its popularity. Tara squeezed past various tables where the diners were overflowing into the side aisles and found a quieter booth in the back. "What do you feel like eating, Ric?"

Ricky thumbed through the extensive menu. "Please don't take this the wrong way, but I'm not into big breakfasts. A bowl of oatmeal and some blueberries and a decaf coffee will be great."

A cheerful-looking server came to them, and she repeated Ricky's order to her.

"And you, ma'am?" the waitress asked.

Tara wasn't at all tempted by the thought of oatmeal—she wasn't a horse. "I'll have the breakfast special, eggs done over easy, and two hash browns."

"Sure thing." She scribbled the order on her pad. "Coffee?"

Tara nodded. "With a side of cream."

"Great. I'll fetch you ladies some water."

"Now, what is it that you want to ask me?" Tara asked after their server pushed her way back through the crowds toward the counter.

Ricky seemed excited simply to be here with her. Tara found her totally endearing, which was ridiculous, but a woman had to own her feelings, even if she had no intention of sharing them.

Ricky looked down and fiddled with her napkin and cutlery. "How about we eat first? After a plate of bacon and eggs you might be sufficiently mellow to agree to what I'm about to suggest."

Tara narrowed her eyes. This was becoming more intriguing by the moment. "Mellow? That's a lovely word. But, come on, spill the beans."

Ricky laid down her fork and sighed. "Okay. I was thinking about your road trip and you having to drive Thunder all the way to Tacoma. It got me wondering how you'll cope on your own."

Tara's stomach dropped. Being here with Ricky had made her temporarily forget how alone she was about to be. "And?"

"*And…*" She looked up and scrunched her nose. "I hit on what I think is the best idea I've had in months."

"You're moving back to Florida permanently!"

Ricky picked up her knife and examined it for smears. "No. Don't tempt me like that. What would you say if I asked you to let me come along with you, to share the driving, and the necessary care and exercising Thunder will need on the journey? I can help you navigate. You know I don't mind doing the messy work either, like mucking him out and carrying water. I'd love to do it."

Tara's mouth fell wide open, but the return of their chirpy waitress delayed her response. She placed glasses of ice water and fresh cutlery on the table. Tara was grateful; if Ricky's fiddling was anything to go by, the ones on the table weren't the cleanest.

"Coffees and food will be along in a minute," the server said.

Ricky grabbed one of the water glasses and took a gulp. "See, I knew you'd hate the idea," she said.

"No, no, that's not it at all," said Tara, slightly amused at

Ricky's apparent hesitation and nerves. "But you've come home to be with your parents, and the last thing I want to do is spoil your vacation."

"This would be part of my vacation. Can you believe I've never been anywhere northwest beyond Missouri? It would be a fantastic adventure. I love camping out. I could bring my tent, the one I used for college and music festivals. I'll explain it to Mom and Dad, and I'm sure they'll understand. It would be completely wonderful."

Ricky spoke the words so fast, Tara could barely keep up. It was as if she had to get them out before her courage failed her. Why did she make Ricky so jumpy? Still, her heart flooded with relief. It was a wonderful offer, and one she certainly didn't want to refuse. But she wanted to make sure Ricky understood what she was letting herself in for. "I would love for you to come. But it's a huge ask. We can't go more than sixty miles an hour, and I reckon it'll take seven days for us to drive to Tacoma, even if we don't take any rest days. Do you think you could cope with my company for so long? I know I have a well-deserved reputation as a hard woman to please, and our past relationship still has a rather large boulder stuck right in the middle of it."

The server came bustling back with a tray laden with food and two large mugs of coffee. Ricky's bowl of oatmeal was large enough to satisfy even Thunder's appetite, and it must've had eight ounces of blueberries piled on top of it. Tara's breakfast, however, was even bigger and looked like enough to feed a trucker. Ricky raised her eyebrows, clearly wondering whether Tara would be able to finish it. But Tara's metabolism had always galloped along faster than the average person's. She might have the frame of a squirrel, but she ate like a wolf.

When they were once again left in peace, Tara asked, "Be honest, what will your parents say? Surely they'll be disappointed if I drag you away as soon as you've come home?"

Ric shook her head. "No, I'm sure they'll be fine, especially when I talk it through with them. My mom said she was pleased that you and I had settled our differences and that I was riding again. I'd want to be home by the Fourth of July weekend though

We're having a whole family get-together."

Tara nodded. "I promise I'll get you home in time for that. When we get back to the ranch, let's plan the route. I have cash in my checking account to cover the fuel, even with the stupidly high prices. Then we need to scout out some RV parks which will accept a horse truck. When I was a kid, I traveled around with my mother every summer but in those days, it was somehow easier."

Ricky mixed the fruit into her oats and bounced on her seat. "I've heard the National Parks have great camping grounds. Maybe we can check to see if we can go through any. And isn't there an online directory about horse ranches across America? People who run liveries or dude ranches would probably let us camp there, and we could let Thunder out to stretch his legs and ride."

Tara began to imagine driving next to Ricky all day and camping with her overnight. Her nipples tightened just thinking about it. The realist in her almost hoped that Ricky would be a crabby and bad-tempered jerk for the entire trip and cure her of her sudden infatuation. Unpleasant as that thought was, it looked increasingly like the only solution.

But more realistically, she hoped that her secret crush might subside as quickly as it had risen and evolve into more manageable feelings of friendly affection, and that she could be of genuine use to Ricky and help her move on from the long-term obsession with the woman who had hurt her. Thrown together night and day, moreover, they were bound to see aspects of each other which would probably repel and appall.

Tara attacked her food with a relish and excitement that was more about Ricky and less about the crispy bacon and tasty runny eggs combo. Between mouthfuls, she said, "Today is Tuesday. We can pick up the box tomorrow and spend Thursday prepping it. How about we aim to leave on Friday morning?"

"Where might we end up on the first day?"

Tara imagined the route in her head. She'd looked at it so many times since the agreed sale that it was practically imprinted there. "I think we can get over into south Georgia. I have a friend with a spread southeast of Atlanta, where we could stay for the first night. She has outdoor pastureland."

"That would be good," said Ricky. "Otherwise, one of us will have to exercise Thunder morning and evening."

"Why do you think I'm pleased you're coming?" asked Tara and winked. *God. I don't wink. When have I ever winked at a woman?* She pointed to Ric's chair. "How's that plastic seat treating your painful muscles?"

"Don't ask," said Ricky. "I hurt all over. I expect you never get this stiff."

Tara shook her head. "Quite the opposite. I've broken most of the bones in my body over the years. You have one knotted-up old lady on your hands." Tara could've kicked herself. Why was everything she was saying and doing so flirtatious? Luckily, Ricky seemed oblivious, though she did seem to think the idea of Tara as an old lady was amusing.

"No, I don't," Ricky said when she'd stopped laughing. "You're not old at all. If I'm as fit as you at forty, I'll be lucky."

Tara accepted the compliment. "Well, I'd like to still know you when you're my age. I'm sure you'll have the same sweet smile you have now. You were a kind child and a bright spark as a teenager, and now I'm sure you're a talented teacher. Tell me about your school and your students. What do you teach?"

"Phys ed. It's what I majored in. When we're on the road, there'll be plenty of time to bore you with my school stories," said Ricky. She shook her head and grinned. "I'm excited to make the road trip with you."

Tara smiled and shoved a forkful of food into her mouth to stop her saying *exactly* how excited she was for the adventure in a *very* different way.

When they'd finished eating and Tara had paid the tab, Ricky drove them back to Meadowlands.

Tara whistled an old country song. "We'll need a pile of CDs to play on the road. Start picking your playlist," she said. "My horse truck has an old CD player, and I'm not sure I'd be able to find the ones Mom played when I was a teenager."

"CDs?" Ricky asked and frowned. "I don't own any CDs. Can you even still buy them? Everything I listen to is streamed from my phone."

Tara tried not to react to being made to feel older than God. If they survived the trip without her making an awful, embarrassing pass at Ricky, it would be a miracle. She'd never been an ugly duckling, but she was most definitely a swan now. There was no point pretending there wasn't danger ahead. The emotional crust on which she walked with regard to Ricky seemed too thin, and the volcano unexpectedly roaring away below was far too close to the surface for comfort. But Tara had never let her head rule her heart, and she wasn't about to start now.

CHAPTER SEVEN

"What are you looking for?" Ricky's mom called to her through the open attic hatch.

Ricky scrabbled about in the roof space with a small flashlight, stumbling over the boxes and crates. "I'm trying to find my old pup tent and sleeping bag. They must be up here somewhere."

"Row took them for Craig when he went camping with the Scouts last year. Sorry, dear. What do you need them for?"

Trust her sister to take her stuff. Some things never changed. Ricky came carefully back down the extended ladder. She had yet to tell her parents about the sudden road trip she was taking, but it was now or never. "Mom, don't panic, but I'm going to ride shotgun with Tara when she takes Thunder to his new home in Tacoma, Washington, and I was hoping to use my old tent."

"When did this happen? I have a whole list of house and yard fix-up jobs I was hoping you'd help me with this month."

Her ever-patient mom sounded disappointed but not angry.

"I know. I'm sorry, Mom. It just came to me last night, so I talked to Tara about it this morning. She can't go all the way to Washington without a co-driver and a groom. It wouldn't be safe, and it would take too long as well for Thunder's comfort. I also thought it might finally put everything to rest, you know? But I'll be back by the fourth, and then I'm all yours for the rest of the summer."

"You really want to become good friends with her?"

"Maybe. Yes, I think I do. She'd make a good friend." Ricky pushed the ladder back up into the roof-space and closed the trapdoor.

"I'm pleased for you. You can probably cope better with her now than you ever could as a youngster. Just don't go falling in love with her again, okay?"

"Mom!" Ricky was stunned by the casual way her mom effectively outed her and floundered about, wondering how best to respond.

"I've known you all your life, remember? And I've seen special girls come and go through your heart since you were eight. None of them ever stayed tucked in there like Mrs. Morris did, so don't kid me you don't still hold a torch for her."

"Mom!" Ricky still couldn't think of anything sensible to say. All her attempts at subterfuge about her gayness had clearly been useless. In a real way, it was a great relief that her mom's world wasn't going to fall apart if she started being honest with her. Did her dad know too?

"Your dad and I, we both understand, honey. We do. So don't worry, we would've fallen over backward in surprise if you'd ever brought a boyfriend home. You can always confide in us as much or as little as you like."

Funny how her mom had just reached into her brain and seen her question.

"But just remember one thing. Tara Morris has been through a rough time over the last few years. She's bound to be vulnerable right now and understandably, she needs someone like you to lean on. Just don't take seriously anything she might say or do on the trip, will you? I'm saying this for your own sake, as well as hers."

Ricky tried to look calm, but she still couldn't bring herself to be totally honest, even knowing how accepting they were. "It's totally fine, Mom. All I want from Tara is friendship. Besides, she virtually told me I'm the polar opposite of her type, so I'm sure there won't be any action in that direction while we're on the road. Okay?" She squirmed a little, not prepared to start discussing sex in any detail with her mom this quickly, if at all. "But I'm so happy to be out to you and Dad at last. I've wanted to talk to you both for years. I just never knew how to bring it up."

Her mom drew Ricky in and kissed her gently. "That's my sweet girl. Just stay safe and enjoy yourself. When are you leaving?"

Ricky smiled. She'd been away too long. She missed this.

She'd missed her mom being sensitive to her every need and emotion. An almost stifling blanket of regret came over her, and she tried to shrug it off. She'd make up for it when she got back. "Friday. As soon as Tara gets her horse truck back from the repair shop, and we've loaded up all the necessary supplies for Thunder. Tara is calling some of her contacts this afternoon, so we can have some horse-friendly places to stay on the route."

"Well, if you're really desperate to use the tent, you'd better call your sister, but she could've passed it on to someone else by now. You know what she's like with helping people out."

Ricky nodded. Yeah, she knew. Looking after people was something they'd all inherited from their parents. She called anyway, just in case, but Row had passed the tent and sleeping bag to a homeless woman and her dog. That didn't bother Ricky, and she enjoyed the chance to chat with her sister for a little while.

Ricky returned to the riding stables the next morning and apologized about not being able to provide a tent for herself as she'd promised.

Tara said, with her characteristic wry smile, "It's not a problem. My mother and I used to bunk together all the time when we were touring the horse shows. There's a double bed, plenty of room. And if I'm being unbearable, you can always go around back, put down a bed roll on the haybales in the spare stall, and sleep next to Thunder. I won't be offended."

She laughed, and Ricky laughed too. But she dreaded the prospect of sleeping next to Tara, hearing her quiet breathing and feeling the warmth of her body right next to hers through the short, sultry summer nights ahead of them. The truck was old, and she was sure there would not be any effective A/C to cool things off either. It would be torture. But to go sleep next to Thunder would look like a deliberate snub and imply she had a problem. Lordy Lord, what should she do? Nothing for now. She simply had to trust in the gods to help keep her hands off Tara. With luck, they'd be too exhausted at the end of each long day's drive to do anything else but fall asleep.

They drove to the car shop and picked up the horse truck, now with its new, safe, expensive front tires.

"Here, take the keys and drive back," Tara said. "I'll follow behind in your car. You need to get used to it before we hit the road with Thunder on board. It has very loose pedals."

Trying not to be too freaked out by the lack of safety of the vehicle, Ricky climbed up into the high seat and fumbled around for the ignition switch. She found it eventually, and then adjusted the mirrors and the driver's seat. Wow, Tara had been right about the pedals. Ricky had to press the accelerator almost four inches before it engaged, and the brake pedal felt equally soft.

She drove the big horse truck down the freeway then exited at the next off-ramp and returned, then drove back through the town for ten minutes before circling into their suburb and finally turning in under the swinging *Meadowlands* sign.

When she brought the vehicle to a stop, Ricky inspected the living quarters just behind the driver's cab, paying particular attention to the double bed which folded out from the wall. It was a standard four foot six, but even if it had been twenty-foot square, she still might not be able to cope. She'd need to turn her back whenever Tara dressed or undressed in front of her. She assumed there would at least be some shower blocks and toilets in the campsites where they'd be staying and so she wouldn't have to watch Tara stripping for a wash.

She spotted the hay and hard feed for Thunder alongside the house. Tara had also stacked a collapsible water bucket and the rest of his gear, like boots to protect his forelegs and ankles, bandages for his legs and his tail, and a soft rug to stop him bruising if he was swung against the padded bars inside the box.

Later they sat together at her kitchen table, and Tara opened up a freshly purchased road map of the whole country. She'd highlighted the entire proposed route. Seeing it in bright yellow and crossing so many state lines solidified the adventure for Ricky. They had an epic expedition ahead of them.

"I'm better with maps, far more than those tiny images you get on smartphones," said Tara. "I think we should take the I-75 north as far as south Georgia. My old friend Bree is expecting us."

FOR LOVE OF THUNDER

"How far is it?" Ricky traced the route with her finger.

"Four hundred and thirty-eight miles. About eight hours' driving, which will be more than long enough for Thunder. We'll take a few breaks along the way. Be sure to pack your swimsuit, Ric. Bree has a pool, and south Georgia is famous for its warm springs."

Natural hot springs weren't going to be the right thing to visit with Tara. Just thinking about it made her hot enough, but she added a swimsuit and towel to her mental list of things to pack. She decided to go shopping to buy some lightweight jodhpurs and new riding boots, along with a few plain polo shirts. If she was traveling as a groom, she wanted to look the part.

They made another plan for Ricky to ride Thunder each morning and by Thursday, she wasn't aching quite so much and had found her natural seat again. Thunder never complained, and he seemed almost cheerful about carrying her on his back. He had no idea of the grueling journey and new life as a stud horse which lay ahead of him. He wouldn't be ridden much, although the new buyer's reply to their email had been full of praise for the video footage they'd sent him, and he seemed more than impressed with Thunder's paces and smooth transitions.

Ricky reminded herself that the whole purpose of the road trip was to take Thunder safely to the other side of the country. It was for love of him she was going, not for love of his owner. But she resolved to do all she could to take equal care of them both. Wanting to make Tara happy, to bring that quirky smile back to her mouth and to her eyes wasn't such a bad ambition, was it?

CHAPTER EiGHT

On Thursday afternoon, Ricky drove ten miles to the Tampa city center, to buy new riding gear. She also withdrew a thousand dollars from her checking account to give to Tara as her first contribution to their travel fund. She didn't expect Tara to fund her expenses like food and site fees as well as her own costs.

The image of that snug little cabin with the double bed in the front of the box came back into her mind, and she worried so much that she splurged on a new pup tent and a summer-weight sleeping bag. She added a new hard hat into her shopping trolley for good measure. It'd been generous of Tara to lend her one, but Ricky never wanted to get so out of practice and so stiff again. Tara had taught her well, and she didn't want to waste that gift. Horseback-riding would always be part of her life from now on.

When she returned to Meadowlands, Tara had almost finished packing the truck.

"I've taken it to fill the gas tank," she said, "and look here, I'm putting a little cashbook in the cab. Each time we fill up, let's record the mileage and the cost per gallon. Then we can see what the whole trip costs."

Ricky smiled at Tara's cute organizational ambition and presented her with the neat roll of fifty twenty-dollar bills.

Tara looked horrified. "No way. I'm not taking your money. I should be paying you for coming."

"Tara, if I don't share the costs, then I'm not coming, so it's your choice. I'm not doing this journey with you and Thunder for any great unselfish reason. It's going to be massive fun, and we're going to have a great time, even though the reason for the trip is sad. I want to pay my own way. Please take the money and use it as and when you need to. Go on! Take it."

Tara scowled and folded her arms, so Ricky rolled up the wad and pushed it firmly down inside the front pocket of Tara's shirt. Tempting as it was, she didn't linger.

But Tara looked even more angry. "I'm not penniless. I accepted your offer to come because I need your horse skills and driving stamina, not to subsidize my trip with your teacher's salary. I don't need this money, okay?"

Ricky scowled straight back. "Right. Then just stick the cash down your boot or wherever, as an emergency backup fund. Let's get to the end of the trip, and if there's any money left, then we can argue again about what to do with it. Maybe we can go further and dip our toes in the Pacific."

Tara gave a theatrical sigh. "I don't remember you being half as stubborn as this. We're clearly not going to get along. Letting you come might turn out to be one of the biggest mistakes of my life."

Ricky began to enjoy this and suppressed a smile. "Fine, I'll just go back home now then, okay? It's a shame, because I've just bought myself a cute little tent, so I don't invade your space in the van. Or should I just drive my car behind you all the way to check you stay on the right road without us ever having to talk to each other at all?"

A whole raft of expressions crossed Tara's face while she seemed to decide how to respond. "Okay, Gates, you win. For now. We'll keep a book of all our expenses and settle up at the end. How does that sound?"

"Perfect." Ricky gave her a mischievous grin, and Tara reached out and pulled her head forward into a neck lock. She quickly released Ricky from the rough embrace though and smoothed down her tousled hair.

"So, why don't you show me all your pretty new purchases you didn't need to buy. I have at least half a dozen riding hats in the tack room. You shouldn't have bought another one."

"We may have an old truck, but if I'm going to be transporting a prince among horses and be a groom for the best riding teacher in Florida, if not the whole country, I need to look the part. I even have new shiny high-top riding boots."

"Big mistake," said Tara. "You'll get terrible blisters."

"No, I won't." Ricky laughed. "But I can see this trip is going to end up being one long argument."

"It won't as long as you let me take charge now and then." Tara sighed and shrugged. "Even if you fight me on everything, it'll still be better than traveling alone. If I have only my company, I'll fall asleep at the wheel in no time. Come on then, Ric, let's finish packing. What time can you get here tomorrow morning? Seven?"

"Earlier, if you like."

Ricky went home happy. She could see a way to be with Tara that wouldn't entail her turning into mush under her boots. Tara clearly liked a bit of a fight now and Ricky was used to difficult and argumentative teens; she'd developed enough self-confidence and assertiveness to take her on.

She packed her backpack, remembering to add a swimsuit and a couple of pairs of shorts to her small collection of clothes, and charged her phone. She slipped in a pair of running shoes and a towel. The leather front seat of the horse truck was likely to be hotter than bare legs could stand.

Her farewell to her parents next morning was short and sweet, involving lots of kisses and promises to keep in touch with regular texts and calls. Her mom, caring as ever, rose with her, made her coffee, and sent her off with a package of leftover sandwiches from Happy Buy.

"Call me every night, if only for a few minutes. I know you're all grown up but thinking about you with Tara and that big horse takes me back to when you were young. I never worried when you were down at the stables because I always trusted Tara to look after you, but I'm concerned about this trip. Two women on such a long journey. Anything could happen."

"Mom, we'll be fine. It's not the Wild West. Tara's a member of AAA. The worst that can hit us will probably be a flat tire."

"I wasn't thinking about the age of the horse truck so much as your other challenges," said her mom quietly.

"Everything's going to be fine." Ricky kissed her and headed out for Tara's place.

Thunder was dancing on his toes and full of beans as she mounted him and started to circle the riding school. After a few minutes of walking to stretch out his back muscles and ease him into movement, she nudged him forward, and they cantered around the manège for almost half an hour, changing legs and direction every few circuits.

Thunder had spent most of his life in the disciplined environment of sandy riding schools, training grounds, and racetracks, and Ricky hoped that his new home would include freedom to range over wider pastures. In that respect, Ricky saw Tara's experience as similar to her horse's. For the last fifteen years, she had been teaching youngsters to ride, day in and day out, penned in within the confines of a riding school and with only a few pupils who had shown sufficient enthusiasm and talent that she could foster beyond the basics. Many children would have loved to come riding if their parents could have afforded it. But the increased costs now meant that it was strictly for the very wealthy.

Now that she had no business to run, Tara would at last be free to do something else. Ricky really hoped she would also find happiness with someone better than monstrous Marcia, someone who would appreciate her beauty and her talents. She tried hard to be unselfish about it and vowed that if Tara met anybody on their road trip who looked remotely worthy of her, she wouldn't stand in her way. Loving someone as much as she did meant that she had to want the best for Tara, not for herself.

That sounded fine in theory. She just hoped she wouldn't have to put her best intentions into practice any time soon. Then the woman in question strode out of the house and stood by the corral watching Ricky ride past.

"You're daydreaming again, Ric! I can tell, and so can Thunder. He's been waiting for some aids from you to tell him what comes next. See how his ears are twitching back and forth?"

"You're right. Sorry, Tara." Ricky pulled up and walked Thunder over toward her. "I just wanted to give him a good workout, but I got lost in thought."

"Who were you thinking about? Was it your unobtainable

lover, the woman you were telling me about last Sunday?"

"Yes, in fact I was." Ricky hid in plain sight. It was far easier than lying.

Tara looked into her eyes. "Forget her. From what you say, she's not worth it, Ric, trust me."

"How would you know?" Ricky asked, half amused that Tara was belittling herself without realizing it. "I think she is, worth it, I mean. I know I don't stand a chance with her, but she's worth a hell of a lot more to me than you might understand. She's completely wonderful."

Tara looked rather downcast and shrugged. "I guess I'm in the wrong for a change. Now, can I have one last ride on my boy before we pack up and leave?"

"Of course." Ricky jumped down and handed over the reins. Thunder nodded his head up and down and tried to nibble at Tara's hair. They loved each other so much, it was almost painful to watch, knowing they would soon be separated.

She watched Tara effortlessly mount up and swing away, and then she pulled out her phone to take pictures. Tara wasn't the only one who enjoyed seeing Thunder in action, but Ricky took a video for the even more important reason of catching Tara riding. It meant that she would have something of her forever, something she could treasure when they eventually parted, as they inevitably would.

CHAPTER NINE

Thunder looked alert and interested as Tara led him to the front yard and showed him the horse truck, his home for the next week or so. He'd perked up as soon as she'd taken the leg bandages into his stall and wrapped them around his pasterns and fetlocks, then added soft traveling boots. He'd be warm wearing all this paraphernalia in summer, but his legs would be fully protected in case of a fall, or if God forbid, they were involved in an accident.

He probably thought they were heading out to a show. She wished she could explain what was about to happen. But maybe it was for the best that she couldn't. Best that he couldn't share her misery for the next three thousand miles.

Like the star he was, Thunder loaded easily into one of the compartments in the back of the box. Tara turned on an old transistor radio and placed it in one of the storage compartments in front of him. Music always seemed to soothe him, and the voices would keep him company. She closed up the back ramp and went to grab her kitbag from the kitchen, lock up the house, and find Ricky. She'd stayed behind to muck out Thunder's loose box for the final time and push a wheelbarrow full of the last load of droppings and straw over to the muckheap at the end of the property. When Tara returned in a couple of weeks, she wouldn't have to face too many reminders of her lost boy. All she would see would be a clean, empty stall, not his droppings still hidden in the straw.

It was typical of Ricky to be so thoughtful and to go the extra mile. Driving with her would be the one silver lining to the clouds hovering over the forthcoming trip. Ricky had said she wanted them to have a great time on the road. But right now, Tara wasn't certain she could ever feel happy again.

The thermos and picnic box on the kitchen counter reminded her to make up a decent amount of coffee for them both and to take the sandwiches she'd prepared for their lunch. The simple tasks kept her from focusing on losing Thunder.

Ricky came up behind her and washed her hands thoroughly in the sink beside her. "Have we packed the bucket, broom, and mop to keep his box clean as we move along?" she asked.

"Of course. I've gone right through the check list. The coffee is ready as well, to put into the thermos. Use the bathroom, and then let's go. Thunder is already waiting for us."

Tara watched Ricky go into the downstairs bathroom and once again thanked her lucky stars that Ric seemed well on her way to forgiving Tara for her actions ten years ago. She vowed to keep telling Ricky how beautiful she was and how well she rode. Both were heart-achingly true. The way she moved and spoke and the way her eyes danced when she was feeling happy entranced Tara more and more each day. She loved looking at her, at her generous, sunny smile, and her short mop of wavy hair, which curled so attractively around her ears, skirting her collar. It was a deep chestnut color, not so different from Thunder's own coat.

Ricky had delicate features and a much softer face than Tara. Her mother had once explained the origins of her angular bones and high cheekbones, saying they were inherited from a Cherokee ancestor of her father. People had called her good-looking when she was young, but she didn't rate herself highly anymore.

Marcia had managed to make her feel ugly and boyish. Even when they were lying naked in bed together, Marcia would perpetually come out with small insults—that her breasts were too small was a favorite jibe—and she never made Tara feel anything like a goddess.

When Ricky was a teenager, Tara had known she had a normal teenage crush on her. It was impossible not to see it. But she assumed Ricky must now have grown way past that, into a woman with far more sensible tastes. Ten years of ignoring the existence of her former teacher had certainly sent that message to Tara loud and clear. And now she had her own middle-aged and even more senseless crush in return. She wondered who Ricky's secret long-term love object was and decided instinctively that if they ever met, she'd hate the woman on sight. She was sad for Ricky's sake that she still seemed smitten by someone so unworthy.

After Ricky emerged from the bathroom, Tara moved in herself and then changed her clothes for something clean and reasonably decent. Tara pulled down all the blinds against the unremitting Florida sun, turned off the water, and closed the inner doors. They were finally set to leave.

Tara took the first shift behind the wheel. Ricky had stowed their luggage neatly behind their seats and sat on a towel on the passenger side of the big bench seat in the cab. They turned out onto Route 75, north out of Tampa, and joined the traffic heading toward the border with Georgia.

Ricky stretched out her legs and leaned back against the worn leather seatback. Tara kept her eyes on the road, but she could tell Ric was looking at her rather intently, and it made her uneasy. "Do I have peanut butter on my cheek from breakfast?" she asked.

"Sorry!" Ricky jumped a little and fixed her eyes on the road. "I didn't mean… I mean—"

"Yes?" Tara was amused by Ricky's unexpectedly flustered response.

"I just enjoy looking at you."

"Oh. Right." Tara had no idea what to say to that and decided to ignore it.

Ricky wriggled slightly in her seat. "Sorry. It's just your profile is very, you know…watchable. You must've heard that many times before. I've never sat to the right of you like this before, so I never noticed. I won't mention it again."

"Since we don't have a DVD player, all I can offer is my normal grumpy face for your amusement." Tara smiled, turning slightly to look at Ricky. "But I have to say, being with you does cheer the world up for me. Maybe you'll even manage to cure me of my miserable tendency to scowl and snap at everybody."

"Eyes forward, Mrs. Morris!" Ricky said, as if they were about to smash into another car. "I'll just shut up now, okay?"

Ricky was clearly embarrassed, and as much as she looked

super cute, Tara thought she should help her out of her hole. "We do have music. Pull out the CDs and choose something. Something road trippy."

Ricky scrabbled about in the old string bag of discs and pulled out one by k.d. lang, who remained a firm favorite with Tara.

"This album is called *Sing it Loud*. What's this like? Is she any good?"

"You've never heard of k.d. lang? I think she's the best singer in North America. She's Canadian from the plains of Manitoba or some place."

Tara couldn't believe Ricky hadn't heard of her. It emphasized their age difference more than anything else. "Play it," she said. "Consider it the beginning of your musical education."

"She definitely looks butch," said Ricky as she looked at the cover.

"My God. She was, no, *is* iconic. The first openly gay woman singer to successfully invade the red-necked ranks of country music. Haven't you even heard her version of Leonard Cohen's "Hallelujah"? What about "Constant Craving"?"

"Nope. I'll put her on then, okay?"

"Please do. I see I have a lot of musical coaching to undertake on this trip."

Ricky laughed, and they got over the slight awkwardness surrounding her admiration of Tara's imperfect profile. They pressed on through the northern countryside of Florida, keeping mainly to the right outside lane, and Ricky marveled at all the trucks loaded with citrus fruits passing them.

"I remember there used to be an orange-juice processing plant toward Gainesville," said Ricky. "It's a horrible, smoke-belching factory. I almost feel sorry for all the oranges going to get squashed there."

Tara laughed. "How can you feel sorry for an inanimate object?"

Ricky shrugged. "I can feel sorry for anything: an orange, a tree, even you."

Tara gave Ricky a sidelong glance, and Ricky winked. "I'll let you have that one. But orange season was over back in early

April. That fruit must've been in cool storage for months. But when we get up into Georgia, the early peaches will be coming in. Have you ever had peach pie? It's to die for."

"Tell me again where we're heading," Ricky asked.

Tara wondered why Ricky hadn't responded but didn't press in case it had something to do with Ricky's unrequited love. The last thing Tara wanted to do was have a conversation about her again. "My friend lives near Juliette. It's a small town close to Macon, home of Otis Redding. It's where they filmed *Fried Green Tomatoes*."

"Is that another song I should know to continue my education?"

Tara couldn't believe her ears. "Where have you been living, on another planet? *Fried Green Tomatoes at the Whistle Stop Café*. It was coded, certainly, but it was definitely a lesbian movie. It was based on a book by Fannie Flagg, and it really spoke to my generation."

Ricky still looked blank.

This was no good at all. How could Ricky call herself a lesbian and not know all this stuff? "Kathy Bates. Jessica Tandy. Mary Stuart Masterson."

Ric shook her head. "They're just random names to me. Sorry. I've never had much time or inclination to watch films or television. I've been too busy either coaching or training. Even the modern stuff has mostly passed me by."

Tara felt about ninety, despite Ric's reassurances, and decided to change the subject entirely. "So tell me about your own girlfriends then. Tell me about the sort of women you like."

"You can't honestly expect me to talk to you about that."

Ricky sounded so genuinely shocked that Tara gathered she must have misjudged their level of friendship and had way overstepped the mark. "Sorry, honey. Let me put a different question out there then. I want to learn about the current scene for you younger women. Who are your heroes? Who do you follow? If you don't want me to know about your private life, tell me about the rest of it."

"It's not like that," Ricky said and touched Tara's forearm briefly. "I need to adjust to this new reality, where I can talk to openly to you about sex. I know you were wonderfully honest with me, but I'm still shy. Just give me time, okay?"

"Of course. I'm sure I can squirm all your deepest and darkest secrets out of you by the end of the trip."

There was a big fat silence now from the seat next to her. She'd probably gone far too far again.

Ricky coughed. "I really like this album. She's good, isn't she? I see what you mean."

And they both sat back and let the haunting twang of k.d. lang's syrup-laden voice entertain them in companionable silence. Tara still knew nothing about Ric's taste in women, and that bothered her. Ricky might favor big-busted, blond, bubbly types. Under ordinary circumstances. Ricky would probably give Tara a wide berth. But these weren't ordinary circumstances.

CHAPTER TEN

Tara pulled into a large rest area near Jennings, just before the Florida/Georgia state line, and drew the horse truck to a halt in a quiet corner away from other trucks and RVs. "We need more gas, and I thought it was time we checked on Thunder and maybe switch drivers?"

"Sure." Ricky was glad of a break from being a well-behaved passenger and jumped down onto the worn paving of the asphalt lot. They both walked to the back of the box and cautiously lowered the tail gate. Thunder looked around at them and snorted as if to say, "Well, that sure was boring. Are we there yet?"

"Not quite, boy," said Tara, almost as if she knew what his twitching ears had been asking. "How have you been doing back here?"

Ricky heard quiet music playing from inside the storage locker. "You've given him some music?"

"Yes, it always seems to soothe horses. I'm going to back him out and walk him around for a few minutes. Could you put another wedge of hay into his net and check his water?"

"Sure." She watched Tara and Thunder stroll away in the bright midday sunshine and thought how good they looked together. He was bending his head toward Tara and nuzzling her as they headed for the trees surrounding the large gas station complex. The woods stretched all around them for miles.

She decanted some more water into Thunder's traveling bucket and replenished his hay net, hung high above, so there was no danger he could catch his foot in it. Then she waited for them to return.

When Tara emerged from the trees, she seemed subdued, and Ricky could tell the reality of selling Thunder was beginning to get to her. They re-boxed him and closed the ramp. When they drove over to the fuel pumps and put in another ten gallons of diesel, Ricky winced at the price.

Tara pulled out her little red cash book and made an entry. "It's gone up even from yesterday."

Ricky wondered what she could do to cheer Tara up. "Do you want to eat our lunch here or as we drive?"

"Let's eat as we go." Tara motioned to the cab. "You drive, and I'll take care of the catering. There are two chilled Cokes in the cooler in the living cabin."

Ricky wrinkled her nose. She didn't want ten spoonfuls of sugar, thanks. "Any chance of a diet Coke?"

"Sure."

Ricky climbed into the driver's seat and adjusted the mirrors slightly, while Tara climbed in the other side, a picnic bag in front of her.

"I made subs. Ham salad, okay?"

"Sounds good. Thanks."

Ricky was happy to be behind the wheel, and they entered the flow of traffic heading north. Ricky ate as she drove and turned the stereo back on to replay k.d. lang's album.

"Her voice is sultry, isn't it? But smoky as well. I can tell why you like her."

"What do you like to listen to? Expand my mind into the current music scene," Tara said as she ate her sub roll more slowly than usual.

"Okay. When we stop next time, I'll pull together a playlist on my phone. There are loads of current lesbian recording artists, some I really like."

"Like? Give me some names."

"How about Girl in Red? Janelle Monae? Sophia Wang? And if you like country, there's Lily Rose."

Tara looked completely blank at all the names.

"Not a good feeling, is it?" Ricky asked, enjoying the turnabout in knowledge. "I think we can educate each other on this trip."

"Yes, maybe. I don't know any of the artists you've just mentioned. To take a new view of everything is always good. Just being alongside you is rejuvenating somehow. You have such a fresh energy, so different from my own right now."

Tara seemed to look a little brighter, but the sorrow was still deeply etched in her face.

"Feed on it then. Hook your wagon onto mine, and I'll do my best to cheer you up. I don't like to see you so down. You should be flying."

"It's been a bad time, I can't deny that. But I want to be happier, I really do."

"Let's help each other have a good time then. You're so far ahead of me in nearly everything. It feels good that there are some things I can teach you—in music, I mean." Ricky had so much to offer that Tara might never be interested in, sure. But as their relationship deepened, she would get to know Ricky as an adult, an active lesbian woman for whom sex would always be a central part of any relationship.

As soon as they crossed into Georgia, the heat seemed to grow even more suffocating and gaps between the trees grew smaller until they were driving through thick woodland. There were lakes on either side of the freeway, and the air was damp. Sweat began to drip down Ricky's neck. She pushed some errant hair from her eyes.

"I'm sorry. The A/C is shot, isn't it? I should have thought to add it to the things I needed them to service before we left. Let me help."

She reached across with a small disposable wipe and gently ran it across Ricky's neck from ear to ear. It tickled slightly, but the faint scent of the cologne was attractive, and Tara's touch stirred Ricky's arousal. She shivered slightly, flexing her shoulders.

Tara smiled and apologized. "Sorry, honey. Did that feel too cold against your skin?"

"No, it was nice. Just right."

Tara pulled another wipe from the package. "Here, take this and smooth it over both your palms. It will cool you down."

Ricky took the wipe then handed it back to Tara. "Can you help? I can't take my hands off the wheel."

Tara wiped her hands one at a time with the sweet-smelling wipes and seemed somewhat reluctant to let them go. The touch of her hand was electric.

"Thanks, they were beginning to stick to the old steering wheel. Can I have that Coke now?"

"Sure."

"We need to keep drinking water as well. It's so easy to forget and become dehydrated."

Tara unscrewed the lid and passed a bottle over before opening her own. They drank the soda.

"I've decided that even my addiction to k.d. lang has been sufficiently fueled." She put in a CD of Emmylou Harris, and the mood lightened.

After another hour, they swapped seats again, and Tara turned off the I-75 to drive toward Juliette. Tara had given her the address, so Ricky put it into Google Maps to guide them to their first stopover.

They would soon complete the first leg of their strange, intimate journey. Ricky wondered if Tara felt anything like she did, becoming more uncontrollably attracted toward her companion by the minute, and not knowing what the heck to do about it. Of course she didn't. No one, let alone Tara, could possibly be so misguided.

"I think it's up ahead," she said, keeping her eyes on the phone screen.

"You're right," said Tara. "I recognize the signs."

Ricky sighed deeply. If Tara *could* recognize the signs she was giving out, this trip would be infinitely more fun.

CHAPTER ELEVEN

A t last!"

Ricky was relieved when Tara turned into the driveway of what looked like an extensive estate. A circular driveway took them to a large two-story house with wings spreading out on each side, and an adjoining guest wing on the right.

"Have you been here before?" Ricky asked.

"Once," said Tara. "But it was more than a decade ago. Bree's husband, Rob, was in grad school with my ex. But I've stayed friends with Bree since. Back in the day, I coached their daughters for the show-jumping circuit, until they grew up and lost interest. Bree said we'd be welcome to stop over. But Rob has run off with someone else."

Ricky was secretly relieved. She preferred just to be in the company of women if they were to stay with strangers. "Thunder will be relieved to be out of the box."

"He's not the only one."

Tara pulled up and gave a soft toot on the horn. The front door opened to reveal a substantial woman in her late fifties, suntanned, with bright bottle-blond hair and wearing sandals below a loose kaftan.

They walked toward her, and Tara was immediately enveloped in a generous hug. Ricky hung back.

Bree then turned to her with open arms. "You never said she was such a beauty, Tara. Come here, kid, and let me give you a hug. I'm Bree, and you're both more welcome than a shower in springtime. It's been far too long, Tara honey, really it has. Let me show you where you can unload and give your horse some freedom for the night. Then we can share a few drinks and chill by the pool."

Ricky was embarrassed that Tara had been briefing Bree about her and wanted a few minutes alone to regain her composure. There was a stable block a hundred yards to the right of the property, with a generous pasture running alongside some woods. Ricky offered to drive the horse truck across to it while Tara and Bree followed on foot. She settled uncomfortably into the cab, her shirt stuck to her back with perspiration from the long hours they'd spent on the road. She couldn't wait to shower and cool off her inappropriate feelings about Tara. Ricky pushed the motor back into drive and heard Thunder moving his feet around in his stall. He was obviously getting restless and eager to be released. It had already been such a long hot journey for him, and there were so many more days ahead.

Tara had Thunder out of the truck in no time, hitched his halter rope to Bree's fencing post, and then began to relieve him of his traveling boots, leg and tail bandages, and light rug. He stamped his feet and shook himself, clearly happy to be out of all the gear. Ricky began to roll the bandages up again neatly ready for the following day.

"Here, let him run free in the paddock," Bree said. "I've already filled the drinking trough up with fresh water."

Tara walked Thunder into the enclosure, turned him back toward the closed gate, and unclipped his head collar. "Here you are, boy. Five-star accommodation for the night. Have a good roll and enjoy yourself."

He stood for a moment, sniffing the air as though he was getting his bearings, then he lowered his head and began cropping the sweet grass in the meadow as though he'd always lived there.

Tara came back to join them. "Well, we've made it, Ric. Day one accomplished and only seven to go."

She gave Ricky's neck a squeeze to relieve the tension there, and on her shoulders, a move which Bree observed with apparent interest. She leaned into it for a moment and then casually moved away from the embrace.

"Let's get you women a cool drink," Bree said.

She led them across her pristine lawns. A water sprinkler whirred gently in the background. Ricky looked at her phone as she walked. "We've covered just over four hundred miles because we came up the I-75. It says it would have been shorter if we'd gone cross-country, but some of those back roads might have been pretty rough going."

"You're the navigator," said Tara. "I'm leaving it to you to plot our route each day from here on. I know I marked the map, but let's take the odd detour if it leads to quieter country."

Ricky looked back at Thunder and smiled. He looked happy. "You think Thunder is going to care whether or not we take the scenic route?"

"I'm sure he will. The freeways are full of fumes and the constant noise and vibration of passing trucks. He'd love more peace."

"I'll do my best," said Ricky. "I'll try to find somewhere nice for him to get exercise along the way. If you give me the list you have of possible horse-friendly places, and I'll call ahead each morning."

"Well, I think you're both real brave going all that distance with a horse." Bree tugged at Tara's sweat-soaked shirt. "Maybe you'd like to take a shower then we can all chill in the swimming pool with a cold drink. Nobody uses it any more except me."

"Our bags are still in the truck," Tara said. "I'll go back and get them."

"No, let me," said Ricky quickly. Before Tara could argue, she sprinted back to the horse truck to pull out their two small suitcases and even smaller backpacks. When she caught up to them again, Tara and Bree seemed to be talking about something serious.

"So Rob has left for good, just like Geoff? I'm so sorry, Bree. How are you doing all alone out here?"

Ricky joined them, but it didn't stop the personal nature of their conversation.

"Yep, nothing like the power of a bad example," Bree said and huffed. "He's moved to Atlanta. Told me this place was way too quiet without the girls, and he wanted some fun before he got too old. He remarried earlier this year to a young physical therapist who treated him when he damaged his knee playing golf. She can't be more than thirty, and he's going on sixty-seven."

Tara rubbed Bree's upper arm in sympathy. "I don't really blame Geoff for leaving me. I never had any enthusiasm, you know, for the physical side. But you have two daughters. How have they taken seeing their dad marrying someone nearer their age than his?"

Bree shrugged. "They hated him at first, but you know girls and their fathers. Rob managed to charm them, and they see him regularly now. They're away at college most of the year, building their own lives. I'm getting used to living alone, and I quite like it. I love this place, and I have my dogs for company."

As if on cue, two spaniels rushed out of the door and enthusiastically jumped up to lick everyone they could reach. Ricky gave Tara her luggage and waited to be directed to where she'd be spending the night.

"I've put you both in the guest wing," said Bree. "You have adjoining rooms, with a shared bathroom. I wasn't sure, you know, how things are between you." She tilted her head and grinned. "And whether you wanted to sleep in the same bed or not."

Ricky didn't know if she or Tara was the most embarrassed that Bree might presume they were together. Tara simply laughed it off.

"No, honey, I wouldn't be so forward as to ask Ricky to share my bed, not just yet. She hasn't been on speaking terms with me for ten years, but I am trying to wheedle myself back into her affections. I couldn't help noticing she's bought a one-girl tent and a sleeping bag for places where we can't get rooms."

"I…I didn't mean…" Ricky went hot with shame at the thought of Tara catching on to why she'd bought the pup tent. But more than that, Tara was thinking she might ask her to bed down with her in the future? Mind-blowing.

Tara smiled and put her hand on Ricky's shoulder. "Shh, no need to explain, Ric. I totally understand. Bree, two rooms will be great. And Ric, honey, why don't you take the shower first? I'm going to sit out front on the porch and chill for a while."

"How about a nice cold beer to help, then?" Bree went over to her fridge and pulled out a couple of bottles. "I'll join you. I want to hear all about Geoff's departure and why you need to sell Thunder. I bet you're more broken up about that than losing your ex."

"There's no comparison, Bree, none at all. Husbands can be bought for two cents, but parting with Thunder is truly breaking my heart."

Ricky backed away into the guest suite, only too happy to hide her blushes. She took a short, cool shower and changed into a light tank top and a pair of shorts over her swimsuit. If there was a chance to swim in Bree's pool before dinner, she would take it. After a few moments stretching out her weary shoulder muscles, she made a quick call to her mom to say they'd arrived safely in south Georgia.

"How's the trip going so far?" her mom asked, a slight note of concern in her voice.

"Fine, absolutely fine. We're staying with a friend of Tara's, somewhere near the place where they made a film about green tomatoes."

Her mom laughed. "I remember that one well. Kathy Bates was wonderful. She smashed up some bimbo's car in the opening scene. It is an iconic lesbian film. You should watch it."

Ricky raised her eyebrows. "Mom!" Was she now going to have to listen to unending lesbian-friendly comments for the rest of her life? "I'd better go. I'll try and call you every evening. Love you, Mom."

She heard Tara enter the room next door and put her head around the door. "The bathroom's free. Thanks for giving me first dibs."

"It was the least I could do," Tara said. "You earned it. I can already see there's no way I could've made this trip without you. You're a star."

Tara stood close to her in the narrow doorway.

"Don't be too sure. I'm no saint," said Ricky. "Wait till you catch me at my worst when we're tired and hot, and we don't have a wonderful hostess like Bree to look after us. It's early days yet."

Tara reached up and pushed Ricky's hair back from her face

with both hands, then gave her ear a little pinch. "Don't worry, Ric. I know you're no saint. You've been sulking for ten years, God damn it. But you're back again now, and I agree we should have a good time on this trip. Well, as good a time as we can on such a sad mission."

Ricky looked into Tara's smoldering dark eyes and wanted to kiss her so bad, just as she had at their reunion at Meadowlands. She managed to control herself and exhaled, gently blowing upward, so her annoying curls lifted off her forehead and no longer needed help from Tara's gentle fingers. "I'm sure we'll have some adventures. Enjoy your shower. Will I see you in the pool?" she asked, moving back slightly.

Their eyes locked for a second, before Tara looked away. "We will. And I'll join you for a swim shortly, don't worry."

Bree was already in the swimming pool when Ricky stepped through the double doors onto the wide patio. She floated around on an inflatable chair with a convenient cup holder in which she'd deposited a large plastic tumbler of white wine. She wore a white swimsuit splattered with large red roses, not something Ricky would ever have chosen, but on Bree it looked kind of glamorous.

"Come and join me, honey." She waved Ricky over and indicated a poolside table on which there was a variety of iced drinks. "Fix yourself a drink first though. There's beer, wine, or a Bellini. I've made up a pitcher."

Ricky removed her tank top, pants, and sandals and left them on a chair. Then she poured herself a peach Bellini over ice and carried it down the shallow steps into the pool. The two spaniels were now lying flat out under the oleander trees, snoozing in the shade, and bees were buzzing through the bougainvillea bushes.

"This is so great! Thanks, Bree." She waded through the turquoise water as far as Bree's floating chair and then sank below the surface to submerge her shoulders. The cool water was absolute bliss after the intense heat of the late summer afternoon.

Bree smiled at her obvious delight at being in the water. "Just what you two girls need after such a long drive, I'm sure."

The pool wasn't deep, only a level five feet or so, and Ricky stood on the pool floor and leisurely sipped her drink as Bree bobbed lazily around next to her.

"Tara will be out shortly," Ricky said.

Bree nodded. "It's good of you to have agreed to come with her on this long trip, honey. Tara told me all about it, how you offered even though you'd come home to see your family for the summer."

"It was no sacrifice," said Ricky. "I'm pleased to help, and I'm excited. There's lots of the country I've never seen. And I love Thunder. I remember him from when I was a kid, and he's still just as wonderful."

"I hope I didn't offend you suggesting you and Tara were an item."

Ricky shook her head, gulped down the rest of her Bellini, and set the glass down on the side of the pool. Then she did a little back flip into the water and swam a couple of lengths. It cooled her off sufficiently to give her the courage to swim back toward Bree and try again at a less cringe-worthy conversation.

"You have a neat technique going on there," Bree said as Ricky emerged from the water, droplets shaking off her hair.

"I should hope so. I teach swimming, well, most sports, so I should be able to crawl." Ricky grinned and lifted herself out of the water to sit on the pool edge beside the floating chair.

"Not horseback-riding though?" Bree asked. "Tara said you were once her star pupil."

Ricky had no idea how to respond to that. Had Tara also mentioned that it was her behavior and insults that had stopped Ricky from riding for ten long years? She recalled Tara's words. *"You've been sulking for ten years, God damn it."* Was that true? Was some blame for their shredded friendship due to her own stubbornness? She'd thought of herself as the wronged victim for so long, any other interpretation of their ruptured relationship had never entered her head. Tara had tried to apologize and make up; her mom had emphasized that more than once.

So maybe Ricky's own stubbornness had blocked off what might have been a reconciliation years ago. She banked that thought and decided not to dwell on it. It was too sensitive.

"You know, what you said before, about misunderstanding our relationship?"

"Yes, honey."

"How do you know Tara is gay? When did she tell you? She told me a few things about it before we set out but said she hadn't explained to anyone else the real reason for her divorce."

Bree laughed. "Tara didn't need to tell me. Her body language when they visited here said it all. She could hardly bear her husband to touch her. I gave them the guest suite when they came, and there was no way they weren't going to use both rooms. Only one person in that marriage was enamored with Geoff Morris, and it sure wasn't his wife. Then I heard Geoff mouthing off to Rob as well, saying his wife liked playing around with other women. He made a joke of it, used a vulgar expression. That's when I decided I disliked him."

"Oh, I see."

"Yes, it wasn't a nice thing for him to joke about, but I could easily imagine how Tara might well be gay. Their marriage was heading nowhere. Whereas with you…"

"What?"

"It's plain to see; Tara can't keep her eyes off you. I've sensed something hot running between you since you arrived."

The quickfire analysis stunned Ricky. Bree sure did shoot from the hip. What could she possibly say in response, other than pretend that the woman was way off course? She'd never been a gifted liar. She'd better say something though, because she couldn't very well jump in the water again and do another few turns around the pool just to avoid answering. That would look too obvious.

"You're wrong about us, I'm afraid, Bree. After ten years apart, Tara and I hardly know each other. We're making the road trip because of Thunder. He's brought us together, and we're committed to the journey for him, not for each other."

Bree smiled knowingly. "Sure, Ricky, if you say so. My mistake. And I'm sorry if I upset you. If you're not with Tara, I bet you have a girlfriend waiting for you."

"Not anymore. I split with my last girlfriend six months ago."

Bree smirked, and Ricky realized she'd fallen straight into that little trap. She'd just outed herself to Bree, floating about in her plastic chair, all innocence and peroxided bonhomie.

Bree chuckled. "Don't let my big mouth bother you, honey. When you get to my age, you tend to call everything as you see it. Now, get me another drink, if you wouldn't mind. There's a sauterne, the open bottle's over in the ice bucket."

Ricky grasped the opportunity to move away from Bree's all-seeing gaze. She grabbed the proffered plastic tumbler and went to pour her hostess a new drink. It was almost a relief to see Tara walking across the yard toward them. She stopped by the drinks table, a vision with a lithe tanned body in a high-cut black swimsuit. Ricky averted her eyes and looked at the drinks table. "Would you like a Bellini?"

"No, thanks, they're far too sweet for me. I'll take some of that white wine, thanks."

Ricky kept her eyes firmly on the bottle she was pouring from. She could sense Tara's body heat, even after a cool shower. "I'll bring it to you in the pool," she said, trying to get Tara as far away from her as possible.

"Enjoyed swimming in the pool?" Tara asked. "Your hair's soaking."

"Hm. It was great."

Tara didn't move away but reached across and drew her finger along the back of Ricky's neck, catching the drops of water falling from her hair. It was just a tiny gesture, but it fired Ricky up with hot lust and made her shiver. She looked up fiercely and caught Tara's eye. "Bree was convinced we were lovers. We have to set her straight."

"Do we?"

"Tara, don't tease me. You know I'm not..." She wanted to say that she wasn't strong enough to cope with how she felt about Tara but fell into silence.

"Interested? I know you're not, sweetie. And maybe you'll probably never trust me again." Tara sighed. "But I hope by the end of the trip, you might begin to like me at least. It's getting rather cramped, squashed up here in the doghouse."

She sounded so funny, Ricky laughed. Tara had broken through the awkwardness, and she could relax. "Of course I like you, Mrs. Morris. I like you a lot. And no way are you in the doghouse anymore. I'm just having to learn to see you as a friend and not my brilliant but aloof teacher. Here, take your wine, and that one's for Bree. I'm going to pour myself a second Bellini. I love peaches, and I don't mind prosecco."

"I must remember that," said Tara and walked away, a glass of white wine in each hand.

Ricky could have sworn Tara gave a slight sashay to her hips as she went. Oh hell, if Tara was going to start teasing her, how would she survive? The hazard of a deep, dark bog of unrequited love lay ahead of her, one she was determined to avoid at all costs.

They stayed in or around the pool until the shadows from the tall cottonwood trees lengthened, and the evening drew in. Bree fixed them chicken parmesan with a spinach salad for supper. But by nine thirty, it was proving impossible for Ricky to keep her eyelids open. "Sorry, I think I'll have to turn in. I'm so tired."

"No problem," said Tara. "I'm going out to check on Thunder and won't be long myself. Goodnight, Ric, sleep well."

"I'll walk the dogs out with you," said Bree.

"Thanks again for everything," Ricky said to Bree before retiring to her room. As Ricky prepared for bed, she could see the two women with the spaniels at their heels strolling off together in the moonlight toward the stable block. They seemed to be having quite an animated conversation, but she couldn't hear a word. She hoped it wasn't about her and Tara again.

As soon as her head hit the pillow, she drifted into an exhausted sleep, hoping her dreams wouldn't include Tara. Hope was a dangerous luxury though.

CHAPTER TWELVE

I'm taking us all out for breakfast," announced Bree early the following morning as Tara emerged from her bedroom in search of some coffee.

"Oh?"

"Yes. We can't have Ricky visit Juliette without sampling our famous fried green tomatoes, can we?"

Tara walked over to the open kitchen door and was more than relieved to see Thunder still safely in his pasture. She whistled to him, and he pricked up his ears and snickered back to her. She'd never had a horse like him, and she was sure she never would again. He really was her best friend. He was her *only* friend really. Yet again she cursed her own stupidity to be reduced to such a dire financial situation that she had to sell him to survive. She'd let him down so badly.

Something else as well had happened overnight to lower her spirits. Just as she was sinking into a deep sleep, her phone had pinged. She focused her vision and had the nasty shock of seeing Marcia's name flashing in bold for a second time. Her first text had come when they'd stopped for a break in north Florida and even though she hadn't opened it, seeing Marcia's name had made her sad and anxious. Tara had turned off her phone at once and thrown it across the room. What the hell did Marcia want after two years? It left fear in her mind and made her heart race. It also prevented her sleeping again until well past two a.m.

"Here, I've made a fresh brew," Bree said and handed Tara a cup of coffee. "Why don't you go on a trail ride with your horse before we go out to the café? There are some fine forest trails all around here you can access straight from the house."

"I might. I need to ask Ricky what she thinks. She's the timekeeper and journey manager."

"I'm what?"

Ricky came through the door, and Tara immediately felt better. Something about seeing her lifted her mood. "In charge of our itinerary. I was just telling Bree. But now you're up, I'm sure we have time to take Thunder off for a trail ride through the woods. It'll give him some stimulation before he's boxed up for the day. Then we're kindly invited out for breakfast."

"The Whistle Stop Café does a fine breakfast," said Bree. "But it's only seven fifteen. You'll have plenty of time to fit in both before you go on with your journey."

"Cool. I'm up for that," said Ricky. "I'll run behind you, Tara. I like to get in three miles or so every morning."

Tara looked Ricky up and down; she believed it. "Okay. I'd offer to run partway, but I know if you ride Thunder at anything faster than a trot, I'll never keep up. These days, I'm nowhere as fit as I once was, not like you anyway."

"Let's not start the morning with another disagreement," said Ric. "I love to run. You can give me a head start if you like and chase me through the woods."

Tara swallowed hard. The thought of chasing Ricky made her own heart race.

They both got ready and spent a hard hour exercising around the woodland trails. They turned Thunder out to graze for another hour and returned to the house. Tara retreated to her bedroom to change into some light linen slacks and thought again about how much happier she was within herself having Ricky here with her.

Ricky could certainly run. She'd sprinted through those woods like a deer outrunning the hunter, and Tara wondered how a real pursuit of her might go. What would it take to capture Ricky and to steal her heart from the annoying mystery woman who seemed to hold so much power over her?

She washed her face and briskly brushed back her hair, then looked in the mirror. Stupid woman! Only a fool would expect anything remotely romantic to happen on this trip. She'd been subtly flirting with Ricky just to test the waters, but there had been no visible response to any of her endearments. She wondered why such inappropriate thoughts had occurred anyway. Ricky certainly hadn't encouraged them.

Like Ric had said, she was obviously still trying to negotiate her way out of viewing Tara purely as a crabby riding teacher, the woman who had fat-shamed her once and who might suddenly revert to being horrible and do it again. She totally understood why Ricky didn't trust her and didn't want to share anything personal, let alone talk about girlfriends. But Tara still had hopes Ricky had meant it when she had said Tara was on the way to being forgiven. That was something to build on.

Bree drove them into the center of the tiny town to where the café used as a set in the film still stood, elevated between two streets. They went inside and were warmly ushered toward a table. As the food kept coming, and Ricky seemed to take a healthy interest in her pile of fried, breadcrumbed green tomatoes smothered in white gravy, Tara relaxed enough to enjoy her own breakfast. If they kept riding, neither of them would need to count calories along this road trip at all.

They were ready to leave Juliette soon after ten, and Tara took the first driving shift. Thunder, if not enthusiastic, seemed now to be resigned to be rugged up again and to wearing his protective shin pads and boots, and he loaded quietly. As she swung out of the drive, she glimpsed Bree waving them away from her front porch in the mirror, and she gave a little toot of farewell back.

Despite the mysterious message from monstrous Marcia—she liked Ricky's term immensely—Tara felt a little less on edge than before. She drove while Ricky consulted her ever-present phone. It seemed her whole life was held within the little gadget, and Tara had a weird feeling of jealousy about it. Her own phone could happily be thrown into the nearest river for all she cared, but she wanted to be inside Ricky's, her name top of the list of Ricky's contacts, her picture used as a screensaver, all her texts sentimentally saved in messages.

It was a completely infantile desire, and she was ashamed of it. What had happened to her over ten years' separation that young Ricky had morphed into an object of sexual desire? Her promise to herself to stop fantasizing had been impossible to keep. Not only that, but Tara also felt the heat growing between her legs at the thought of lying with Ricky in the horse truck cabin, zipping her out of those shorts, pulling down her panties, and caressing those long, tanned legs.

"Lily Rose?"

"What?" Tara jumped in guilty shame. Ricky's voice jolted her back into the present.

"Lily Rose. She's a popular gay country singer. I think we could start with her. I'll play you 'Green Light' on my phone."

"Okay," said Tara. She just hoped Lily Rose wasn't too mawkish. Then she remembered something she'd forgotten from earlier trips in the RV. "I think there might be a way to connect your phone into the truck's audio system. If you look, there's an old manual and a cable of some sort somewhere."

Ricky rummaged through the glove box and pulled out a battered and creased little booklet. "Is this it?"

"That's it. It's probably been in there twenty years, but take a look, and see what it says."

Ricky flicked through the pages and eventually found a way to plug her phone into the sound system, and they were treated to Lily Rose for thirty miles. With a name like that, Tara had imagined the singer to be all blond curls like Dolly Parton, but the lyrics and her voice bore no resemblance to Dolly.

"She has long hair, but it's always tied back and stuffed under a baseball cap. There's nothing girly about Lily Rose."

They drove on.

"Bree was a nice woman," said Ricky out of the blue. "No one could have been kinder."

"I agree," said Tara, "but I didn't like the way she embarrassed you by implying anything untoward was going on between us. I'm sorry if that upset you."

Ricky squirmed a little in her seat. "It didn't upset me. I took it as a compliment that you might feel that way about me, that I might be someone you could care for."

Tara pondered whether there was any possible encouragement contained in this comment and considered pushing a little further.

"Let's head back to the I-75 and take the ring road around the outskirts of Atlanta. I thought we might stop for lunch in Marietta, off to the northwest. It's supposed to have a *Gone with the Wind* museum and with a name like yours, I thought we should give it a try."

Tara huffed. "You know *Gone with the Wind* but not *Fried Green Tomatoes*?"

"Everyone knows *Gone with the Wind*. It's an American classic."

"One which helped perpetuate a whole load of myths about slave owners and conditions on the plantations. What I most remember was Vivien Leigh chewing on that raw turnip. It fed into generations of people's fantasies about the Old South and the Confederate cause."

"I've noticed a few of their flags as we've come through south Georgia."

Tara shook her head. "Yeah, people's memories are easily mixed up with myths that they've been told or invented themselves for comfort. It's called false consciousness. As Americans, we seem particularly prone to it."

Ricky sighed. "Memories can be a curse. Sometimes I wish I had amnesia about a few things."

Tara felt yet another pang of guilt. She knew just what Ricky was saying. She wished they could move on, once and for all. This was like picking at the scars of an old wound, but Ricky clearly wasn't done with her yet.

"I know memories can be partial though," said Ricky. "I've been trying to adjust mine, after you talked about the good times we once had with Thunder. I'd kind of blocked them out."

"I know," said Tara, turning off the back roads onto the interstate highway again. "And I understand. But let's not lose the good times. Do you remember when I took two or three of you girls to Tampa Bay Downs with Thunder in this truck, and we ran him right around the track. I'll never forget the look on your face when you galloped him for the first time."

"Yeah, and how you shortened my stirrups and taught me how to stand in the saddle to keep the weight off his back, just like a race jockey. How he flew!"

"He ran faster than thirty-five miles an hour as a three-year-old.

You looked so good together. It was a happy day."

"It was. Who were the other girls who came with us? I'm sorry I don't remember."

"To be honest, neither do I." Tara searched through her memory to come up with the names. They'd been good girls, nice young riders, but it was strange that the only person she recalled was Ricky. It was hard to admit it, but she had to say, if only to herself, that Ricky had mattered. She had always mattered, and now that she sat beside her, a beautiful, fit, warm-hearted young woman, she worryingly mattered more than ever.

"Wouldn't it be great to get another young colt and bring it up to be a racer?" Ricky asked.

Tara didn't permit herself even to think that far into the future. "Horseracing's a brutal sport in many ways and a sure way to lose money. Money I don't have. No, let's just hang on to memories of the good old days."

They made it into Marietta by midday, and Tara insisted Ric take time out to explore. After their inevitable tussle of wills, she went off alone, clutching her phone, for an hour's visit to the famed Gone with the Wind Museum.

In the meantime, Tara unboxed Thunder in the RV park and let him nibble the grass on the end of a lead rope. It was only day two of their road trip, and Tara was genuinely shocked by the speed at which her faintest stirrings of attraction toward Ricky seemed to have crystalized into a far darker craving.

Maybe it was the constant thudding of the famous k.d. lang song, "Constant Craving," which she couldn't get out of her head. Maybe it was triggered by Bree's casual assumption that she and Ricky might be lovers. But something had prompted that ludicrous fantasy to invade her dreams, first at night, and now in broad daylight. Tara scratched her head and tried to think how she could chuck such nonsense into the trash can where it clearly belonged.

But no magic solution seemed about to offer itself. She would have to fight this ridiculous longing by willpower alone. Surely two women who both happened to be gay could enjoy each other's company without sex rearing its head, couldn't they?

Sex with Marcia had often been ugly, and Tara now didn't even know if she could face any relationship like that again. But Ricky was so different. With her, Tara could imagine sex being as sweet as cherry pie. But there she was, falling into the fantasy again. It just wouldn't work. It wouldn't work at all.

Ricky came strolling back wearing a cheap straw cowboy hat, which made her look adorable. She carried a Subway paper bag.

"Salami, cheese, and pickles or chicken salad wrap?"

"Chicken, please. I'll grab a couple of Cokes from the chiller. Bree refroze the icepacks for us." Tara looped Thunder's rope around a handy branch, and they sat down together nearby on the grass. "How was the museum? Up to its reviews?"

"Yes. Busy, even after all this time since they made the film." Ricky chewed on her roll. "Oh, I bought you something else. Here, look at this."

She offered Tara a small paper bag.

Tara extracted the contents, a postcard, and saw Tara written in old-fashioned script along the bottom of the photo. It was of a large classic Southern mansion.

"This was the house which was the model for the film set," Ricky said.

Tara turned over the card and saw Ricky had written *Beautiful. Just where I'd like to spend the rest of my life.* She bit her lip, wondering what on earth Ricky meant by that. "No, you wouldn't. These old places might look good on the outside, but they generally have far too high maintenance costs."

"Speak for yourself," said Ricky. "They might just need a little TLC. I think this one would be well worth the effort."

"Drink your Coke before it gets warm," said Tara to close down this dangerous little chat. But she tucked the postcard into her shirt pocket and thought long and hard about Ricky's words and what they might or might not mean.

They finished their lunch, offered Thunder some water before reloading him, cleared up all evidence of their picnic, and prepared to rejoin the road to the north.

"Should I take over?" asked Ricky before they climbed into the cab.

Tara considered the offer but felt she needed something to take her mind off all her inappropriate thoughts and feelings of lust. "No," she said, "I'm fine. Let's press on toward the Tennessee border. Then we can switch when we next make a gas stop."

The arrow on the tank was slipping way down past the quarter-full mark when she finally saw a filling station where the price of fuel didn't look too outrageous. They pulled in and moved to the back of the line.

While they waited, a noisy gang of bikers roared in opposite them. Revving their huge bikes, the dozen or so guys seemed to delight in making as much noise as possible as they jostled each other for a place at the pumps. The hairs rose on the back of Tara's neck.

As a horse rider, she'd never cared for bikers, who were generally pests and often rode too close, even revving up deliberately to scare the horses. Thunder stamped and moved about in his stall. Motor bikes and pigs were his two great hates, and she wanted to march right over to the helmeted men and confront them. She put her hand on the door handle, about to leap out.

"Leave it to me," said Ricky quickly. "Look, the next gas pump is free already. Just start refueling. I'll go and talk to them on the way to the cashier's booth."

They moved the truck forward to the diesel pump and got out of the cab. Tara watched as, without any hesitation, Ricky strode confidently back across the forecourt and gave the bikers the broadest of smiles, along with a definite swivel of her hips.

She spoke loudly enough above the revving of their engines that Tara could just hear the start of the conversation.

"Hi, guys, could you do us a huge favor and not rev your bikes? We've got a racehorse on board, and we don't want him kicking his way out of the box and causing an accident. He could do a lot of damage to your bikes."

Tara didn't catch any of what the men said in reply, but they immediately cut off their engines. Ricky seemed to be enjoying herself. There was laughter, and she took off her straw hat and waved it about. Then she paid at the window, so Tara had the green light to begin refueling.

Tara felt a stupid pang of jealousy. The girl was flirting with these yahoo types far longer than necessary. Tara was still busy filling their truck, so she couldn't intervene, but she was so caught up with monitoring the situation across the way, she pulled out the nozzle too quickly and spilled some diesel over her hands.

"Ric! Get back here! I'll need to go wash this fuel off."

She knew it came out wrong, too strident, too bossy. But Ricky, obliging as ever, strolled back to her and smiled.

"Sorry, I was just thanking the bikers for being quiet."

"They're supposed to shut off their engines anywhere near the pumps. You didn't have to be quite so charming."

"I know, but as my mom always says, you catch more flies with honey than vinegar."

Tara sniffed. "I don't want you catching anything from those guys. We should give them a wide berth. Wait here, please. I'm just going to use the restroom."

"Yes, ma'am," said Ricky.

She grinned but had made her point. Tara realized that she'd been talking as though she was somehow in charge of Ricky, which was stupid. Ricky was probably more in charge of her and most certainly boss of her heart.

CHAPTER THIRTEEN

Ricky took the wheel while Tara filled in her little fuel journal, sitting on her cotton jacket to protect her thighs from the hot leather of the cab seat. The afternoon was limbering up to be a real scorcher, and the shades on the windshield offered little protection against the sun's glare.

Whenever she wasn't driving, Tara far too easily lapsed into a miserable silence, clearly dwelling on losing Thunder, so Ricky tried to keep her talking.

"We have another hundred or more miles to go before Nashville, by way of Chattanooga. Want some different music? Glen Miller and the "Chattanooga Choo Choo" or I could give you a taste of The Girl in Red?"

"No, not now, Ric." Tara stared out at the lush greenery. "This used to be Cherokee country. Did you know I'm one-eighth Cherokee in a straight line down through my father, grandfather, and great grandfather? The name on my birth certificate was Ross."

Ricky was at a loss to understand the significance. "Um, yes? So?"

Tara looked as though Ricky ought to know. "The original name for the central district in Chattanooga was Ross's Landing, after Captain John Ross, who later became a famous chief of the Cherokee nation. He set up the first ferry crossing over the Tennessee River. It's a family legend that he's a direct ancestor of mine, though I'm not sure if it's true. I don't know how many children he had or how many survived. They were terrible times. His wife was one of the four thousand or so Cherokee people who died on the Trail or Tears in 1838."

"That *is* something I've heard of," said Ricky. "We covered it briefly in an American History class I took as a junior in high school."

Tara tutted. "Yep, I bet though that all you received was a brief, sanitized version of the many forced death marches of the southeastern native peoples, driven at gunpoint away from their homes after farming and caring so well for the land for tens of thousands of years. When I was in high school, the expulsions never even got a mention. They tried to make us believe that the land was virtually empty scrub, just waiting for British settlers to take it over and start cultivating it."

Ricky veered right and drove them down a side road away from the pounding roar of the twenty-first century traffic and pulled up, glad of a rest. "You have some strong opinions, don't you? More than most people. Do you feel that these are your ancestral native lands then? I remember learning about some sort of landmark court case, *The Cherokee Nation versus the State of Georgia,* wasn't it?"

"Some sort?'" said Tara. "You obviously didn't have to pass many history classes to get your teaching certificate."

Ricky could sense Tara's irritation at what she admitted was a pretty flimsy engagement with the reality of nineteenth-century American history. But Tara was on a roll here, and what had started as a grumble was rapidly gaining traction into a full-on rant.

"It was a brutal exercise in ethnic cleansing. Other groups were expelled starting in 1829, but in 1838, the last of the great Cherokee nation were burned out of their farms and driven north. They had to walk more than a thousand miles in terrible conditions, starved, frozen, forced even to pay extortionate fees to use ferries and river crossings." Tara shuddered. "More than four thousand died on that last winter trek to north Illinois. You should read about it. People might think the Civil War was bad, but this was as bad, if not worse. It was an attempted genocide of a whole nation of different peoples."

Ricky felt hot with shame on behalf of all white people and wondered how to respond without getting her head bitten off. "All this, and slavery too. It makes you permanently uncomfortable being white."

"Well, whites weren't the only ones to have slaves," Tara said, a little more softly as if she'd realized how harsh she sounded. "The Cherokee had them too. As many as five thousand black slaves went on those treks north along with the Cherokee. That was the way many black people escaped the South before Emancipation. Having suffered so much, many of them were freed at the end of the trail and headed toward new cities like Chicago to work in the mills and meat-packing stations. Many joined up as soldiers on the Unionist side and some ended up as cowboys as well." She glanced at Ricky and gave a half-smile. "Did you know that? The truth is far more cowboys in the Western states were either black or Indigenous American than white. It was considered such a rough, dirty job. There's some real history that you won't find in many school textbooks."

Ricky was interested in history but even more in the psychology behind Tara's passion for it. "Do you feel Cherokee in your bones? Do you feel the pain of past times?"

"Sometimes, more these days than I used to. To be honest, I never did as a child. Like you, I was never taught most of the facts, and I never went to college like you did. It all seemed so remote, so long ago. I've done a heap of reading though since Geoff left. It's become a passion of mine. Lately, when I feel a great melancholy come over me, I wonder if there isn't truth in the notion of inter-generational trauma, that pain and distress can be felt through the DNA of past lives."

Tara had stopped looking so angry and just looked sad. Ricky decided she had to lift Tara's spirits. The woman had enough in her own life right now to make her low. She didn't need to take on the sufferings of all her forebears. "I bet you got your skills on horseback from the Cherokee," she said, "and that's a good thing for me."

"As far as I know, the Cherokee were mainly farmers and homesteaders," said Tara. "They lived in villages and towns and grew crops. It was the Spanish who introduced horses, more to the Western tribes."

She obviously liked to disagree on principle. Ricky didn't want to encourage her to stay so grumpy. "Well, whoever it was, without horses, no one would have built the America we know today. Let's drive up to the summit of the state park in Chattanooga and look at the views. From there, according to my road trip app, you can see right across the old Indian country over three states."

Ricky pulled over and rerouted the GPS on her phone, which was a good substitute for the non-existent one in Tara's horse truck.

"You and your phone! Don't you ever get off it? And don't say Indian, it's First Nation or Indigenous American. I thought you'd have known, being all PC and modern."

Ricky tried to keep her own expression impassive. "Right. Sorry. Now, I've reset the GPS. Can you hold the phone up so I can see it, and we'll be up in the mountains in no time?"

Tara didn't move. "Why? Climbing up all these hills unnecessarily will just waste fuel."

"Just do it, Tara, okay? When we get up there, you'll be glad we did." This was getting ridiculous. Ricky wondered which of them was acting like an adult, and which one was being a brat.

"All these apps. How do you ever manage to keep track of them, or do you have an app for that as well?"

Ricky didn't answer, and Tara finally took the phone and held it aloft so Ricky could see. They went back onto the highway and the Google Maps app took them to the top of Fort Mountain State Park overlooking Chattanooga and the surrounding country. They left the stifling cab and enjoyed the breeze at the top of the hill. The views were amazing.

"I forgive you for being right, Ric," Tara said quietly. "This was so worth seeing. You know, you're damned difficult to fight with."

The penny dropped. "What, despite your best efforts to make that happen? Why have you been so moody since we refueled?"

Tara shrugged. "No reason. I just felt grouchy and wanted to poke a stick through the bars of your happy cage a bit."

Ricky raised her eyebrows, an art she'd perfected when dealing with troublesome teens under her care.

"If you really want to know, I didn't appreciate you flirting with those bikers. I know, I know, I was being stupid, but it seemed so easy for you to be charming. You had them eating out of your hand, and it's gotten progressively harder for me to even stay civil with folks these days. I was just a little jealous. I guess I'm better with animals than people."

Her candor undid Ricky's best efforts to be stern, and she burst into relieved laughter. "If this is the way it's going to be from now on, I'm going to start issuing forfeits every time I see you pull a grumpy face. I'm not President Andrew Jackson, okay, so don't take the whole Trail of Tears out on me."

Tara perked up somewhat. "Ah, so you do know some US history then?"

"Of course I do, and I also recognize low blood sugar when I see it. Let's make a pitstop when we get past Chattanooga and get some cold drinks and carbs. Then we can drive on to the horse ranch I made reservations for near Clarksville. It's not far after Nashville, and we should be there by dinner time. They said we can turn Thunder out in a pasture of his own, well away from all their mares."

"When did you organize that?"

"In Marietta, while I waited in line at the museum. I forgot to tell you before. I did it all on my phone." She thought Tara would berate her for not telling her all this rather important information earlier, but she was quiet for a few seconds.

"What sort of forfeits?"

Ricky grinned and tapped her nose. She decided to invent some good ones for future use. Let the punishment fit the crime, and Tara obviously liked playing games. Her bad mood had lifted, and she obediently held the phone in place so that Ricky could navigate them around Chattanooga and back out onto the Nashville road going north without any further difficulty.

But as they continued, Ricky couldn't help wondering why Tara had been jealous. The guys were old, overweight, and paunchy. How could she be jealous of them, or of her? It made no sense.

They made it to Clarksville by the end of a long hot afternoon, and Ricky pulled over as soon as they'd left the highway. "Can you drive, so I can concentrate on navigating the last five miles or so?" She was surprised Tara had let her take the wheel at all, to be honest. She'd been in a funny mood from the start of the day, and whenever Ricky caught the look on her face in repose, she still seemed troubled and restless, constantly crossing and uncrossing her legs.

But now she jumped out happily enough and ran around the front of the truck. Ricky went in the opposite direction and peeped in at Thunder, who seemed to be dozing on his feet. He'd been tied up in the box since Marietta, so she was glad he'd have a nice paddock to relax in overnight.

Tara buckled up and turned on the engine.

"If Thunder is happy in his quarters, and there's decent security at this place, maybe we could go into Clarksville and look for some place to eat dinner downtown. What do you say?"

"I think I'm tired of the road," Tara said. "Let's maybe call for some pizza on the way and eat it in our camp."

Ricky tried to remember how many facilities there were. The woman on the phone had said they were welcome to park and stay the night, but she'd also mentioned something about it being a dude ranch with guests, so maybe she could provide them with a cooked meal.

"Well?" Tara asked. "Are we going to stay here beside the road for the night or what?"

"Yeah, sorry. Let's see." She consulted her phone. "Yep, we take this for another half mile, then turn left."

They arrived at the dude ranch, and Ricky was pleased to see it had several corrals and small horse pastures where they could release Thunder. Tara was on a tight budget and wouldn't want to spend more on their own accommodation than was needed. "If you sleep in the van and I use my tent, maybe we can use their shower block. And we can see if they'll supply food for weary travelers," she said.

"I'll go in and negotiate," said Tara, parking up. "Wait here with Thunder, please."

Ricky was happy to let her go. It was good to stop moving at last, and she stood outside to let the wind ruffle her hair and take some of the heat from her body. They were out of the deep woods of south Georgia, but the air still felt thick and heavy, as though it might rain soon. While she waited, she looked up Clarksville on her phone to check the local weather report.

Crap. Now she knew why the city had sounded familiar. Two disastrous tornados and a huge flood had hit it within the last twenty-five years. One tornado had almost flattened the city in '99, the floods had wiped away part of the center in 2010, and another huge tornado had hit again in 2018. She didn't like the sound of that at all and looked up at the sky. Was it her imagination, or were the storm clouds already gathering? She looked on her phone again. There were no flashing little red lights or tornado warnings, but it said precipitation over the next twelve hours was 90 percent likely. The sooner they made camp the better.

Tara came out of the ranch office holding some paperwork. "Good news. We can camp over on the far side of the property, and the woman gave me a site plan. We can release Thunder, close by, and for ten dollars each we can eat supper with the current guests. I made reservations. This place is perfect. Well done."

Finally, something she'd done right that they wouldn't disagree over. "Let's get Thunder unboxed and turn him out. It looks like rain, so I'm glad we can stay here for dinner instead of going into Clarksville for food."

Ricky wondered whether to warn Tara any more about the recent history of Clarksville's scary weather but decided against it. Tara's mood was thundery enough, and she wondered what the night would bring inside the truck, let alone outside. She was learning the woman was like a bear when she had an empty stomach.

CHAPTER FOURTEEN

Tara knew she'd been a complete pain in the ass since they'd left Bree's place, but she was determined to make it up to Ricky. She checked the odometer on the box as she drove it down the road to their destination; they'd covered nearly three hundred and seventy miles since Juliette.

Not so far, when she thought how much farther they had in front of them, but a hell of a trek if you were a browbeaten, badly shod Cherokee back in the early nineteenth century. The weight of her connection with those times had somehow gotten under her skin, literally, she supposed, but it didn't excuse her churlish behavior toward Ric, who had been amazingly patient with her. She was determined to do better this evening. At some point she would have to look at her phone again. But not now, not yet.

Ricky pointed to a nice flat area not too near the trees and within a short walking distance to the shower block and toilet facilities that wouldn't be too daunting at night. "Let's park there, okay?" Tara positioned their truck with the cab facing back toward the buildings and the paddock where she'd been told to turn Thunder out.

In no time, they'd unwrapped his traveling bandages and socks and released her lovely boy. She led him over to the grass and set him free. He bucked and snorted, executing tight turns around the paddock, as if he wanted to explode with energy after a long day in the box.

She checked the water trough provided, which looked clean and full of fresh water. The grass in his enclosure was okay, not too lush and rich in protein, so ideal for him to graze off and on through the night. Horses had a delicate digestive system, so needed to eat little and often. As they'd done earlier, if she and Ricky rode him for an hour in the morning, he should be able to cope with the stress of another day on the road.

She hoped that they might make it as far as Kansas City, still short of halfway to Tacoma, but getting there. Crossing the prairie states should be relatively straightforward, if deadly dull, and the sooner it was done the better.

Ricky, a good groom as ever, had mucked out the box as best she could and left the doors and windows open to give it a good airing. Tara decided to be helpful and went off to get a mucking-out wheelbarrow from the main Dutch barn and also to find out where she should put their straw and droppings.

When she reached the big barn, she stepped inside and walked straight into the middle of a class in stable management. A young guy was teaching an assorted group of people how to muck out a stall and refill it with sufficient straw to make a comfortable bed for a horse.

His students all looked up and stared at the newcomer as she approached, every one of them dressed in brand new immaculate Western gear, some of their plaid shirts still had the creases from their packaging. It had to be their first day on the ranch.

The young man in charge tipped his hat toward her. "Hi, are you the lady with the horse truck? Mom said you were staying the night."

"Yes, don't let me interrupt. I just need to borrow a wheelbarrow."

"Sure. Take one of the ones outside." He turned to the group. "This lady's taking her horse all the way from Florida to Seattle. She'll be joining us for dinner. It's at seven, ma'am. We bang the gong by the back door fifteen minutes before to warn everyone to come to the cookhouse door."

"Wow, Florida to Seattle," said one youngster, standing next to someone who was probably her mother. "That's a long way."

"It is. Three thousand, four hundred miles to Tacoma, near Seattle, to be exact, but don't let me stop you all. I just need to know where to dump the muck from our box."

The girl who'd commented started to giggle. "Oh, gee, I thought you were riding all that way. Stupid or what?"

Tara gave her a small smile. "One or two guys have crossed

the USA on horseback in recent times, but it took them nearly a year, and they used more than one horse. Now, the muck?"

"Yeah," said the first guy. "Around the back, over to where there's a red painted dumpster. You'll see it if you go through here and out the far door. See ya later."

Tara strode off as directed and found the wheelbarrows and the place to dump the stable droppings, then more slowly she began to walk back, pushing the barrow with a pitchfork balanced on top of it. She stopped and leaned on the fence to enjoy her favorite leisure activity, watching Thunder enjoy himself. It restored her nerves and lifted her mood within minutes.

He was sniffing the air in that way he did, figuring out which other horses were in the vicinity and whether any of them were mares in season. Castrating male horses was the industry standard for this business—a stallion could cause havoc in any yard—but when you looked at it from the horse's point of view, it was still such a cruel thing to do.

The sex drive was fundamental to all living things, and Thunder wouldn't be Thunder without his. Hers was certainly central to her, damned annoying though it was right now. She supposed she too was being 'marish' with Ric.

Ricky had already erected her little tent next to their van. When she made it back, Ricky almost glowered at her.

"Where have you been? I've been worried about you."

She seemed alarmed. Tara shrugged. "I only went to get a wheelbarrow, and I met the group of our fellow guests. Most of them looked as though they wouldn't know the front end of a horse from the back. Then I stopped to watch Thunder. You would've seen me if you'd looked up."

"Just let me know next time, okay? I don't like the idea of you wandering off on your own."

Tara was annoyed and amused in equal amounts. Her earlier grumpiness had apparently jumped host straight over into Ric's pretty little head. "Oh, don't you, miss?"

"No, like I said, I was worried."

"What about? That I might fall into a pit of stable manure and never be seen again? There aren't many places to get lost in around here, so lighten up, honey. Now show me your tent. Did it cause you trouble putting it up? You seem less than happy after your efforts."

Ric seemed to jump a little when she called her honey yet again, but then she offered Tara that gentle smile which could turn her insides to melted caramel.

"You got me there," Ricky said. "I expected it to pop up out of its bag fully formed, but it's way more complicated than that. I still need to peg it out."

"Let me help." Tara took a handful of tent pegs and the rubber mallet which came with them, and they did the job together. Tara bent down further to look inside. "It's small. You'll have much less room in here than you would have sleeping on the bed with me in the back of the cab."

"I'll be fine. The outer skin is all pulled tight now, so the rain shouldn't get in."

"How do you know it will rain?" She sniffed the air. "I agree the air pressure seems heavy."

"On my phone, that annoying gadget you seem to despise so much," Ricky said. "Where's yours, by the way? If you'd had it on, I could've called you and not been so worried."

Tara wondered where Ric had picked up the idea that she needed a new mother figure in her life. "Sheesh, you're right on track to becoming a control freak. How old am I, Ric?"

"Forty?"

"Yes, I turned forty last Sunday. So maybe I can look after myself, right? Stop worrying about me."

"I only do it because I—"

"Yes?"

"I…look, I care about you, okay?"

Tara smiled at the way Ricky made something nice sound so troublesome. "That's sweet, but—"

"It's not sweet at all!" said Ricky. "And I'm not your 'sweets!' I just care, plain and simple. And I feel I should be the one responsible for the road trip going smoothly. I know how upset you are about having to lose Thunder, so I can't expect—"

"Oh no, stop right there, *honey*," Tara said. Ricky wasn't going to deny her the right to use those affectionate little tags if she talked about caring for her. "No one needs to be responsible for another adult. We're only responsible for ourselves, *our* actions, *our* words, *our* thoughts, and I've obviously worn you out today by my failings to control any of mine since this morning. I'm sorry if I upset you, truly I am. Come here, Ric. Let's not fight. Let me give you a big hug."

She managed to draw Ricky in for the first real hug they'd ever shared. It was a tight, awkward embrace, but Tara didn't let go for several seconds, not until Ricky softened in her arms and hugged her back, just as hard, in return. "So we're good? Good friends and good road trip buddies? And we both care about each other. And that's okay, right?"

Ricky nodded, cradling Tara's head against her shoulder, and they stood like that, in total physical contact, for another fifteen seconds. Tara cursed inwardly when a gong strike disturbed the moment. "That's the fifteen-minute warning for supper. Let's take a quick shower before dinner. We must both stink of the road and the heat."

Ricky nodded again. She seemed to have calmed down from before. They gathered up their towels and wash bags and went over to the women's shower block which was set up with six private showers and separate changing cubicles.

Ricky disappeared behind one glass door, and Tara took another, and the sound of hot running water was soon the only sound. Tara turned her handle all the way to cold and enjoyed the shivering contrast. She recalled the feel of Ric's body against her own as she lathered the soap over her body.

"Are you telling me it was your birthday last Sunday, and you never said a word?" Ricky called out from her own shower cubicle.

"Yes. Sorry. But you turning up to see me was the best present ever." Their separate glass doors were hardly protection against the heat she felt. Tara would like to turn the hugs into a daily happening. It wasn't much, but it might be just enough to survive and get her through the trip, and Ricky's supple, warm, and graceful body was exactly as wonderful as she'd imagined it would be. Ricky left the showers first, and she gave herself thirty seconds' more punishment to tamp down her ardor before wrapping herself in the towel and leaving the cubicle.

Ricky stood at the mirror, drying her hair. "You're right. I'll stop fussing about you. I was being ridiculous earlier. We care because we're friends and road trip buddies, not family. I'll wait for you outside."

Tara heard what she said, loud and clear. Warm, platonic hugs were fine. But as the door banged shut behind Ricky, Tara pulled off her towel, leaned over the vanity bar by the bench, and gripped it as she took in a deep breath. She looked at her naked body and wished it looked better, less scrawny. She wished she could be sexually attractive to Ricky. But it was what it was.

She also hoped, if there was to be a thunderstorm, that it would break soon and lower the temperature. The air felt heavy enough to cut. It must be the weather causing her heart to beat so fast and her temperature to rise, even after a cold shower.

She redressed and pulled on her old shirt, linen slacks, and her comfortable scuffed jodhpur boots. The memory of those city slickers in their store-creased, fringed Western shirts with silver buttons made her want to laugh. She just hoped they would be kind to the horses. She ran her fingers through her hair and went outside to head over to the sprawling ranch house for dinner with Ricky. She felt as hungry as a bear, and not just for food.

CHAPTER FIFTEEN

The evening meal was served family-style, with all the guests sitting down on either side of a long trestle table, which easily held ten people. Tonight there were eight folks on vacation, who had all changed from cowboy dress into smart casual, plus Tara and Ricky, who hadn't changed from anything into anything.

They stood out, but Ricky didn't really care. She'd never meet these folks again, and she'd showered and washed her hair. They should be grateful she didn't stink of horse shit anymore. Tara's reluctance to dress up was rubbing off on her.

They slotted themselves in on opposite sides at the bottom end of the table, and she could feel Tara's foot pressed against hers as they took their places. The cook came down the line, ladling food over everyone's left shoulder onto their waiting plates. She greeted Ricky with a warm smile.

"Hi, honey. We spoke on the phone, but I haven't introduced myself. You must be Ricky. I'm Bet. No, don't try to get up. That's fine. Would you care for some of my chicken and vegetable stew?"

"Yes, please," Ricky said. "It smells delicious."

"First night staple. Country American. Tomorrow it'll be enchiladas, then prime rib, then catfish. The last night is always a barbecue. I work to a plan."

There was just enough left in her stewpot for Tara to receive a couple of generous dollops, and then Bet retreated to the kitchen end of the room to refill her serving bowl. Plates of amazing-looking biscuits were passed back and forth up and down the table, as well as steaming bowls of oiled and spicy collard greens.

To begin with, there was little conversation. The other guests looked tired after their long first day and probably long flights or road trips to get to the ranch, and just tucked into the food. Ricky was ravenous and cleaned her plate. Tara seemed to be enjoying it as well. It was well worth ten dollars.

Bet brought in a large sheet pan of gooey chocolate brownies, smelling delicious, and placed three coffee pots on the table.

"Those are regular, and this one is decaf," she said. "There's cream and sugar in the center of the table, and almond milk for anyone lactose-intolerant."

Ricky smiled to think how, even in rural Tennessee, times were changing and diverse diets were being catered for. "Don't move. I'll get you a coffee."

"Decaf then, please, hon," Tara said. "It'll be hard enough getting to sleep with this heavy air pressure without mixing strong coffee into the bargain."

"Yep, I just saw on the TV that there's a big storm coming in just before midnight. Will you two gals be okay, camping out over by the wood there? I saw you roll up earlier."

"We've got the horse truck, and my friend has her new tent. Thanks for asking."

"Oh, so you two gals are friends then. I thought maybe mother and daughter," said the man sitting next to Ricky.

She stiffened at his stupid remark. "She would've have been a child bride for me to be her daughter. I'm Tara's co-driver and groom."

He smirked at her explanation and didn't seem convinced.

"You might want to take your horse inside and stable him in the barn tonight," Bet said. "The TV weather station said we should expect two inches of rain later, with plenty of thunder and lightning in the bargain. My son Paul will find you a stall."

"Thanks, but no," Tara replied. "My horse has been cramped up in a truck for more than eight hours, and he'll have to be confined again tomorrow. I think I'll leave him out if you don't mind. It's not like we don't get heavy rain in Florida. He's used to bad weather."

"As you please, but these summer storms can get mighty intense."

"Are we in Tornado Alley here?" asked Ricky, not surprised that Tara wasn't interested in cooping Thunder up all night.

"Just about," said Bet. "We had a terrible one through here back in 2018. It blew the roof off our barn on the edge of the pasture and killed one of our best young calves. The tornado picked it right up in the air more than fifteen feet then dashed it to the ground thirty feet away and broke its neck."

Ricky nudged Tara's foot under the table, whispering. "If it gets that bad, maybe you should stable Thunder for the night, just to be on the safe side?"

Tara raised her eyebrow and shook her head. "Oh, I don't think so. He'll be fine. It's not like any tornadoes are expected tonight."

The brownies finally made it down their end of the table, and they took one each. Ricky dipped hers in her coffee and enjoyed its rich, chocolatey deliciousness. Bet was certainly a good cook.

"Shall we leave the others to it and retreat to the van?" asked Tara quietly. "We can play some more music on your phone before we turn in for the night. I'm really not in the mood for company."

Ricky could see how weary Tara was. Tara had clearly been troubled by something all day, and Ricky couldn't quite understand what. She must be as tired as she was though, from the long drive and having to listen to the inane chatter from all those loud Bostonian and New York accents. "Yep, good idea. Let's do that," she said and rose from the table. "Sorry, folks, we're leaving you. We've got a long drive tomorrow and need to get up early to exercise our horse in the morning before we set out."

The other diners seemed revived by their meal and were revving up to make a much longer night of it. They let Tara and Ricky go without protest.

"Here, why don't you take the last brownies?" Bet offered the plate as they headed for the door.

Ricky refused. Her shorts were already feeling tight around the waist.

"Thank you," Tara said as she took two. "We'll have them for breakfast. Are there any good trail rides around here? I imagine there must be, this being a dude ranch and all."

"Sure are. We've got maps." Bet indicated to a box by the door. "Take a copy from there. You can ride for more than three miles over our own land and then on toward Fort Campbell. It's a large military base, home of the 111th Airborne Division, so don't worry if you hear planes take off at the crack of dawn."

Ricky held the door open for Tara, carrying the map in one hand and two brownies in the other, and they slipped out into the night. She could just sense that as soon as they had gone, folk around the table would be discussing them. Two women traveling together and wanting to go to bed early to be apart from anyone else? It was inevitable people would assume they were gay. She could just imagine that young girl asking, "Mom, were those two ladies…you know?"

It wouldn't be the first time. She'd had a similar response more than once when she'd been on vacation with previous girlfriends. But this time they'd all be wrong, wouldn't they?

CHAPTER SIXTEEN

It wasn't raining when they left the ranch house but by the time they made it back to the horse truck, it was practically torrential, and they jumped into the cab to avoid getting soaked. Tara turned the two chairs around so they faced the bed to make a small sitting area.

"Up for a game of cards?" she asked, placing the brownies behind her on top of the dashboard.

"I thought you didn't want company?" Ricky asked. "Aren't you going straight to bed?"

"It's scarcely nine. Let's play for a while. You're not 'company' anyway."

"So what am I?" Ricky kept it light, but her heart yearned for a deeper connection with this beautiful, and often exasperating, woman.

"You're a wonder, that's what you are," said Tara. "Come on, here's a pack. You deal. Let's play something simple, like Gin Rummy. My mom and I used to play cards every night when we were on the road. It settled my nerves and took my mind off whatever competition I had the following day."

"For sure. It'll get us in the mood for nodding off. We can use the bed as a table." Ricky cut and shuffled and cut. She'd played cards and shot dice for hours with friends in her college dorm and was something of a card shark. She dealt them seven cards each, put the rest of the pack on the bed in front of them, turned over the top one, and placed it beside the pack. "My dad taught me this game. We used to play every Sunday evening when I was eight or nine."

"How is he doing?" Tara asked, her interest seeming genuine.

Tara knew both of her parents from way back. Theirs was a small community. "Not so good," said Ricky. "He gets so bored, sitting at home in constant pain. If he could cope, I think he'd like to go back into construction. He used to build amazing houses. He even told me he wished he could buy some of your land and build some great homes on it." Ricky smacked herself on the head when Tara glanced away. "Sorry, that was totally insensitive of me."

"Don't worry about it." Tara picked up the three and dropped a seven of hearts. "I'm used to the idea now. I'd happily sell it to him if I could."

They played until Ricky grew bored. "This game is for babies and old ladies. How about a few hands of poker? I'll play you for pennies."

"Texas Hold 'em?"

"Why not? Even with only two, poker is fun…unless you put your shirt at risk."

"Strip poker is even more fun," Tara said lightly.

Ricky saw a definite gleam in her eye. "Mrs. Morris, well, I do declare! What might you be suggesting?"

Tara dropped her eyes down on the table and said nothing. She reached into her purse slung over the seat and pulled out two handfuls of loose change while Ricky dealt the cards.

"Let's say quarters are thousands, dimes are hundreds, and pennies are tens. Here's a pot to start with." Tara dropped a handful of coins onto the bed. "We'll take half each."

"Okay, plenty of funds. No risk of having to strip then." *Don't even go there, Ricky.*

They played for an hour. Tara was good, but Ricky was better. She always knew when Tara was bluffing. Her final hand of four queens was the strongest of the evening, and she scooped the pot.

"I win. You can keep this and buy me lunch tomorrow." She pushed the little pile of money back across the bed. "It's getting late. I should turn in."

She thought of her tent, where her sleeping bag was unrolled, ready for use. Tara put the playing cards away in their pack, pulled out the bed, and covered it with a fresh white sheet. Then she opened the overhead locker and extracted two pillows and a light summer weight duvet.

"Sure you won't join me, Ric?"

Was this a straightforward question or a proposition? "No, I'll be fine outside." It was a downright lie. She was sure she'd ache with unrequited longing all night, but she was damned if she'd admit it. They stood awkwardly in the tiny space, each waiting for the other to say goodnight. "Um, goodnight then."

Tara stepped back to let her push past her and opened the cab door for her. Their breasts nearly touched as Ricky squeezed past, feeling almost combustible.

"Goodnight, Ric, darling. Sleep well."

Ricky breathed in the scent of her, a mixture of hay, and leather, and a touch of something unique. She ran from its allure out into the rain and scooted across the two-yard gap to her tent.

She pulled herself in backward, slipped out of her sandals and shorts and left them by the door flap, which she zipped shut. No rain was coming in through the tightly stretched tent fabric, thank God, but it was super sultry inside, and she pulled off her T-shirt and bra before wriggling down into the summer weight bag.

She looked up into the darkness, listening to the hypnotic beat of the rain above her. Rather than stay awake half the night, she could feel herself falling asleep in minutes, the uncomfortable hardness of the ground beneath her outweighed by her exhaustion after a long day, and a whole load of frustrated passion. Being in love was so damn tiring.

It felt like a mere five minutes later when an almighty flash of lightning woke her, illuminating the tent like a flare. But when she squinted at her watch's neon display, it said 12:48, so she'd slept for more than an hour. The rain was still drumming on the canvas and Ricky started to count. "One, two three." Then came an almighty crack of thunder. "Wow, the storm's coming right over us."

She heard the cab door open and called out to Tara, "Are you okay? Anything I can do?"

"No, stay there," Tara said. "I'm just going to check up on Thunder. He'll hate this storm, being in a strange place. I was wrong not to stable him."

Ricky struggled to push down her sleeping bag and get her

clothes back on. "You'll be soaked in seconds. You can't go off in this on your own."

"It doesn't matter. We have towels, don't we? You stay there in the dry."

"Not a chance," Ricky said. "We'll go together. I'll grab my flashlight and follow."

Tara for once didn't argue but headed straight off across the field. She had already started to run but Ricky soon caught up, able to see her figure moving through the storm ahead of her. Tara had undressed out of her trademark shirt and pants and was now wearing some sort of shift over bare legs and boots.

They passed under pouring rain and were both drenched in seconds. They could see Thunder, obviously not happy, prancing back and forth around his little paddock and whinnying loudly. Tara had a lead rope with her. They put their heads down against the rain and struggled through the warm, wet darkness toward him. Another streak of lightning shot across the sky, with a crack of thunder on its heels.

"It's right above us," said Ricky.

Tara whistled to her horse, and it carried through the noise of the weather. Thunder looked up and ran toward them. He seemed to be saying, "At last! What were you doing, leaving me out here? Don't you know I'm a thoroughbred? My ancestors came from Arabia. We don't enjoy standing out in pouring rain getting soaked."

Ricky grabbed his mane and pulled his head around toward them while Tara clipped the rope onto his head collar. In the darkness, he looked like a hugely powerful horse, looming above them, but he followed quietly enough for the long walk toward the barn, even though the thunder and lightning continued to unnerve him.

Bet's son Paul was already in the barn, checking up on all his own horses. "Good idea. I'm glad you changed your mind. Put your horse in the end stall, well away from all the others, him being a stallion and all, and for the quarantine rules which we should observe when a new horse comes on the property."

Ricky hadn't thought of that, but Tara seemed to know what

he was talking about. They walked him into the far stall, where Thunder gave an almighty shake and covered them with another shower of water.

"You did that on purpose, didn't you?" Ricky asked him.

Tara took off his lead rope and halter. The stall was already prepared, clean and comfortable, with a two feet depth of straw on the floor. It was top class horse lodgings for the night, and Thunder seemed much more settled now he was inside out of the rain.

Tara twisted a handful of straw into a wisp and used it to dry him off. But then he shook himself again and covered her with bits of straw as well as water. Ricky had to laugh. She guessed they must both look like scarecrows.

"Thanks, Paul, you've prepped the stall great." Ricky fastened the stable door bolt and set the kicking catch at the bottom, while Tara petted Thunder over the half door. She exchanged a grin with Paul and then started to wring the water out of her sodden T-shirt, twisting it up and squeezing out a puddle onto the floor.

"Hey, don't stop on my account," he said.

Ricky had paused, thinking maybe that wasn't the best thing to do in front of a man after midnight. He seemed to be flirting with her but in a funny, completely relaxed way.

Tara stepped between them. "Right, I think we're done here. We'd better return to our horse RV and get out of these wet clothes right away. Thanks, Paul, and good night."

She took Ricky's arm and gave her a deliberate little shove in the small of her back, prodding her forward out of the barn. Ricky made no comment until they stood together just by the truck. The thunderstorm still surrounded them, making it hard to be heard.

"Come inside the cab and get dry," said Tara. "The rain will have to stop soon. I'll make tea and then we'll try to start the night over again."

They climbed onto the horse truck. Tara took off her boots, and then began to pull off her nightshirt.

"Don't stop on my account," Ricky said. "So, what was that about? Do you intend to frog march me away every time a man looks in my direction or pays me a compliment? I don't remember asking you to be my babysitter on this trip. And if Paul didn't guess we were gay before, he sure will now." She wanted to lightly but firmly remind Tara that she wasn't a child anymore but a woman of twenty-six. She was also not Tara's wife or girlfriend—much as she might want to be.

But Tara looked at her with eyes suddenly as hot as coals. They were both dripping wet from head to foot, but it was almost as though steam was coming off her. Ricky shivered. She kind of sensed what might happen next before her brain could put the thought into anything like words.

Tara stopped undressing and let her shift fall back into place. "A babysitter? As if. If you knew how I feel, then you'd understand. I've been like a cat on hot bricks all day over you, couldn't you tell?"

"What?" Ricky's mind did a couple of double-flip somersaults, wanting to believe, trying to grasp what she was hearing, what she thought Tara might mean. "You mean?"

"Yes. I know, I'm sorry. I didn't dream this would happen when we first set out. It's out of line, but what can I say? I'm burning up here."

"Oh."

"It seems all resistance is futile."

"Resistance against what?" Ricky asked, hardly able to speak. She could feel her powers of language disappearing through the floor. Tara emitted such powerful vibes, and the air around them seemed alive with pheromones.

"My need to do this."

Tara reached out and pulled Ricky toward her, cupped her cheeks, and brushed her lips softly against her own. She moved in further and kissed her hard. Her mouth tasted of chocolate and coffee, with undertones of wild rainstorm, and overtones of red-hot woman. She held Ricky's head in her hands and pushed her back against the inside of the truck.

Her touch electrified Ricky's body. She couldn't believe the sheer joy of realizing that whatever she felt, Tara was feeling it too. She melted immediately, wrapping her arms tightly around

Tara, and dared to kiss her back.

It was happening… It was finally happening.

Ricky could hardly bear the happiness. It was almost too painful. All these years, she had pined for this woman without hope, and now she was in her arms. She couldn't process it, except to think it was perfect.

Except it wasn't, not quite. Their wet clothes clung to wet flesh. Ricky tugged at Tara's nightshirt. She wanted to see more of her body, wanted to feel her, wanted to be inside her. "I need you too, so much," Ricky whispered.

"Just a kiss. That's all I'm asking for," Tara said, her quiet voice sinking even deeper into a whisper.

"We need to get out of these clothes." Ricky lifted Tara's nightwear and slid her hands under it. Tara flung back her head and gasped as she closed her eyes. She flipped Ricky backward onto the bed. Tara might once have been the unobtainable ice queen who drove her crazy, but now she was setting them both on fire with her heat and obvious desire.

"No, no, just a kiss," she whispered.

No way did her words match her actions. Ricky slipped out of her tank top and bra, then pulled off her shorts and underwear in one quick movement. It was too dark to see, but she wanted Tara to touch her everywhere and take whatever she wanted.

"Oh, honey, come here." Tara gently lowered herself into Ricky's arms.

They seemed to meld together in a perfect fit. Tara kissed her face, then began to move all around her jaw line, taking little nibbles and licking her.

There was a faint ping on Tara's phone, but it seemed to have the effect of a fire alarm and activated the sprinkler system in Tara's head. Her hand went still, and then she slowly withdrew and shuddered.

"Sorry, forgive me," Tara said. "I don't know what came over me."

"What's the matter? Why stop?" Ricky panicked. Had she done something wrong? Was this not what Tara had wanted? She kissed Tara again, wanting access to her body, to make love to her however she wanted. Every woman was different, every lover had different needs, different turn-ons.

Tara kissed her in return but far less fervently than before. She ran her fingers across Ricky's back but seemed to want to slow them both down. Then she put up her hands and gently pushed Ricky backward.

"Let's just lie down here on the bed for a while and listen to the rain."

They lay in an embrace still damp with unspent passion as well as from their soaking by the rainstorm. Ricky could feel the beat of Tara's heart against her own. Her heartbeat slowed back to something sensible, but she didn't understand why Tara had suddenly gone into reverse. "Tell me what you like. Tell me exactly how to please you," Ricky whispered in Tara's ear and then kissed it.

Tara squirmed and chuckled. "No, I'm so sorry. It's not you, it's me. I shouldn't have kissed you like that. I certainly shouldn't have thrust my hand down your pants. It's so wrong."

"What?" Ricky lifted herself up slightly and rested her elbows either side of Tara's head. She couldn't see her face in the darkness, but she gently smoothed back Tara's hair and ran her fingers down the edge of Tara's cheeks and along her lips, learning her face by touch alone. "What do you mean? This isn't wrong. It's right. It's perfect. You're perfect. I want you inside me."

Tara's response came in the form of a sob, and Ricky felt wetness against her fingers. "Tara, what's wrong? What have I done to upset you?" Ricky realized that there was no guarantee that Tara would be feeling the same joy as her. The sex she had craved so ardently minutes earlier was maybe a source of pain as well. Something wasn't right, that was for sure. "Don't cry. Just talk to me," she whispered. She kissed away the salty tears, and Tara didn't protest. Instead, she clung to Ricky even harder. But she still didn't speak or stop crying.

CHAPTER SEVENTEEN

Lying in Ricky's arms and weeping, Tara didn't have the mental clarity to explain the feelings in her heart that were at war with, and yet complicit in the sexual chaos running through her body. These feelings made no sense to her, so why would Ricky, bright and sensitive as she was, even get close to understanding them?

Tara's head was a complete mess. She was sabotaging what, for normal people, would have led to hours more of total bliss and physical intimacy. But if Ricky made love to her as she clearly wanted to and Tara so desperately longed for, it was bound to end in complete failure. As soon as Ricky entered her, she would freeze, and close up, and maybe even have a panic attack. She could only give love, not receive it, and even the love she gave wouldn't satisfy anyone if Marcia was anything to go by. She knew in her bones that the new message that had just arrived would be from her as well. It had shot an arrow straight through her libido, knocking her little songbird heart right out of the trees.

Something wicked and basic had driven her desires to pull Ricky into her bed tonight and make love to her, and now, when she'd given in to the longings of her heart, the lust in her body, and Ricky had turned into a firecracker and almost jumped from the bed with her response, Tara knew she must be punished to atone for it. The Pavlovian responses she'd learned so well under Marcia's sadistic tutelage were already kicking in.

But how to let Ricky in on her secret? That despite longing to make it happen, climaxing for her was a forbidden pleasure? How to explain that Marcia had effectively rendered her incapable of normal lovemaking? It had taken years of consistent pressure, with subtle and not so subtle cruelties, but after eight years Marcia had destroyed Tara's ability to find release. Ricky would never understand; how could she? She was a normal, healthy, balanced person, not a wicked, withered witch who had allowed herself to become terrorized by an abuser like Marcia.

Because Marcia had found Tara irresistible, despite claiming to be a happily married straight woman with three children, she had to punish her in bed and out of it. It was all Tara's fault, so Tara had to pay.

She had nothing sensible to say. For now all she could do was weep. Ricky, having been so full of joy before was now also clearly distressed for her and with her.

"Tara, honey, what's the matter? Don't you realize that I adore you?"

Tara tried her best to stop crying. She was making a complete fool of herself. "Pass me a tissue, could you, my love?"

Ricky pulled down the box from the shelf above their heads and passed her three large Kleenex. "Here, let's stop the flood. We're going to dry those tears, and then you're going to tell me what this is all about. Please, just talk to me. Help me understand."

Tara blew her nose and patted her eyes. The torrent of tears had sprung from somewhere deep, and she despised herself for letting them happen, making herself look such a mess, so ridiculous, when she'd been the one to initiate sex in the first place.

She was no more in control of her emotions now than she'd been ten years before. She'd ruined their friendship then, and now she was ruining their love affair before it even started. The gremlin ghost of monstrous Marcia was sitting on her shoulder, whispering obscenities into her ear.

Ricky sat up, wrapped herself in a towel and handed one to Tara.

"Here, take off your shirt, get dry, and, for now, stop taunting me with your beautiful body. I'm going to make us both hot tea," she said.

She picked up a bottle of spring water, filled the kettle, and turned on the stove.

Tara wondered at the practical wisdom of her. "Hot tea at two a.m. to chase away the blues? Thank you, honey,"

She wrapped up in the towel and sat on the edge of the bed. Ricky waited for the water to boil and prepared their tea.

She carefully opened one tiny sachet of sugar and sprinkled a little into each drink. "Just enough sweetness to boost your adrenaline and calm mine. I've just been kissed by the most beautiful woman in Tennessee tonight, and I need to get over the happy shock."

Ricky was blatantly sugaring her up to make her feel good, but she was comforted to know that at least Ricky hadn't run screaming from the truck, crying for help, and that her responses had been genuine.

"So you enjoyed it?" Tara asked. "That's a comfort at least."

Ricky passed her over the mug of tea. "Enjoyed it would be an understatement. Tara, this was shaping up to be the happiest night of my entire life. You were glorious, a rain goddess. I just wish we hadn't stopped."

Tara looked down into the swirling, tobacco-colored liquid and took a sip. Her eyes hurt. She felt as little like a goddess as any woman ever could. She had known from the start that she could never deserve Ricky, and she was even more convinced now. "I'm sorry. I'm just so, so sorry."

"Drink your tea. Look, I'm drinking mine."

Ricky was managing her, like a paramedic treating a trauma victim, but she didn't have the will to fight it. She wanted to tell Ricky that if she thought she was in love with her, her heart compass needed immediate readjustment. Tara didn't deserve love like this, didn't deserve any love. She wondered where to begin. But it was late, and they needed to sleep. She pulled open a drawer, took out a clean night shirt for herself, and handed one to Ricky.

"Here, wear this, and lie down. Don't go back out in the rain to that wet tent. Let's just sleep for a few hours. It must be past two."

Ricky shed her towel and quickly pulled on the cotton T-shirt. Tara ran a wet washcloth over her eyes to soothe her tears, and then changed. She lifted back the top sheet and let Ric lie down first. Ricky pushed herself against the back wall and tugged

Tara's hand to lie down next to her, holding her close so they could spoon. She felt Ricky's breath gentle on her neck. Ricky moved her arm around Tara's waist and gently held her close. Tara turned out the light.

"Good night again," Tara whispered, and Ricky responded by a squeeze around her middle and a gentle kiss on the back of her neck. Tara lay and listened to the rain. She couldn't hope to sleep. Everything she'd wanted had been about to happen, but her past hadn't allowed it. Fear, despair, and a tiny glimmer of hope battled for supremacy inside her brain, but as the pain settled and her tension was released, she cherished this present reality, this now. Ricky was in bed with her. She hadn't returned to her little tent but was here, holding her close, so how could she despair? Whatever the morning might bring, it couldn't take away this illuminating flash of joy. She loved Ricky, and for now, she knew Ricky loved her back.

CHAPTER EIGHTEEN

When Ricky woke, it took a while for her to surface. She gradually became aware that the storm had finished, and daylight was coming through the windows. For a moment, she couldn't get her bearings, before she realized that, yes, she had spent the second half of the night with Tara, chastely. All her good intentions—or wimpy determination depending on how you viewed it—not to risk close proximity had dissolved in last night's rain. Of course, she and Tara had slept together but as she clarified in her muzzy brain, after sharing tea, they had lain down and slept. *Slept*, and nothing else.

Their session of kissing had proved hotter than either of them seemed to have been prepared for or could deal with, especially Tara. They'd kind of come to an understanding on that, even if Ricky wasn't sure about much else. She had loved the kissing, but Tara had seemed almost in pain. She'd whimpered as if she was hurting from some physical wound. Lovemaking shouldn't be like that.

And where was Tara now? Ricky was alone in the bed, and the mattress beside her felt cold. She looked at her watch. Eight already. Tara must have dressed and left to take care of Thunder. Perhaps she'd already saddled him and taken him out on the range, galloping her way out of the raw passion which erupted so quickly yesterday, and which she had found so hard to deal with.

Ricky swung her legs around and stood up, crouching slightly to avoid banging her head on the overhead locker. She looked down to see she was wearing Tara's nightshirt and her own skimpy underpants. For someone who had wanted to avoid embarrassing intimacy, this hadn't been the best idea. She looked around to find her clothes and located her T-shirt draped over the sink and her shorts and bra down by the side of the bed. She shoved them on and ventured out into the heat of the summer morning.

Everything was steaming. What had fallen as rain was now rising up again from the meadowland as thick curls of white mist. The sky was white too, with low clouds almost touching the top of the surrounding trees but before long, they would disperse to take them into another hot day. She padded barefoot across to her tent and retrieved some clean undies and a towel, grabbed her shower gel, and headed off toward the washing facilities in her sandals. There was no sign of Tara or Thunder near the barn, so she assumed that they were out on a trail ride somewhere.

She could detect no sign of movement from the ranch house either. The pretend cowboys and cowgirls inside were on vacation after all, presumably still tucked up fast asleep in their cozy bedrooms under their patchwork quilts, probably imported from somewhere east of Singapore.

Ricky made it into the toilets, relieved to have the place to herself, and then stood under a hot shower and let the steaming water pour down over her head. She allowed herself some space to think through last night.

Tara had started it. She'd kissed Ricky. Yep, she'd definitely started it. It was a gift from the gods. Ricky hadn't had to make the first move, which was amazing, given she'd been convinced that she would leap in uninvited and embarrass them both by groveling at Tara's feet, feet shod in those adorably scruffy, brown jodhpur boots.

Tara had done the hard work, risked all to come out and say she had the hots for Ricky and needed a kiss, and left Ricky reeling. This marvelous, austere, beautiful woman had wanted her so badly, she'd appeared not to be able to help herself.

And the kiss. What a kiss, well, multiple kisses. If it had been up to Ricky, she would've given Tara the full works and made love all night if she'd wanted it. But Tara had pulled back. Had it been such a bad idea? Tara had probably seen the pitfalls. They had a job to do. They should stay as friends, work partners, not romp about like sex-obsessed teenagers.

But Ricky wished they had done more. Oh yeah, she wished that badly. She was sure that having great sex would turn Tara into a frisky demon lover, full of confidence and empowered. Ricky would have gladly taken it all on. Tara would want to lead, naturally, and Ricky would happily follow. So why all those tears? Why had she said sex wasn't *allowed*?

And what now? How were they supposed to continue as though nothing had happened? Or would they talk it out? Judging by the way Tara had shared so much with Ricky when they'd reunited, Tara had no trouble talking. When it came to intimacy, it was crystal clear that Ricky was still too shy to dare confess how she'd pined for Tara for years.

She had layers of vulnerability barely covered over where Tara was concerned. She loved her too much, more than ever now that she had tasted her and felt her soft kiss. If Tara and she were to move into a full-blown sexual relationship and then break up, as they inevitably would, or when Tara eventually rejected her again, Ricky could hardly bear it.

By the time Ricky emerged from the shower, she had ninety-nine percent convinced herself she was grateful Tara had stopped when she had, and that it had been simply an affectionate fumble, not even a one-night stand. She went back to the truck to make coffee and think about where they'd be heading today. Did they have time to explore Clarksville? While she waited for Tara to return, she would read up about the city on her phone.

***

Tara rode hard across the surrounding countryside on Thunder. She'd hoped to find clarity and peace of mind through the activity, but as they cantered along a wide off-road track beyond sight of the horse ranch and into the misty uplands, Tara's mind was as cloudy as the landscape around her, and her heart seemed as bumpily unsteady as the trail beneath Thunder's hooves.

She steered him to one side of the trail to keep out of the deepest mud and risked riding him along the grass verges, watching out for gopher holes, which might trip him up.

Her head was in a mess. Why, oh why, had she lost her mind and assaulted Ricky like that? It was tantamount to sexual harassment. But the sweetness of her mouth, the warmth with which Ricky had responded, let her in, and had held her—what had that meant? Tara decided to hope for the best and interpreted it as evidence she was finally forgiven for being such a witch when Ricky had been a girl. Ricky hadn't been disgusted, hadn't angrily shoved Tara away and told her to lay off.

She'd kissed her back, shown great kindness, and even seemed like she was as hot for it as Tara had been. But Ricky was young, and fit, and sexually active. She didn't need to be in love to enjoy sex. And then, bless her, she'd made tea. She'd agreed to stay in the cab to comfort Tara after that embarrassing display of tears and had slept the sleep of someone with a clear conscience, untroubled by demons.

Tara had lain quietly beside her, so grateful, but so fired up and anxious about Marcia's texts that she'd been awake and trembling for much of the night and was sure she'd barely slept for more than an hour. She'd listened to Ricky breathing gently beside her through the remnants of the storm. She'd wanted to turn, to wrap her arms around her, and explore Ricky's beautiful body. But of course, it could never be.

Tara was used goods, too old, a survivor from a miserable failure of an abusive relationship. Besides, didn't Ricky still have her secret love controlling her own heart? Tara still hated the thought of that woman, the one whose presence had obviously contributed to Ric's earlier breakups. If she ever got her hands on her, she was tempted to take a horse whip to the bitch. How dare she not respond to such a lovely woman? What had she done to hurt her so?

Thunder, feeling softer ground beneath him, quickened his pace now. Maybe this trail reminded him of his youth, and Tara realized she was doing something she had chided Ricky for often enough, daydreaming when she should have been fully focused on controlling her horse. He had the bit between his teeth and was beginning to pull hard into a full gallop.

She saw the trail steepen ahead and took advantage of it to attempt to regain control. She shifted her legs away from his sides, no longer urging him on, but deliberately telling him to slow down now, to drop from a gallop into a lope and then into a trot. "Whoa, there you go. Steady boy, steady."

She used the well-worn words as an additional aid, coupled with body language, leaning right back, and applying gentle pressure onto the reins, alternatively one side and then the other, so his mouth eventually softened and he began to act sensibly again, not running away with her like a headstrong colt.

It was good to know he still had some speed in him, but a headlong dash up an unknown and rutted trail wasn't the right way to see how fast he could gallop. She had no idea what lay over the brow of the little hill but just before they reached the summit, Thunder finally decided to oblige her and responded to her instructions by applying some brakes.

They gradually slowed back to a walk as she wanted, and she made sure to keep him steady as she looked at the view before descending into the next fold of the countryside. Tara could see the way back to the ranch. It would add a mile or two to her ride, but it would be good for them both to cool down slowly and not lose control again.

As she rode the back the long way to the ranch, Tara gave herself similar advice to what she'd tried to tell Thunder. *Keep it steady. Don't lose control. Think before rushing over fences and galloping straight for Ricky like a crazy teenager. Don't jeopardize that precious friendship by acting badly. Accept your limitations. And most important of all, make sure there's no more frantic kissing!*

She eventually arrived back to where they were camping.

Ricky was making pancakes. She waved a bottle of maple syrup at Tara and looked relieved. "I was about to send out a search party. Thank God you're not dead in a ditch somewhere."

Tara laughed, glad that there was no obvious atmosphere to deal with. Ricky was acting as though nothing had happened between them, and that suited her just fine. "No, not dead. I'm fine. So is Thunder. Stop worrying and save me some of those pancakes. I'll just unsaddle him and turn him out to cool off for an hour." She dismounted and walked Thunder into his enclosed little half-acre pasture again.

Tara decided to let what had occurred in the dead of night stay there. They had another long day ahead of them and five hundred miles to cover. "What happened to the brownies for breakfast?" she asked when she returned.

"I thought we could save them for the road. I decided a pancake breakfast might be what we both need. Okay with you?"

"For sure." Tara sat down and tucked into a plate of pancakes and syrup. They tasted divine. So Ricky could cook as well as everything else. She tried not to think about that too deeply.

"Coffee?"

"Yes, please. Now tell me all about Clarksville. I can see you've been making notes."

"Sure have," said Ricky. "Ever heard of Wilma Rudolf?" And she started to elaborate. As Tara half-listened, she tried hard not to focus on the way Ricky's mouth moved, how she wanted that sweet mouth against her own, how she yearned to be wrapped in those strong arms and enveloped in Ricky's love. They had another long day ahead of them, sitting together in the cab. Tara's heart began to beat faster at the thought of it.

CHAPTER NINETEEN

Ricky watched Tara munch her way through the pancakes, reassured by the obvious healthy state of her appetite. Two hours' stable duties and hard trail-riding had obviously done its job in clearing her head and hopefully settling the grief and nerves which had erupted after their little tryst in the small hours.

While she'd waited, Ricky had done her own share of chores, hanging up a clothesline, and trying to dry out their clothes. The humidity in the air wasn't making things easy. She was now firmly in teacher mode and wanted Tara to be as impressed as she was to have discovered the famous athlete Wilma Rudolf had come from Clarksville. "She was America's first black female Olympian and the first American woman to win three track and field gold medals in a single Olympics. She had polio as a child and spent years learning to walk again before becoming a champion basketball player and then a sprinter."

Tara shook her head. "I know the name, but I'm afraid I couldn't have told you anything about her."

Ricky grinned. "Don't worry. I'm sure most people have forgotten just how great she was. It was back in 1960 when she broke the Olympic record in Rome. But someone recently made a documentary about her, specifically to be shown in schools, and I've played it for my students to inspire them. Half the students in my classes are young black girls who need a strong and high-achieving role model. Apparently, Wilma was one of twenty-two children, born into poverty. It just shows what you can do if you focus and put your mind to it."

Tara cleaned up the syrup with her last pancake and took a long swig of coffee. "You're a sprinter, aren't you? I remember your mom telling me you'd won the state championships for two hundred and five hundred meters when you were in college."

Ricky raised her eyebrows. Tara and her mom must have kept in close touch for years, not just for a month or two after she'd quit the school. "Mom seems to like polishing the cups, and she has them all on display, which is kind of embarrassing. But I don't run competitively anymore. I much prefer teaching these days."

"You would make a superb riding teacher. You're so calm and gentle. I wish…" Tara pushed her plate away. "What else have you found out about Clarksville?"

"This city was founded by General George Rogers Clark, and he was the brother of William Clark, of the famous Lewis and Clark, the explorers who opened up the Oregon trail. Aren't we following along in their footsteps all the way to Oregon?"

"More or less, I guess." Tara shrugged. "I expect General Clark was sent here to persecute the local tribes. I think we'll hear the same story in every state we cross. Anyway, from here on, we cross out of Tennessee and head into Kentucky. If we can, I'd like to make it most of the way to Kansas City before we stop for another night. Can you reserve a campsite while I pack up and prepare Thunder?"

"Yeah, of course," Ricky said. "How was he this morning after the rainstorm?"

"Too full of oats, which must be what Paul has fed him. He ran like the wind and nearly yanked my arms out of their sockets. I had trouble holding him."

"I can't believe Thunder could ever be that naughty," said Ricky. "He's always so gentle with me."

"He would be, especially when you were young. He never takes advantage of novices. But with me, he acts up sometimes. He knows I'll always forgive him. Horses are born to gallop. I don't begrudge him the odd breakout."

"We all need to break out now and then," said Ricky softly. Tara met her eyes, and they looked at each other in silence for a few seconds. By silent mutual assent, it seemed that they'd moved on from what had happened between them overnight. The door was shut on that whole thing. For now.

They broke camp at ten, and all that remained of their stay at the ranch were a few tire marks in the wet grass and a couple of square yards of flattened ground where Ricky's tent had stood. It was still wet, but she'd rolled it up as best she could, collected the pegs, and shoved it all into its bag.

Precisely what the sleeping arrangements would be for the nights to come was still to be worked out, but she'd located an RV park five miles short of Kansas City and had reserved them a site with electricity. Thunder would have to sleep in his box, but the site guide indicated the place was animal-friendly, and there were plenty of hiking and horseback-riding trails nearby.

"Five hundred miles. Should I take the first shift?" Ricky asked. From the deep shadows beneath her eyes, it was clear that Tara hadn't had much sleep, and she already looked weary.

"That sounds good, if you don't mind. I might just lie down behind you and get some shuteye."

Ricky took the keys from her hand, climbed into the driver's seat, and they set off. Tara grabbed a pillow and lay down on the folded bed. When Ricky took a quick look behind her after ten minutes, Tara was fast asleep, her hair falling across her face, and her arms folded under her head.

Ricky knew the day's route, more or less, and had propped her phone up against the dashboard to give her up to date guidance about the state of the traffic ahead. She would need to recharge her phone as soon as they stopped for the night, but it should last the day.

She followed the I-24 north toward St Louis, skirting the huge lakes in southern Kentucky until they came out of the South and entered the Midwest. Clumps of trees were everywhere still, but the spaces between them were larger, and the horizon lay farther away.

She kept her foot on the pedal with just enough pressure to maintain a constant speed of fifty-five. On the straight, flat road, the only challenge was to stay awake as the miles rolled under them. Huge intercontinental trucks were the most frequent vehicles to pass her, sometimes flashing their lights impatiently at her sedate progress.

To keep herself alert, she tuned the radio to a local channel.

Country music, as bland as bathwater, seemed to be the only thing on the menu, but it was pleasant enough and wouldn't wake Tara. Thunder was listening too, safely lodged in the back. She wondered if he had any favorite artists.

The mists had cleared, and the sun soon beat down from a hard blue sky. Ricky stopped for fuel, which she paid for with her own card, not wanting to disturb Tara. She also bought a couple of bottles of Coke from the cooler in the filling station. She pressed the cold plastic to her forehead and enjoyed the feel of the cold against her cheek. Then she opened it and took a glug or two before setting off again.

It felt good to be quiet and just drive, but as she pressed on through this strange country of endless farmland, wheat, soy, and the occasional massive grassless lot full of dairy cows, she began to think. The upshot was that she decided not to give up on Tara. She would keep working to unpack whatever weird collection of conflicting emotions and anxieties might rest inside the person sleeping behind her and try again to draw her out into some romantic fun and games.

One thing she was sure of—Tara hadn't been faking it. Ricky could tell Tara had fallen for her bigtime; she'd wanted her, she'd been full of lust and passion, and yes, maybe even a little in love, and Ricky wasn't going to let her slip back simply into riding-teacher mode.

There might be more than a few glitches to smooth out but for the first time in her life, Ricky knew exactly what she wanted, and just like Wilma Rudolf, she was going after it. There was no question of giving up the race like some wimp. By the end of the road trip, Tara and she would be lovers. Ricky would make it happen, whatever it took.

At one o'clock, signs for St Louis began to appear along the highway, and Ricky decided it was time for a break. She signaled right and pulled the truck into a service area just outside the main city boundaries. Tara had slept all the way into, through, and out the northwest corner of Kentucky, but when Ricky pulled up the horse truck and engaged the parking brake, she woke up with a start, almost falling off the bench.

"Hey! What happened?"

Ricky turned in the driver's seat. "Great! Now you're conscious again, you can treat me to lunch. Remember that was the deal when I won the poker game last night?"

Tara rubbed her eyes and groaned. "How long have I been asleep? It feels like hours."

"It is. Three and a half, actually. You missed Kentucky, and we're almost in Missouri, heading toward St Louis. I've had a lovely quiet time moseying along, but I could do with a pitstop."

Tara pulled twenty dollars from her jeans' pocket. "Here, take this and go get us some hot food. I'll stay here and guard Thunder. St Louis? I never would've guessed."

"I picked up some drinks earlier." Ricky passed a bottle to Tara. "Here's one for you. I'll be back shortly." Ricky went off in search of the restrooms. Tara asleep was manageable. Tara awake, on the other hand, looking extremely kissable with her hair sticking up and her cheeks pink was a challenge that might be harder to resist. Kissing was the least of what she wanted to do. Her body clenched whenever she thought of the gentle curve of Tara's breasts and the perfect round tightness of her ass.

When Ricky returned twenty minutes later with a bucket of fried chicken pieces and some corn dogs, she found Tara sitting cross-legged on the dry grass, her head buried in their map. She'd tethered Thunder to a long rein attached to a corkscrew post, and he was cropping what little grass there was around their spot.

Tara looked up at her and smiled. "According to the odometer in the cab, we've covered over eleven hundred and sixty miles since leaving Tampa. That means we're over a third of the way there. What day do you think we're likely to arrive? I should send a message to Eric Carson in Tacoma to give him an ETA."

"Not sure." Ricky didn't want to think about this trip ending. "Here, as you missed out on Kentucky, I thought you might like some fried chicken. Let's eat, and then we'll look at the route you drew so we can calculate the distances more accurately. It depends how far we can pound the highway each day." Ricky passed Tara a napkin and a piece of meat. You couldn't beat it for greasy deliciousness when you were hungry. Tara seemed to think so, anyway. It wasn't long before she was reaching for more from the paper bucket.

Tara patted the ground beside her. "Come and sit by me. The grass is dry. I don't think they had the rain here which we had back in Tennessee."

Ricky sat down on the grass and nestled close. Body language to show she found Tara utterly attractive might get the right message over rather than venturing into the dodgy swamps of conversation. They ate lunch, and Tara didn't move. But she seemed happy.

"No fries then?" she asked and pouted. "I thought they were included in these deals."

I thought you'd say they were too fattening." She laughed at the absurdity of that idea, given the chicken in its heavy batter must be loaded with calories. "Why don't you have a corndog if you're unhappy."

Tara took it. "How could I be unhappy with you to cheer me up all the way? You're a huge comfort, and I'm sorry I spoiled everything last night."

"You didn't spoil anything. Don't say that." Ricky pulled Tara into a headlock and pretended to wrestle her. It was really an embrace in disguise, but it reconnected them physically and conveyed love…she hoped.

"Stay here while I go pee." Tara jumped up. "I also need to wash my greasy fingers."

Mission not accomplished. When Tara emerged from the restrooms, they reloaded Thunder and traveled on across the state of Missouri toward the great river. Tara drove, but the only thing she said for the first fifty miles between St Louis and Kansas City was, "You've obviously refueled while I was asleep. Give me the receipts, and I'll reimburse you."

Ricky sighed. Tara sure did know how to talk dirty.

CHAPTER TWENTY

We're halfway across Missouri, the 'beating heart of the Midwest.'"

"You think so? It looks like it needs some resuscitating." Tara kept her eyes on the road ahead, the IS-74 which ran straight as a die east to west across the state from St Louis to Kansas City. They were well over a hundred miles into it now, and the small towns they had passed looked pretty weather-beaten and rundown. This was prime tornado country, and she kept her eyes peeled for any looming storm clouds on the horizon. Ricky remained a fount of information, pulling up nuggets of trivia from the encyclopedic depths of her iPhone.

"Yep, that's what the state tourist site says, though why it's called the Show Me State, I can't imagine. What's there to show us? Two great big cities with country farms and beef lots in between. But it says here Missouri's big on brewing and wine making. A quarter of the population are of German descent, so they grow a lot of grapes for Riesling type wines. It also says it's one of the most liberal states for alcohol consumption because of that, so we can get drunk tonight if you want to. They brew a heck of a lot of beer around here too."

"I thought Missouri was more a center for the French Creole people and its own version of their language. My great-grandmother on my mom's side was Missouri Creole. Her folks left St Louis back in the nineteenth century and moved down to Louisiana."

Ricky looked at her, as though she was trying to detect any French forebears. "Yeah, I can imagine that. Cherokee on one side, French on the other. You'd look wonderful in Paris fashions. Natural chic and all that."

Tara swallowed a laugh and almost choked. "You're full of it,

Ric. I'm the least stylish person on the planet."

"No, you're not. You have everything, face, figure, that 'Who gives a shit?' attitude. I think you're gorgeous."

A warm flush rose up through Tara's cheeks. The cab suddenly seemed hotter than normal. She lowered the window to her left to take in some fresh air.

"And I hope you realize, I wish you were mine. I mean, *really* mine," Ricky whispered, her voice husky.

But it was a firm and definite statement, an honest confession. "Oh no, honey," Tara said before Ricky could say any more. "Please don't. I'd be so bad for you. You don't deserve that. You're worth so much more."

"Tara, listen." Ricky switched off the radio and turned to face her.

Tara couldn't handle the face-to-face, so she scowled a little and looked firmly ahead through the windshield.

"I want to show you just how wonderful you are and find out why you have such a lousy self-image. It's not how I remember you when I was a kid. You shone with self-confidence in those days. We all believed you could do anything, and you could. You were a fantastic horsewoman and riding teacher, and we all had a crush on you. You must've known."

Tara gritted her teeth, like a horse fighting against its bit. She resisted hearing all this positive affirmation. She knew Ricky had always looked up to her, starry-eyed, as did several girls each year who went through the riding school. But thankfully, their obsession with both her and their horses usually gave way to a fascination with boys, sometimes virtually overnight, and then, as often as not, she'd be left with bewildered parents and a neglected livery horse to sell. "Having to study for college" had been the most common excuse. So many good animals had been discarded once the initial enthusiasm had waned.

Ricky was different, of course. Her parents, even before the accident, could never have afforded to buy her a horse of her own, but she was a true devotee of all the animals on the ranch. She never grew tired of being around the horses and would clean tack and muck out stables for hours just to be near them.

"Yes, of course I knew. It came with the job, a natural phase most young teenage girls go through, but you all grew out of it. I know you would have, too, sooner or later, even if I hadn't accelerated the process." She thought that reminder would shut Ricky up, and she *was* quiet for a few moments.

But then, Ricky said, "Tara, you're so, so wrong. Maybe not about the other girls but certainly about me. I never stopped loving the stables and all the horses, even though I couldn't ride there anymore, and I never stopped loving you. Can't you see that?"

Tara heard the words, made her poor brain interpret and process them. "You mean…"

"Yep."

"What are you saying? That I'm the woman you can't get out of your head?"

"Yes."

Tara gripped the steering wheel until her knuckles whitened. "That's bizarre."

"I know. But it's true. I kept hoping I'd grow out of it, that I'd get over you. I tried to shake you off. I tried for ten years. But I never have."

"You talk like you had a dose of the flu."

"More like I was held under an unbreakable spell. That's why I came back to see you as soon as I arrived home last week, to see if it still held me captive."

Tara sneaked a look at her sideways and gave a half smile. "Don't say it. I can tell where this is going. A spell cast by a wicked witch?"

"I did call you that sometimes. But I never meant it, apart from the fact that you've always had the power to enchant me, and that hasn't changed."

Tara slowly began to catch on. "But you stayed away so long. All those years without a word."

"I know. Once you've been burned, you tend to stay away from fire. I thought I couldn't face pain like that again. But everything's changed, hasn't it? Last night you showed me that you feel the same, or that you could, that you wanted me. Don't deny it. I can work on that, Tara. I can build on it. I have a chance here, and I'm going to stick to you like a burr in your coat, under your saddle."

"Burrs are damned irritating. They'll make a horse buck like fury."

Ricky seemed amused rather than discouraged. "I know. I'd like to see you bucking and fighting me off. I reckon it could be a lot of fun to wrestle with you and chase off your demons, to make you submit to being happy."

Submit. The word took Tara straight back to Marcia. Ric's revelation made her feel so warm now, so dangerously overheated, that she quickly opened with her left hand the bottle of Coke she'd asked Ricky to haul out of the chiller and took a long swig from it. The bubbles danced on the roof of her mouth, and took her back to her childhood, when excitement had come so easily, when it had been easy to be happy. Once again Ricky had managed to flip the dark clouds above her head so they were all silver lining. Was she finally being allowed into the sunshine? "I hated that woman, you know, the one you said you loved, as soon as you told me about her. I wanted to take her out in the back yard and whip her ass."

Ricky looked puzzled. "Who?" Then the penny dropped. "Ah! When I said there was someone in my life I'd loved for a long time, a woman I couldn't escape?"

"Yes." Tara's vision swam with the possibilities of what all this meant for them both. "I couldn't bear the thought of you in love with someone who had hurt you, who had the power to make you pine like I'd pined for Marcia. I wanted to punish her and tell her to leave you alone."

"I'm sorry, Tara. I was teasing you, just a little, trying to tell you how much you'd meant to me. But it *was* you, Tara It was always you."

Tara's breath caught in her chest as she thought through the implications of this piece of unexpected information, this little bombshell. Then she said, "Even so, now I know, I still hate myself for making you so unhappy. I hate me for that. I deserve punishment, not love."

"Stop that!" Ricky gently touched her thigh before withdrawing quickly. Her tone was almost sharp. "Don't keep hating yourself."

Tara felt the clouds gather once more. "I can't help it. I don't expect you to understand. You have no reason to despise yourself the way I do. I want to be the sort of woman you might think I am, but you have to believe me, Ric, that woman you thought you loved, she's not here anymore. She's been lost, and I have no power to bring her back. I can never make you truly happy, even though I want to. So we shouldn't try to be more than friends. You have to believe me on this." There, she'd laid it out as best she could, maybe not in all the gory detail but surely clear enough for Ricky to get the message. Only three days into the road trip, and they were already enmeshed in a whole barrowload of emotions, all her fault.

If only they could push their feelings away and just stick to the task at hand. Speaking of which… "What about this campsite you've found for this evening?" she asked. "Tell me about it."

Ricky was clearly surprised by the abrupt change of subject, but she wasn't totally fazed by it. What she thought about Tara's little lecture, she didn't say.

She answered, "Yep, it's just this side of KC, a few miles off the main road near to a park. When we stop for gas again, I'll call and confirm we're on our way. I've reserved a site with electricity, so we can cook ourselves an evening meal under the Missouri skies."

"Tara said, "We'll stop at the next service station. I need some water for the radiator, and I want to check on Thunder. I think he acted up this morning partly because he's bewildered and upset by this journey. He doesn't understand what's happening or why we're going so far. I'm going to ride him quietly for an hour again this evening if I can."

"There are worse things than being upset," said Ricky. "And none of us really know where we're going, do we? We'll all find out by the end of the road, I guess. But there's one thing I am dead sure of—"

"What?"

"We're going to get there together, all three of us. You, me, and Thunder. We're a team, and Thunder is our boy. I'm getting you through this, this depression, your weird self-hatred stuff, whatever you want to call it. Whatever it takes, whatever you need, okay?"

Tara's first instinct was to try to shake her off once again, to push Ricky back for her own good, but in reality, her words were like a cool spring of water to a thirsty cowboy crossing the desert. It wasn't just a preference to have Ricky near, it was a damned necessity. She sighed. "Okay. You win. Let's not fight over it. For now, I'll let you think better of me than I deserve, but what happens on the road trip stays on the road trip. I won't hold you to any commitment after it finishes."

Ricky pulled off her hat and reached over and kissed her gently on the cheek. "Sure, Ms. Morris, whatever you say. That's good enough for now. But let's go back to what we agreed at the start. This trip is about having some fun as well as covering the miles. So why don't we concentrate on that for a while. I can show you a real good time if you only let me."

"I see a sign for a pull off up ahead," said Tara gruffly. "Let's see what the Show Me state can show us in roadside catering, huh?" Then she signaled right and moved into the gas station complex.

Tara had a good idea of what Ricky's promise of a good time might involve, and it made her toes curl up in her boots. Perhaps she could give herself a pass out of purgatory for just a little while and let Ricky take charge of the entertainment.

She still hoped that the farther they got from Florida, the looser the hold over her those memories of Marcia might have, but those unanswered texts had her doubting that. She still didn't even want to think about them. She dreaded having to check her phone and discover they'd been joined by a fourth.

"You're impossible," said Ricky. "We'll park up in the far corner over there. Thunder will be safe in his stall for thirty minutes. Let's go in together and take a coffee break. I can see a store, so we can stock up on food for dinner. How about I fix you a nice spaghetti and meatball supper tonight, accompanied by a bottle of Missouri Riesling? How does that sound?"

"It sounds great." Tara smiled as though she meant it, which she did.

chapter twenty-one

They pulled into a cheap and cheerful RV park in western Missouri, ten miles before the state border. There were a few trailers pulled up near them. But apart from a few children who gathered around Thunder, on a long tether out beside their truck, and asked lots of questions about him, no one bothered them at all. The kids' father came over once, stared at them in silence for a moment or two, and then ushered his children back into their own RV. There was no more rain, and the heat lifted slightly, so the night was much cooler.

As promised, Ricky cooked Tara an easy, filling supper of spaghetti and meatballs, and they'd finished the bottle of not bad white wine between them. After they'd together tucked Thunder back to sleep in his box, Tara had just looked at her in silence but seemed kind of hopeful, in a vague way.

Ricky had put up her tent beside the truck, mainly to dry it off after the rainstorms of the night before, but it ended up not being used that night. They both undressed demurely into the same cotton nightshirts they'd worn before, then Tara unfolded her bed and set the sheet straight. She cocked her head in that bird-like way she had, and Ricky knew what she wanted.

"What are you saying? You want us to share the bed, but no sex? How about any kissing or touching? Tara, you sure know how to tease a girl."

"I know. I don't mean to be like this. But you won't want to lie on the hard ground, surely. Let's just sleep next to each other. I promise I'll keep my hands to myself."

"You're nuts," said Ricky. But they both knew she wouldn't be able to resist the invitation. "You climb into the bed first tonight though. I'm not letting you disappear at dawn without me knowing about it."

Tara sat down on the bed and swung her feet over. She pulled herself backward, lying down close to the wall, and seemed to be holding her breath.

Ricky felt they were playing some game, whose rules she didn't pretend to understand. If Tara wanted to be an idiot and torture herself though, then she'd have to let her. Eventually she must surely be sensible and realize they should be lovers, that sex was good clean fun, and as they had the hots for each other, Ricky would be more than okay with that idea. But maybe Tara's head wasn't quite there yet. She'd give her the benefit of the doubt.

She lay down beside her and then reached up to switch off the little light above them.

"Goodnight, Tara," she whispered.

"Goodnight, Ric."

They started by lying back-to-back, just hearing each other breathe. Then as if by mutual understanding that this was both unbearable and ridiculous, they both turned at once, and Ricky quietly moved across into Tara's arms. She lay her head on Tara's breast and felt the beat of her heart, heard the sigh of contentment as she wrapped her arms around her and gently tugged Ricky close.

"Good night again," Ricky whispered after a few minutes, cuddling in. But Tara had already nodded off, and Ricky guessed it was how they'd stay all night.

When Tara climbed over her to get out once the sun was up, Ricky realized they'd both enjoyed more than seven hours' uninterrupted sleep. Maybe it was the wine, or maybe it was because they were perfectly suited for sleeping together. Ricky had always been more than a little restless with her previous girlfriends, often leaving their beds to sleep instead on a sofa, or in some cases, slipping away back to her own apartment entirely to give herself some space.

"You're not really here, are you, Ricky? Your body may be, but your head is off somewhere else. I don't get it, really I don't."

That's what Ricky's last love had said, and Ricky didn't get it either, except that there had often been three in the bed—girlfriend, her, and the shadow of Tara Morris. But now, with just Tara, the real Tara, every minute they spent in each other's company was precious, and she loved sleeping with her.

"Where are you off to?" she asked, gently helping Tara climb over her.

"Where do you think? I won't be long."

"I'll make us some coffee while you're away and look in at Thunder."

"Let's take him out for a ride together when I get back."

"Great. I'll run along beside you like I did before."

Tara rolled over her, pulled on her Levi's, grabbed her towel and washbag, and headed off to the washroom. Ricky glanced at her phone to see it was already 8:15 a.m. She dressed quickly in T-shirt and shorts and followed Tara out of the truck. She walked around to the stable end, looking in through the side door to check up on Thunder.

He seemed fine, lying down on the straw, but then, as ungainly as a foal, he scrambled to his feet. Ricky decided to let him graze on the tether while she cleaned out his stall, but first, she performed her regular routine of slow stretches to limber up her arms, legs, and neck. He watched as though he found her antics funny. He tossed his head up and down, and she could see he was telling her about his empty hay net. "Okay, come on. I'll get your breakfast."

Tara returned, showered and looking as fresh as a daisy, and Ricky took her turn to freshen up. Then they saddled up Thunder, and Tara rode him while Ricky did a three-mile run all around the park. They skipped breakfast, other than a quick cup of coffee, and then packed up and left.

Kansas was terribly boring. Ricky didn't want to insult the state. The Wikipedia guide on her phone listed dozens of notable people who'd been born there. But most of them seemed to have left as soon as they could get away. Only Dorothy in *The Wizard of Oz* seemed to have wanted to get back home, for some strange reason of her own.

The first challenge was passing through Kansas City. "There's no easy alternative to the I-70," said Ricky, "but it passes right through the city center."

"Let's do it. We ought to see where the Missouri and Kansas rivers meet."

"It'll be a big confluence."

"Confluence?" Tara asked, clearly amused.

"Yes. When two mighty rivers combine."

"I know what it means. But what do you know of confluences?"

"You and I, we're in a confluence. This road trip could be the confluence of our two lives. I've been thinking—"

"Don't think, honey." Tara shook her head. "It will only lead to heartbreak."

Ricky huffed and bounced in her seat, irritated. "Why are you so infuriating? Why won't you let me say I love you?"

"Because I have your best interests at heart, that's why."

"But we at least need to talk it through. You weren't pretending, back in Clarksville, were you? You wanted to make love, but something stopped you. Don't bury it in the sand. We have to discuss it."

But Tara played her usual trick of deflection. She could have been a great field hockey defender the way she could send any approaching ball skidding right away from the goal. "If you like confluences, let's stop here and look at one. There's an off for Kaw Point Park up ahead."

Tara indicated to Ricky where she should pull over, and they parked conveniently next to a woman running a coffee shack by the overlook. Tara left the truck and went over to her. She came back with two coffees and some cinnamon rolls in a paper bag.

"Here. A late breakfast for you."

Ricky took her offerings and guessed that heavy conversations were off the menu again.

"The Lewis and Clark expedition set out from around here. Imagine if they could come back today and see how things have changed in just two hundred years," said Tara.

Ricky sipped from her paper cup took a bite of the delicious, freshly baked cinnamon roll and looked across the river at all the impressive facilities and historic buildings. "We learned about their expedition in high school. I did a senior year project on it.

They were so brave and planned everything well. That's how they survived."

Tara sniffed and put on her "You don't know the half of it" face. "But they couldn't have made any progress without their Native American guide and translator, a young woman married to the French-Canadian trapper they hired to lead them. They passed through fifty separate First Nation tribes, if can you believe that. The whole country was populated, not empty as we're expected to imagine today."

"I remember there was an Indian translator, but I don't remember her name or her tribe."

"One never does, does one?" Tara still sounded somewhat caustic. "Her name was Sacajawea, and she was Shoshone."

"I do remember she gave birth on the journey. That's something else people don't often mention." Ricky kept chatting, mainly to fill the silence if Tara wasn't going to let her talk about the most important things. "States have funny names, don't they? I wonder why Kansas is called Kansas. After this Kansas river, I suppose."

She rolled her eyes at the inanity of her ramblings. She didn't want to talk about this stuff. She wanted to talk about the amazing connection she and Tara shared.

"Let's get back on the road. We have a long drive ahead of us today."

Tara led them back into their truck and Ricky pulled away, her twenty minutes in Kansas City leaving her with more questions than answers. Tara sat peacefully beside her, now that the danger of talking about anything real had passed. She was quiet, but not fast asleep as she'd been the previous morning, and she hadn't been argumentative as she'd been between Juliette and Clarksville. Ricky guessed she might be powering herself up to say something though. She was learning to read Tara better every day.

When Tara did speak again, it was more American history. "Most states are named after the Indian tribes which their settlements destroyed. The Kansas River is named after the Kanza peoples who used to live and farm along its banks, only for a few thousand years, mind you. Not much history worth preserving when the settlers wanted to take over and plow up their lands. Now it's just an urban sprawl. Our modern cities are so monochrome, don't you think? All strip malls and paperboard houses. No wonder the tornadoes do such damage. Look around you. Tepees were better built."

Ricky decided not to argue back. She would never have guessed how churned up Tara was about the fate of America's indigenous peoples. It was beginning to sound like one of her father's old vinyl records with a scratch on it, which kept jumping back to the same spot. Of course, she had a point, and Americans' indifference to their country's history was exactly why Tara was so passionate about it.

She drove the truck on westward, and the landscape soon became fields of wheat as far as she could see. It reminded her of her childhood story books. "The settlers didn't have it easy, did they? I read all the *Little House* books when I was a kid."

"I know. Tough lives. Can you imagine breaking the soil on these prairies by hand? It killed the spirit in so many people. Their horses weren't strong enough to pull the plows through the rock-hard grasslands. They worked them into the ground, and they even built their houses from earth sods as well."

Ricky nodded. "And how did the women cope in those long dresses and petticoats, and giving birth without fresh water in all that heat in the summer and freezing under blizzards in the winter? It's incredible so many of them made it west at all, tough cookies."

Ricky was thinking once again about the young woman translator on the Lewis and Clark expedition. Someone who'd been edited out of history. She'd died in childbirth on the trail, only in her early twenties. She'd been younger than Ricky.

"Did you and Geoff ever want children?" Ricky knew as soon as she'd said it that her attempt to bring Tara back into a more cheerful present had touched on another raw nerve.

"Not to begin with, but he changed his mind. I didn't. Besides, I don't have the hips for it. What about you? I bet you'd make a great mom."

FOR LOVE OF THUNDER

Motherhood wasn't something Ricky had spent any time thinking about. "Gee, I'm not sure. I mean, I love babies, but I love all little things, puppies, kittens, foals, piglets even. But to be a parent, that would be a whole different thing." She blew out a long breath. She hadn't expected Tara to turn the line of questioning onto her, and she wasn't prepared at all. "I would love a family, but it would have to be with someone who would be my life partner, someone who wanted children as well. Gay marriages are accepted in so many places these days, but there are still challenges and prejudices and laws are changing and being rolled back all the time. I'd need someone to make me a lifelong commitment, before I'd even consider it."

Ricky hoped that Tara would take the bait and offer her own services as a trusty life partner, but no such luck.

Instead she seemed troubled by the words and just said, "That's sensible of you."

Then they both lapsed into silence for a long time. There was nothing worth discussing out of the truck windows. Sky, wheat, corn, soy. Playing I Spy would get pretty tedious out here. It would have been an ideal opportunity to go deep into their relationship, but Ricky guessed Tara simply couldn't bear to.

"Can we put on one of your CDs?" she asked finally, fearing the silence would deepen too much. Tara nodded and slipped a disc into the stereo. Celine Dion entertained them for the next forty minutes or so. She claimed her heart would go on and on, just like the damn road, thought Ricky.

"Look, there's a sign for a town up ahead," said Tara after another long stretch. "Let's stop and get some lunch. You've been driving for hours. I'll take over this afternoon."

They turned south off the I-70 and drove for a few miles. The town they pulled into could have popped straight out of a Mark Twain novel. The main street was lined with white clapboard houses—some made cheerful with dusty pots of geraniums in front—. There was a small school at one end of the main drag, and a much bigger, modern church down at the other. The battered old city sign named it Emerald Springs and said there were 1,268 inhabitants. Ricky couldn't see any springs though, emerald or not. The place looked to be in a permanent slumber, the essence of middle America in the heat of mid-summer.

Ricky looked down at the trip mileage on the dashboard. "Hey! We have to celebrate. We're crossed the midway point on our trip. Sixteen hundred miles. From here on we're on the home stretch."

"Hardly," said Tara. "We've got much more challenging driving ahead of us. I can't relax until we're driving into Tacoma. But I agree, we should have a little celebration. I'll buy you an ice cream if we find somewhere to eat."

Mary's Place, the one eatery, looked open and welcoming enough, so they parked outside and went in. Ricky could see Tara relax, knowing she could keep watch on Thunder through the window.

A pleasant, but slightly austere gray-haired woman came over to greet them in the otherwise empty diner. She handed them menu cards and showed them to their seats. Ricky looked at the lunchtime options. She knew to avoid the salads, which would be probably tired and limp and so loaded up with mayo that they'd have more calories than anything else on offer. It was also too hot to eat fried anything.

"What would you like?" asked Tara. "My treat."

"No, you bought yesterday's lunch, remember? Let's go Dutch. I'm having a sandwich and iced tea. You can buy the ice-creams for after."

Tara went for a steak and salad and ordered iced tea as well.

"Unsweetened, please. Just lemon."

"Sure."

The woman wasn't nearly as effusive as the servers had been in Florida and Georgia. Maybe Kansas folk were more reserved. But after she'd brought them their ordered food, she returned later to ask how they'd found it.

"It's great, thank you."

"Traveling a long way?" She indicated their vehicle through the window. "I see you have a horse truck outside."

"Yes, we're heading to the Pacific northwest. We've come from Florida," said Ricky.

The woman whistled. "That's a hell of a distance."

Ricky nodded. "We know. We reckon we've just made it halfway right now. We are selling my friend's horse."

"Oh, would it like some water?"

This was unexpected. Ricky looked over at Tara.

"Yes, thank you," said Tara. "We have some big bottles that are full, but I have another empty container which I'd be grateful to fill."

"Bring it in afterward. I'll be happy to oblige."

"It's somewhat quiet in here, even though you seem to be the only place in town to get a meal," said Tara.

"Yep, there used to be three more diners and a commercial hotel when I was a girl. But that was over forty years ago. Most of the remaining businesses around here went bust in 2008 with the crash. Our population has almost halved since then."

"Did you have to get a new sign?" asked Ricky, amused by the exactitude of those tiny city population signs.

"No, that one at the edge of town dates from ten years ago. I reckon we only have around six hundred folk living here now. The high school senior class had just twelve students graduate this year. We held the ceremony on the town green last month."

"So, are you Mary, as in this is your place?" Ricky saw the café owner wanted to talk a little more, and she was always interested in people and their life stories.

"I am. I'm on my own now. My partner died in June last year from COVID."

"I'm so sorry," Ricky said, wishing she hadn't pried. "You must miss him very much."

Mary stood erect and seemed to be assessing them both. "Her. Yes, I do miss *her* very much. She was my world. Tess, or TJ, short for Teresa Jane. She taught history in the high school and caught COVID from the kids. No one on the school board wanted them to wear masks. Dozens of folks took sick, but she was the only one who died. She was only forty-nine."

Tears filled her eyes, and her voice broke. She was obviously heartbroken. Ricky impulsively jumped up and put her arms around her, and the woman allowed, and even seemed to enjoy, the spontaneous hug.

"I'm so sorry." Mary pulled out of the embrace. "I don't know what came over me. I rarely talk about personal things to customers and certainly not to strangers." She picked up a paper napkin to use as a Kleenex to dry her eyes.

Tara smiled. "Don't worry. Ricky has that effect on everyone. Five minutes in her company, and you hear yourself telling her your deepest secrets. But she'll carry what you say in her heart. It's as big as a suitcase, with a huge capacity for caring."

Ricky grinned, surprised at Tara's sweet reference as a general-purpose consoler. "I guess there aren't too many gay people around here," she said.

"No. But I was raised here. TJ and I met in St Louis, and it was love at first sight. You know, like when you just have to be together." Her eyes lit up, as though she could almost see TJ in front of her.

"My father was the Methodist minister here for many years. TJ applied for the teaching post in the high school, because it seemed right for me to return home. My father needed me to nurse him through his last years, so we both moved back here from KC to live with him. The town eventually came to terms with the truth of our relationship. People spout ignorant and prejudiced remarks so easily when they don't know anyone personally, but when it's the minister's daughter and the local history teacher, somehow it's different, easier to accept. We almost became a landmark, you know, Emerald Springs' own local lesbians."

"Well, I wish you all the best," Tara said, bringing the conversation to an end. "I'll just go and get the water container. Can I have the keys to the truck, honey?"

Ricky handed them over and squeezed her hand as she touched her. Her extra word of endearment didn't go unnoticed. Tara left them, and Ricky suddenly wanted Mary to know she had someone other than her immediate friends she could call, if her sadness ever became overwhelming. "Here, let me write down my phone number and e-mail." She pulled out a pen, scribbled the information onto another paper napkin, and then handed it to Mary. "My name is Ricky Gates, and I'm a high school teacher from Florida. Contact me anytime.”

“Thanks. I might just do that.”

Tara re-entered the restaurant with the five-gallon water bottle, and Mary took her into the back kitchen to fill it with fresh, cold water. Tara settled the bill quickly, so Ricky couldn’t muscle in.

“You’re so lucky to have each other,” Mary said. “Hang on to that. You never know when you might lose the person you love. I never dreamed Tess would go before me. Life is so fragile.”

Mary, like Bree earlier in the week, had made a pretty big assumption, but Ricky was astonished when Tara’s firm arm came around her waist and felt a kiss from her on the cheek.

“Trust me, Mary, I know,” Tara said. “I do know how lucky I am.” She tugged at Ricky’s elbow. “We must press on, I’m afraid. Is there a gas station anywhere near town? Our thirsty old wagon will need some more gas shortly.”

Mary gave them instructions, and they left her standing in the doorway of her little restaurant.

“Wow,” said Ricky after they pulled away. “What did you make of that? Do you think we were supposed to stop there? She obviously needed someone to talk to.”

“Yes, I think we were. And the Universe’s message was for me as well. I do need to hang onto you now that I have you back in my life. I promise I’ll try not to drive you away any more by acting even more weirdly than normal.”

“Don’t forget what I said to you,” Ricky said. “I’m going to stick to you like a burr caught in a horse’s fur. No amount of brushing is going to drive me off, so don’t worry. But she only opened up because she assumed we were a couple. Why do you suppose that was?”

“Get out the little cash book to make a note of the fuel price,” said Tara. “Let’s see how expensive it is in Kansas.”

Ricky pulled out the book and the ballpoint pen and resumed normal duties. She had grown used to Tara’s quixotic methods of deflection, changing the subject whenever Ricky got too personal. It was like a constant game of tennis. She was lucky if she got the ball back over the net, let alone in the right part of the court.

Tara drove them along the exact route Mary had recommended, and they went through the now twice-daily ritual of filling the truck. It was so expensive, it was like pouring liquid gold into the tank. At this rate, they wouldn't have enough cash left over to ride a Greyhound bus home. Flying might even be cheaper.

But she'd worry about that another day. The way it had turned out, their trip across Kansas hadn't been so boring after all. Ricky realized she'd referred to Florida as home rather than New Jersey. Sticking to her like a burr would mean moving home to Tampa and changing jobs unless Tara moved up to NJ.

Ricky wondered about the implications of that, but really there was no question. She decided to follow her heart wherever it led, and right now that depended entirely on where Tara ended up living. Whatever else the road trip had or hadn't achieved so far, easing Tara out of her heart certainly hadn't happened. She was more in love with her than ever.

CHAPTER TWENTY-TWO

They made it over the border into Colorado sometime after six, and Tara was more than happy to say adios to Kansas. "So where is our campsite for tonight?" she asked as they pulled in off the I-70 to change seats, and Tara emerged from zombie driving mode into being interested in the navigation again. While she'd been driving, Ricky had called several RV parks, because no horse ranches seemed available in this part of Kansas.

Ricky changed the angle and position of the driver's seat and adjusted the mirrors before putting the truck into drive again and setting off. They still had miles to go down this endlessly straight road.

"I just got confirmation back from a place in Burlington, close to the I-70. We'll be there in less than an hour. I don't think we can expect Thunder to tolerate the box much more tonight."

Tara nodded. "That's for sure. He must be going crazy with boredom." She unfolded her big map. "Give me an idea where to look."

Ricky glanced over and stabbed her finger in the center of the page. "See, we're heading for Burlington, not far from the border. We'll be there soon."

Tara looked more closely. "Good. I see it. I'm kind of getting I-70 road fever." She wasn't joking. The heat and the long stretch of gray highway through monotonous country had given her quite a headache.

Ricky laughed and said, "Sorry, I guess I should apologize on behalf of middle America's highways. I think we'll be on it again all the way to Denver and beyond. We'll be starting to go right through the mountains tomorrow, and it's the I-70 all the way. But it's supposed to get pretty. It's the best route from Denver through to Salt Lake City. Have you ever driven through the

Rockies? I'm getting excited just thinking about them. The next few days are going to be spectacular."

Tara opened a new water bottle and took a long swig, then passed it across. "I'm looking forward to the higher altitudes as well. The air has to get cooler the more we climb. Today has been stifling. But, no, I've never driven these routes before."

Tara worried about Thunder standing in his box all day, and when they stopped and were shown to their site, as far away from other park residents as the manager could arrange, she pulled down the tailgate ramp and took him out into the fresh air as quickly as she could. She saw her fears had been justified; all four of his pasterns showed swelling, and his fetlocks were too warm.

"Is he okay?" asked Ricky, looking equally anxious.

"His legs are swollen from too much standing. I'm not going to ride him, but I'll take him for a long walk right now. There seems to be a quieter access road which leads alongside the park and under the highway off into some areas downtown."

"Take your phone with you and call me if you need me," Ricky said. "I'll clean out his stall and set up camp while you're gone."

Tara wondered if this would involve putting up the little tent or not. "Why don't you call your mom?" she asked, hoping Ricky would spend so long on the phone that she'd forget about setting up separate sleeping arrangements. Last night had been so sweet, just as much physical connection as she could cope with, but she wasn't going to beg for the same deal tonight.

"I will. I forgot to do it last night. She'll start to worry if I leave it any longer. It's so good to know we're halfway there."

Tara found it hard to agree. Every day took them closer to Thunder being taken away from her, and this lovely dreamtime, drifting northwest across America with Ricky would soon end as well.

She removed Thunder's traveling boots and tail bandage and gave him a good brush-down while he enjoyed a drink of water. Then she set off with him at the end of a loose lead rope, so he could enjoy the evening air and take a look around. He was such an intelligent horse, interested in everything. She just hoped there wasn't a pig farm at the end of the dirt road. Like most horses, he'd always hated the smell of pigs.

While they walked, Tara did some hard thinking. She needed this headspace and an hour away from the intensity of being with Ricky. She wanted her so much but felt the constant need to resist showing it, in case Ricky should fall any deeper in love with the useless, emotionally damaged woman she was travelling with.

It was like having long-COVID. Tara hadn't totally recovered from the virus which had been monstrous Marcia. The memory of their years together burned like internal scar tissue, constantly flaring up and irritating her soul, undermining all her efforts to recover and be happy.

And now there were the repeated text messages from Marcia, something she still hadn't shared with Ricky. They were the reason Tara didn't open her phone or check for other messages. Why had Marcia been repeatedly trying to contact her? It had been a horrible shock to see that familiar name come up as the sender. She hadn't opened any of them, but they'd been the main cause of her inability to enjoy what should have been such a beautiful night together back in Clarksville. Ricky hadn't understood why there'd been all those tears, but she'd been so lovely that Tara had summoned the courage to ignore the messages.

She felt even daring to do that had been dangerous. Marcia had been so dominant in her life that even now, she had a default reaction to respond immediately to any communication. Then there had been another incoming text that morning and three voicemails in one single day. This was turning into a crisis.

Tara had switched off her phone, pushed it into the depths of her pocket, where the communications lay, burning an ever-growing hole in her self-confidence. Why did Marcia have to message her now, just as Tara was beginning to heal and move on? Maybe she was sick? Maybe she wanted Tara back?

Whatever the reason, Tara knew they wouldn't be cheerful messages, telling her news of how Marcia's kids had graduated from high school or that the family dog had gone in to have his coat clipped. Marcia was poison, so why did an urge to read the messages pound in her head? It was as though those dreadful years with Marcia had hypnotized her into feeling she should respond, come what may.

She was thankful Thunder appeared to have none of this introspective gloom. He was simply delighted to be out of his traveling jailhouse and looked around over the fences as they walked. She was reminded of his days as a young racehorse, stepping energetically out around the paddock prior to a race.

Marcia had often come with her to those races. She loved to gamble, and she always bet on Thunder. He had won several times in his first season, as a three-year-old, and Marcia had done well out of him financially. She'd wanted to be part-owner with Tara, but it was the only thing she had always denied her, cherishing him for herself, even though Marcia had beaten her as punishment.

Secret physical violence had been central to their relationship.

Her bruises had healed okay, but even the thought of Marcia wielding a whip could still terrorize Tara, and her various sly brutalities had crippled her enjoyment of sex and her ability to climax. Knowing Marcia had decided to be back in touch again was horribly frightening.

They walked along rows of pastel-colored mobile homes, which would unlikely ever be mobile again. Folks seemed to have settled down for good in most of them, housing more casualties of the 2008 mortgage crash. Like so many RV parks, the place had long since stopped pretending to be simply for vacation travelers.

The city was so small that before long, Tara and Thunder found themselves walking along Fifth Street and heading across town toward the railway. Huge grain silos dominated the skyline by the tracks like agricultural cathedrals, and Tara finally understood the reason for Burlington's existence. It had been the railway stop for the shipping of all the surrounding countryside's agricultural produce. The trains, though, no longer stopped and the only sensible way in or out of the little town now was to take the I-70.

Tara walked on and mulled over her options to deal with Marcia's sudden wish to reappear in her life. Option one: she could throw her phone straight into the nearest trash can and buy another with a new number. That would solve the immediate problem, but it wouldn't necessarily get Marcia out of her head. Option two: read the texts, swallow whatever Marcia had to say, and *then* dump the phone. Option three: as above but send a scornful message back, demanding that Marcia cease all communication. Tara wasn't sure if she was emotionally strong enough to do that though. Option four: be honest with Ricky and tell her what had been happening and explain why she was acting so weird when it came to sex. If it came down to honest integrity, she knew she could trust Ricky with her life's darkest secrets, and Ricky could hold her hand while she typed a response to whatever was in the messages.

But Ricky was young and not at all driven by demons. The idea of Tara being in thrall to a woman like Marcia must be way outside her understanding. It was so humiliating and negative, and Tara didn't want to have to delve into the depths of her horrendously abusive relationship. Ricky hadn't wanted to talk about her own girlfriends, but Tara was sure she'd never had to deal with someone like Marcia.

Tara was also frightened of losing what respect Ricky might still have for her. Okay, Ricky was still sexually attracted to her, but she wanted more than that. In an ideal world, Tara longed for Ricky's unbridled love, despite everything she had said to drive her away.

The last glimmers of evening light were now fading fast, and the trees beside the trail grew noisy with the constant rasping of cicadas and crickets drumming their legs together and talking to each other with the clattering of wing cases. It was still hot, and the long drought in these parts made the air thin and dry. They had walked further from the RV park than she'd intended, and it was well past time to turn back.

Tara pulled Thunder to a standstill on the roadside. She ran her hands up and down his legs and was pleased to feel the swelling had mostly gone down. She too felt physically rejuvenated. The evening walk had done them both good. The Marcia problem still lay unresolved, though, and by the time Tara retraced her steps back to the RV campsite, she was just as undecided over what to do about all the messages as before.

Thank God Ricky hadn't put up her little tent. She must have heard the clip clop of Thunder's hooves approaching, because she opened the truck's side door and thrust a large glass of red wine straight into Tara's hand.

"Here, hand Thunder over to me and rest your weary legs. I'll take care of him. I've set up the corkscrew tether over there for him, so he can graze a little and lie down outside to sleep tonight if he wants to."

Tara smiled and relinquished the lead rope. "What would we both do without you?" she asked. The sight of Ricky's bright smile and wavy mop of hair was welcome. She was certainly easy on the eye, and Tara, now as always, felt buoyed and comforted just to have her there. "Should I go and buy us something to eat?" she asked.

"No need. I've already cooked a risotto," said Ricky. "Enjoy your wine and then we'll eat. Then I want to talk to you about the next leg of the journey. Tomorrow's trip is going to take us out of the plains and up into the mountains. I've been reading all about it on my phone."

Tara sipped her wine, a California cabernet which Ricky must have bought at the campsite store. Not bad at all. She took a longer second drink and felt the tension caused by Marcia's messages begin to ease across her shoulders. How nice it would be to view her phone as an innocent gadget full of positive information. Hers felt more like a small, injured rat threatening to bite her. She wondered if option one wouldn't just be the best way forward. "Great, Ric. I'll wash up and then fix a salad. We still have lettuce and tomatoes in the cooler, don't we?"

It was a gentle evening, and Burlington was such a small enough place, there were few streetlights to out-dazzle the stars. After eating dinner and washing the dishes in a bucket, she and Ricky lay down together on a tarp beside their truck and looked up at the immense heavens.

"Tell me all about our itinerary for tomorrow," Tara said before she gradually dozed off as Ricky's passion for conveying information played a soundtrack in her ear, long after she'd stopped listening.

"Come on, sleepyhead," Ricky said, reaching down to pull on her arms and make her stand up. "You haven't heard a word I've said for the last fifteen minutes. Let's go to bed. Thunder is doing fine."

They undressed and lay together like women who were used to sharing a bed and being content in each other's arms. Ricky spooned Tara from behind and kissed her goodnight sweetly on her shoulder.

Tara was just grateful Ricky hadn't been aware of the texts and missed calls. Her last conscious thought was that she would stamp on her phone in the morning and leave it in the trash cans behind the restrooms. Whatever it was Marcia wanted to talk about, Tara didn't want to know.

CHAPTER TWENTY-THREE

There was no doubt about it, Colorado was having an exceptionally dry summer. Even though it was only June, the vast fields either side of the highway were turning yellow far too early, and the crops weren't growing high and lush but looked thirsty. Unlike the steamy exuberance of the southeastern states, the air here was dry and the sky almost a metallic blue. They drove a hundred or so miles toward Denver the following morning, and Ricky felt the hot wind run through her fingers as she let her hand hang out of the window.

Tara was back to her usual efficient self, sitting behind the wheel and looking remarkably fit for someone who had been up since dawn, sponging Thunder's legs with cold water and soaking his bandages to keep the swelling down on his lower legs.

Ricky had taken him out for an even earlier morning ride, and where Tara had walked him far more sedately the night before, she'd let him go for a brisk canter. She'd enjoyed being able to ride him in the fresh air, full of the scents of early summer and before the characteristic smell of hot fumes blocked sweeter smells out on the road.

Now she navigated their route west while Tara concentrated on driving through the traffic. It was rush hour, and the 1-70 was filling up with folk heading into work in the bustling city ahead of them. Ricky had never been to Denver, but one of her college friends came from there, and she was excited to see it. Her friend's mom had coached tennis there for years, and it sounded like a good place to live.

She tuned the radio to a local station to see if there was any information about road conditions west of Denver, but she mainly learned about all the places to eat that were advertised in between songs. They were also discussing upcoming rodeos, something never talked about on the radio back in Florida.

Tara was doing fine, as long as Ricky navigated for her. No point expecting her to use her phone to navigate. Ricky thought she'd been right when she said she didn't like to use it. She couldn't remember when she'd seen Tara even open it, and it had never been in plain view. She wondered about that, because wouldn't Tara be interested to know if there'd been any offers on her property while they were on this trip? Wouldn't her realtor need to contact her if any prospective purchasers wanted to view it? But then she probably didn't want to face another reminder that her whole life was being turned upside down either.

Ricky was still trying to process an earlier incident with a trash bag while Tara had been carrying buckets of water back and forth and fussing over Thunder's fetlocks. Ricky had been tasked with cleaning up and getting rid of their trash in one of the large dumpsters provided in the park. She had learned as a child never to leave trash bags open, especially on campsites. Anything from a rat or a possum to a big black bear might want to investigate otherwise, and once trash was strewn all over the ground, things could only get worse.

When she'd grabbed their trash to shake it down, she'd been astonished to glimpse the unmistakable shape of Tara's cell phone halfway down the bag, smeared with leftover risotto and tomato sauce, but otherwise intact. She withdrew it and saw that the screen was smashed. It looked as though Tara had taken the tent peg mallet to it in some sort of mad fury.

Ricky had wiped the phone down with a few paper towels, safely bagged it up in case the screen started to splinter and wondered what to do next. Tara clearly didn't want her phone. Had she tried to destroy it, or had she dropped it when she was riding Thunder and he'd stepped on it? Probably she hadn't realized that she could remove its SIM card to put it into a new phone and keep her number. Ricky had gathered enough evidence on the trip to know that Tara wasn't the techiest person on the block.

She decided to wait a while, in case this was something she didn't understand. She picked up the sealed zip-lock bag and carefully stowed it away inside her own backpack. Then she returned to the task of breaking camp, finished tying up the bag, and threw it into the dumpster.

But the mystery had been niggling away in her brain ever since. As they approached Denver and the road began to climb, she decided to tackle the problem with a few sly questions. "Where's your cell phone, Tara? You haven't lost it, have you?"

Tara looked guilty and squirmed in her seat. She laughed. "No, of course I haven't lost it. Why would you think that?"

"I haven't seen you with it for days, and I don't think you've charged it either."

"That's because I don't waste the battery leaving it on all the time." She cast Ricky a sidelong glance. "Unlike *some* people."

"Tell me where it is, and I'll plug it into the cigarette lighter socket. We can charge it up as we drive along." Ricky hoped Tara would come clean, maybe laugh a little, and explain her sudden allergic reaction to her phone.

"No," Tara said brusquely. "No," she said, softer this time. "It's tucked at the bottom of my pack, and like I said, the battery's fine. Don't worry. Now tell me where we're heading. I think the easiest way through Denver is to plow straight through the center east to west. That's what the map seems to show anyway. Is that okay with you?"

Ricky had to admire her nifty footwork. There must be some major issue with the phone for sure, but what was it? Okay, she'd leave it for now, but she planned to tackle it later when Tara wasn't so busy driving. She felt sorry for her and for her apparent need for deceit. Her own phone conversations with her parents were much appreciated on both sides, and she was sad that Tara had no one anxious to hear from her or that there was no one she wanted to contact.

She called her mom while Tara was driving and heard, "If you can, try to visit a place called Moab along the way. It's on the Colorado River, and the rock formations there are incredible. You'll be amazed."

So Ricky took her mom's advice and booked their next site at an RV Park near the resort town of Moab. It would be another long drive today, five hundred miles by road, and it would take them the whole day to do it. Traversing Denver would slow them down, as would driving up the winding wooded hills to the west. But once they were there, they could ease off the next day and enjoy the scenery. Her phone said hiking trails abounded, so she expected there to be plenty of riding trails too. "I think we might cover the distance to Moab today. It's a long haul, but I wondered what you thought of having a rest day there tomorrow to let Thunder relax. We can take him out for the day, pack a picnic, and explore the area. What do you think?"

Tara smiled, all irritation about being quizzed over the phone gone from her expression. "That sounds like a lovely idea, Ric. It's not only Thunder who needs a day off the road. We all do."

"I've also come to the end of my clean clothes," said Ricky. "A trip to a laundromat would be good. I can take your clothes too if you like." She didn't think it polite to ask about the state of Tara's underwear, but they'd been sitting in a hot truck for five straight days, and she knew the state of her own wardrobe. They might benefit from the cool wash cycle along with their clothes. Tara's jeans must almost be standing up on their own. Ricky wondered if she could get her into a pair of shorts. She had the legs for it. Just thinking about them raised Ricky's temperature.

Just before the Denver city limits, they switched drivers. Tara went to the back of the truck to check up on Thunder while Ricky popped the hood to monitor the water and oil levels. Both were okay. She settled into the driving seat, and Tara climbed up beside her. "When we next stop for fuel, I'd like to check the tire pressures. Do you have any wild idea what they should be?"

Tara looked a little bemused. "I don't know.

"I'll call Dad later and ask," said Ricky. "He had several big trucks about this size when he ran his construction business."

"Your father was a good builder with a fine reputation for quality homes. I was so sorry to hear about his accident. When it happened, I came over to see you, but your mom told me you were away at an athletics meet. Did she tell you I'd visited?"

Ricky couldn't honestly remember. "If she did, I was probably still so fired up with hate and shame I probably never even took it in. We were all in shock about Dad's injuries. But it sounds typical of me that I'd selfishly gone off to take part in a race when everyone else was at the hospital."

"Ric, you're the least selfish person I know. Please don't keep beating yourself up."

"How about we both follow that advice, huh?" Ricky reached over and lightly caressed Tara's cheek. It wasn't much, but it was a physical connection to show how much she loved her.

There were really four of them on this trip, she thought. Tara, Thunder, her, and this faithful old truck, who had carried them so far with only minor grumbling. It had never been driven so far all at once in its long life, and she was aware of the need to keep checking the levels. Neither she nor Tara were mechanics, and they couldn't afford any unnecessary breakdowns.

They'd filled the gas tank back in Burlington, and she'd worried about how the column of little figures in the record book was growing. The amount of cash needed for each fill-up seemed to be rising daily. Tara must surely need to break into her eight hundred dollars soon, and Ricky decided to be firmer on the subject of shared costs.

Their road trip continued through Aurora, the large southeastern part of suburban Denver, after she took over the driving. They'd fallen into the pattern of swapping every two hours or so, and every four hours, taking a longer pitstop in a service area and walking Thunder for twenty minutes to ease his legs. It slowed them down even further than their normal sedate pace of fifty-eight miles an hour, but it seemed to work for everyone's mental health.

On the road for hours together, across seven states so far, they had talked of all manner of things, and as it was summer, especially the prospects for various baseball teams. Along the way, Ricky had learned heaps of stuff about Tara, the areas where she was an expert, as well as the things in which she took no interest and knew hardly anything. But it was all general chat, nothing about the inner workings of her heart.

Tara had quizzed Ricky about her college years and early teaching career, her friends, her athletics, where she had traveled, what she had done in her spare time. She had pointedly stopped asking Ricky about her sex life. She wished she would, because they could have gone deeper. But all of it was safe, all of it general information which she'd have found on her Facebook page if Tara had cared to look.

But Ricky, having already searched for herself, knew that Tara had kept well away from Facebook and all the other social media sites. Her online footprint was fainter than a wild mustang's on the hills of Wyoming.

Ricky decided time was running out. She'd had enough of circling each other and avoiding the fat gray elephant squashed between them in the cab. She and Tara needed to talk about personal things, even, if she dared, go straight into their relationship and into the things Tara had told her on that first, revelatory evening back at the stables. Enough of all the deflections.

She wondered if she could use the classic Monty Roberts' horse whispering techniques on Tara. It was an idea anyway. If she could drive her forward to face up to the future until she was mentally exhausted, then she might be able to turn away, seem uninterested, and then let Tara join up with her and open up of her own accord about the things which were really bugging her and clearly blocking their relationship. "Let's talk about next week," Ricky said. "What are we going to do when Thunder is safely installed in his new home?"

Tara looked anxious. "I've been putting it off, you know, deciding what to do next, even how we go back to Florida."

"Well, no time like the present," said Ricky, feeling like she was encouraging her young students to focus on completing their course work and improving their grades. "Let's look at the options together."

"He's almost returning to the place where he was bred," Tara said. "I wonder if the mare who was his mother is still alive and still in Tacoma. Perhaps we can find out and visit when we get there."

That sounded fine, although Ricky had no idea how Tara was even going to call Thunder's new owner, let alone his breeder, without her cell phone. But the conversation was moving forward. She reckoned her horse whispering idea might even work.

FOR LOVE OF THUNDER

They drove straight through the great city of Denver and up into the high hills beyond. Ricky was happy to navigate for herself. Not a problem as following the I-70 wasn't exactly rocket science. As they climbed and the valleys grew narrower, the mountains steeper, and the scenery more dramatic, Tara more often looked away out of the window and stopped talking. What she was thinking about, Ricky had no idea. But she guessed it must be the realization that they were now only days away from losing Thunder, which could only make her sad.

"I think the RV park I reserved has a swimming pool," Ricky said, trying to lift Tara's mood. "That should be fun."

"Yes, sure," said Tara.

But her mind was clearly miles away. Ricky's first attempt at join-up hadn't succeeded. But she was determined not to give up. "About our budget, when are you going to start using my contribution to the finances?" she asked and was pleased when Tara gave her a really angry look, straightened her back, and pulled on the proverbial boxing gloves. Now they were back on track. She loved it when Tara pretended to be ferocious.

CHAPTER TWENTY-FOUR

It was well past seven when they finally arrived in Moab, having driven more than five hundred miles through Colorado and Utah. Tara delegated Ricky to scoot over to the park office and check them in. She'd been driving for the last two hours through some of the most spectacular country she'd ever seen.

It should have been a wonderful touristy experience, but Tara's inner conflicts had seriously spoiled her enjoyment. They'd seen elk grazing beside the roadside, wild sheep with great curved horns perched on the crags, and even a bull moose drinking from a river below one bend. As the road hit the mountains, there were tunnels to negotiate, so she'd needed to concentrate.

The tension of keeping a sane appearance and being reasonably cheerful in Ricky's company, while internally obsessing about Marcia and what she might be up to, had resulted in a tension headache which stretched right across Tara's head from ear to ear. They'd passed through several construction sites and roadwork hold-ups on the way, and Tara felt as though she'd picked up one of the guys wielding a concrete smashing hammer drill and was giving him a ride in her temples.

The not so bright idea of smashing up her phone and dumping it at the campsite in Burlington had simply been like shooting the messenger. She couldn't ignore the obvious truth that Marcia was out there somewhere, on the prowl, like the witch she was. Nor could she pretend she could escape her simply by ducking and weaving. One day she would have to turn and fight, but for now she had neither the courage nor the armor needed.

She'd been poor company all day, and Ricky had been trying all sorts of strategies to get her to open up and spill out all the beans. But the pain was too sharp, too deep, and her self-confidence too close to zero.

Ricky skipped back from the park office, as bright and as breezy as ever, and Tara's heart lifted from its position somewhere near her boots. She loved to look at her traveling companion. She gazed into Ricky's eyes and wished she had the guts to tell her all her troubles, wonderful woman that she was, but she just couldn't. "How did that go?" she asked after winding the window down.

"Fantastic. They were really interested to learn that we had a horse with us, and they've given us a place right at the end of the line, where they say he can stay tethered outside under some trees. The only thing we're not allowed to do, obviously, is make an open fire. Everything is so dry from the drought, it's lucky there are any trees still alive, but we can make camp over there. You drive behind me, and I'll lead the way. They gave me a site plan."

Tara did as she was told and drove at five miles an hour behind Ric, who trotted ahead through the park and found them a great site underneath some trees and next to a water tap. As they unloaded Thunder, she could see he was as weary and stressed as she was. A rest day off the road without moving wasn't only a nice idea, it was essential.

Once they'd set up camp, they hitched Thunder to his revolving tether pole within reach of a large bucket of fresh water. Tara told Ricky that she had a blinder of a headache and was going to lie down in the van until it eased off.

Ricky pulled out a couple of painkillers from her backpack and handed them over with her water bottle. "Dehydration. I've noticed how little you drink. Get a pint or two of water down you and I promise you'll feel much better."

Tara guessed she was partly right. She swallowed the offered Advil along with half the bottle of water and managed a smile. "Don't let me cramp your style, Ric. I'll be fine here on my own with Thunder. You said there was a swimming pool here. Why don't you go and have a swim? I expect it'll stay open through the evening."

Ricky drew her in for a hug and held her quietly in her arms for a moment. Tara could so easily have collapsed into her at that point and broken down. Every one of Ricky's continual small kindnesses made her want to weep. She hoped Ricky would spare her that humiliation by taking a walk.

"Okay, boss," Ricky said. "I might just do that, and I'll look out for something to buy for our supper, as well. How does pizza sound? There's got to be food here."

"Sounds fine, whatever," said Tara. She turned away and went up into the truck into the sleeping area. "Give me a couple of hours, do you mind?"

"Course not. Bye."

Ricky grabbed her swimsuit and a towel and disappeared. Tara was left on her own. She kicked off her boots, slipped out of her Levi's, and lay down on the bed. To start with, the simple act of lying horizontally without moving and with her eyes firmly closed was enough to ease her headache. Tara turned to face the wall and consciously tried to relax, to stop obsessing about Marcia, and think only of Ric's sweet face, her quirky smile, curly mop of hair, and kind intelligence.

But her inner eye wandered south, conjuring up Ricky's perfectly balanced breasts, the flat ripple of her stomach, and the soft curves where her hips joined her long, beautiful legs. Ricky's body was gorgeous. She couldn't think of a single fault. Of course if Marcia was here, she'd find something to criticize. She always had, especially when looking at Tara's scrawny body.

God damn it, Marcia was even invading her current little fantasy. Tara ground her teeth and refocused. *Relax, relax. Think of Ric, relax.* The painkillers and her natural exhaustion took over, and she fell asleep.

When she woke up, the camp was in total darkness, and she glanced down at her wristwatch. Ten thirty? She'd been asleep for three hours! So where was Ric? Why wasn't she here? A stupid feeling of panic shot through her. The guy with the hammer drill had gone away, leaving only a dull ache, but she needed more painkillers. Tara stumbled about in the dark, trying to find her jeans and boots, so she could emerge from the truck, check up on Thunder, and go in search of her Ricky.

She finally located her jeans and pulled them on, and then

berated herself. Of course, if she hadn't been such a damn fool about her phone, she could've called Ricky and located her immediately. What a fool. What a cowardly, pathetic fool. Tara was slipping back into self-hatred again, and her nerves were still on edge even after a few hours' restful sleep. At least Marcia hadn't made it into her dreams this time, and she'd never have to read her text messages now the phone was five hundred miles away.

She turned on the internal light in the cab, located Ricky's water bottle, and took another drink from it, though it was lukewarm and horrible. She thought she'd help herself to another couple of Advil and pulled Ricky's backpack closer. She put her hand inside and felt about for the little package which she'd seen Ricky replace earlier. It wasn't immediately at hand, so Tara shook the contents out onto her bed, and then gasped and swallowed nervously.

Alongside a couple of pairs of Ricky's socks and a rolled-up T-shirt was a plastic bag containing her dirty, smashed-up phone. Ricky must have retrieved it from the trash back in Burlington and bagged it up, like evidence from a crime scene. Anger and shame mounted in Tara's mind in equal measure. Why hadn't Ricky said anything? How dare she retrieve what she must have known had been deliberately discarded? Had she read the text messages or listened to her voicemail? How much did she know and wasn't saying?

Tara sat on the bed and stared at the phone. A dead rat would have been a nicer thing to find in Ricky's backpack. She was paralyzed with indecision and an underlying feeling of panic. Just as she was about to pull on her boots and storm out to look for Ricky, she heard footsteps approaching, and the cab door swung open.

"Hello, gorgeous. How's it going?"

A decidedly buzzed-looking Ricky climbed up to join her. Their faces were less than a foot apart, and Tara could smell the alcohol. "You've been drinking."

"Yep. Only a few beers. What else is a girl to do when her beloved sleeps all evening? I came back to check up on you at eight thirty, and again at nine fifteen, but you were sleeping so hard, I thought I'd leave you. I've been over in the bar playing pool. I whipped those guys' asses, I can tell you. And hey, I've brought you pizza. Hope you like pepperoni."

She clearly hadn't yet noticed the phone. She thrust a food container toward Tara's chest and sat down next to her on the bed, pepped up with pool success and cheap beer. She was obviously feeling playful.

Tara, though, felt like shit. "You pulled my phone out of the trash."

"I did. Why wouldn't I? I'm your friend. I'm here to save you from yourself. You need to tell me what's going on, and why you trashed it in the first place."

Ricky had started by sounding a little defensive, obviously surprised, but Tara saw she wouldn't back off. She would sit there until Tara told her the truth. She stared into those beguiling brown eyes and wondered how to begin.

"Begin at the beginning, my love," Ricky said huskily. "And remember I'm here for you, all for you. No other agenda. You're clearly hurting, and it's my job to find out the reason and then stop it, if I can." She took back the little plastic container and extracted two large pizza slices. "Eat and talk. With your mouth full if you like. You must be starved. But just talk, okay?"

Tara, as she was doing more and more on this trip, took the only course offered and did what Ricky told her to do, at least half of it anyway. She ignored the limp-looking food. "I haven't told you, because I know you'll think I'm ridiculous. But ever since Juliette, I've been getting daily texts from Marcia, my ex."

"I know who she is!" Ricky clenched her jaw. "Sorry," she said softly. "That explains a heap of things. Go on, please. I won't interrupt again."

Tara looked down at the pizza slice, sitting in the food container, dripping with cheese and carbs. She didn't have the slightest appetite for it. "I haven't read any of them, but they kept coming. The only thing I could think of doing was to throw away the phone. I've been so frightened. I can't expect you to understand. You used to look up to me, to respect me…"

Ricky munched through her own pizza slice with cheerful gusto. It didn't quite fit with Tara's mood of tragic self-hatred.

"Sure. I did look up to you, and I still do. More than that, I love you. You're my fair lady, and I'll be your knight. Leave it to me, and I'll get rid of that old stupid dragon Marcia for you. She doesn't scare me."

"Well, she scares me," Tara said, her voice trembling. "She really does. When I was with her, she often used to terrorize me. Her moods were volcanic, and she held such power over me."

"Like how?" Ricky put aside the remains of her supper and wiped her hands on the paper napkin which came with it. "Let me hold you while you tell me everything. She's not here now. I am, and I'll never let her frighten you again."

Tara doubted whether even Ricky would be powerful enough to break such a strong spell as the one which bound her in thrall to Marcia, but she let herself be gathered in and rocked gently on Ricky's shoulder.

"What did Marcia do to you? Let it all out."

So Tara, haltingly, and ashamed even as she did it, began to talk about the regular beatings, the constant put-downs, the sneers and insults. It was a long, humiliating list. "Once, she fractured my wrist by twisting it so hard when I took too long in making her dinner. Then there were a couple of black eyes when she thought I'd been seeing someone else. She was jealous of everybody, male or female, who came to the ranch. Toward the end, she even made me stop taking adult riding pupils."

"My God! The bitch. Where can I find her?" Ricky tightened her embrace. "Sorry. Keep going."

Tara sniffed. "In the beginning, she used to let me make love to her and then make me come. But after a while, things changed. Sometimes after we'd had sex, she would push me out of bed and make me lie naked on the floor beside her, or she'd bring me right up to the point of orgasm, only to slap my face and tell me I was a whore. I was in some sort of torture chamber, permanently afraid and knowing I would never be given a way out."

"My poor, poor baby." Ricky held her close. "She's been gone two years, did you say? Have you not been able to recover?"

Tara shook her head. "She ruined me, Ric. I think she's destroyed me sexually. It's my punishment for ever starting with her. She kept telling me how wicked it was to tempt her away from her husband, that our affair was all my fault, and I should be punished for our sins."

"What total crap," said Ricky. "You've been the victim of severe sexual and physical abuse, and we probably need to find a trained therapist to help you heal when this is all over. I'm not experienced enough. But you did absolutely the right thing not opening those texts and chucking your phone out."

"I did?" It still didn't feel that way. Guilt gnawed at her, just like it did when she and Marcia were together.

"Yep, totally the right thing. You did what you had to. But leave everything to me. If you agree, I'll charge your phone and read the stupid messages tomorrow. You don't need to be there, you don't have to know what's in them, but I think I should, so I can be prepared and to stop this game she's playing before it goes any further."

Tara sat on the bed with her head bowed. She felt like an abused child finally released from the custody of a demonic guardian. Ricky shone with confident energy and healthy anger, and even more powerfully, Tara knew what she said was true.

She had indeed been a victim of a crime, a long series of crimes. She hadn't just been an immoral, feeble failure of a woman. For the first time in years, she began to glimpse a light at the top of the well into which she'd been thrown. She held onto Ric, hugging her as tightly as she could. "Thank you," she whispered. "Thank you so much. I was a victim, not a criminal. I understand now. But maybe I don't have to be frightened any more. Maybe I can move on. Maybe I can become a survivor."

"Don't you think that tonight proves you already are?" Ricky wrapped her arms around her and returned the hug with interest. "Let's go to bed. Let me rock you in my arms."

And Tara let her. Her smashed up, but still operable, phone lay close by, cleaned up and recharging from the truck's battery, and tomorrow Ricky would take care of whatever was inside it. For the first time in more than ten years, she felt safe. Exhausted by all this emotion, she undressed, lay down beside Ricky on the hard double bed and felt her arms comfortingly wrap around her, and then dropped off to sleep almost immediately.

CHAPTER TWENTY-FIVE

Ricky lay on the bed, cradling Tara's slim body against her, and listened to the early morning sounds of the desert birds calling to each other in the nearby small plantation of trees. The guys in the pool bar had told her they'd been without rain all year. Utah had been under drought conditions for the last ten years, and she wondered how the wildlife survived. There'd be no rain again today, that was for sure.

She gently pulled her arm away from under Tara and flexed her hand, stiff and squashed from being lain on all night by this beautiful, lost soul. Ricky had spent the last hour watching Tara sleep and had been processing the revelations she'd heard the previous evening.

She understood so much more now, the paradox of how such a talented, attractive, and confident woman had been reduced to almost nothing by consistent and cruel abuse. There was no softer way of saying it. Ricky's heart burned with fury whenever she thought of monstrous Marcia. She wanted to take revenge for all the misery she'd created, all of Tara's self-hatred and fear of intimacy, and as a side issue, for the way her own life had been impacted by the fallout from their toxic relationship. She just wasn't sure how to achieve it.

One thing was clear. She hadn't lied when she'd told Tara she would be her knight and protect her from any further abuse. However vulnerable and fragile Tara's emotional well-being might be, Ricky was determined to care for her with all her heart until she recovered.

No wonder Tara was scared of sex. If it took years and years for her to heal, then that's how long Ricky would wait. She was setting no limits, no expectations. She just knew she loved Tara unconditionally.

Ricky planned it out rather carefully. She spent the first half hour of the next morning with Thunder, cleaning up his droppings, watering and feeding him as usual, and then she suggested Tara give him a really long grooming session with the dandy brush and curry comb, stripping all the loose hair and dust from his summer coat, and then strapping him down and polishing his hooves with oil. Tara still seemed in a daze after the revelations of the night before and looked as though she'd appreciate basic directions.

"Okay, I can do that," she said. "Just about. But when are we—"

"You're doing nothing. Just give me the access code for your phone and leave it with me. Marcia can't poison me. I'm going to walk over to the camp restaurant, order a good strong coffee and a sweet roll, and sit in a quiet corner. Then I'll open up the messages. I'll find out what her game is, lay that pesky dragon of fear you've got hissing around you, and then report back, with cinnamon rolls. How does that sound?"

"It sounds fine. I'm sorry I'm such a—"

"Don't ever start a sentence with saying you're sorry, my love." Ricky grabbed the phone and turned it on. "Just tell me the code."

"You have to make the shape of an M."

That didn't surprise Ricky. "Like this?"

"Yes. Do you really want to do this?"

"Can't wait, I'm on it now. You get busy with the grooming. We're going out trail-riding all day today, and Thunder has to look his best. Supposing we met some wild mustangs out there in the canyons, and they looked down on him because he wasn't as beautiful as he could be."

This was pretty elementary psychology, but it worked well enough. Tara defensively rubbed Thunder's nose and kissed him. She reached for the box of grooming brushes and started a well-practiced routine, which should take her a minimum of forty minutes.

Ricky slipped the phone into her shoulder bag along with her wallet and strode briskly away before Tara could call her back.

FOR LOVE OF THUNDER

She walked over to the central area of the campsite, where she'd played pool the night before with some guys from Indiana who were mountain biking after graduating from business school.

This morning, the atmosphere in the restaurant bar was quite different. Several families with severely overweight kids were enjoying enormous breakfasts, and she wondered how easily those youngsters would climb up the steep trails and rock formations they'd come to see. The stacks of pancakes in front of them looked like a big enough challenge.

She had some trouble finding an empty table away from other diners, but the servers were pleasantly attentive, and she was seated by a window and soon had the coffee and pastries she'd ordered on the table in front of her.

No point putting it off any further. Ricky took a long swig of coffee and opened Tara's phone. She'd shown total confidence when she'd been talking to Tara, but her terror had been a little contagious. Ricky summoned her inner police officer before scrolling a capital M across the splintered screen. She only hoped the battered phone would still work.

Yep, thank God, it did. The broken screen made the texts in the messenger inbox harder to decipher, but it wasn't impossible. Ricky pulled a notepad and pen from her bag and started to read Tara's messages over the last week. Somehow this made it all more forensic, clinical even. She really did feel like an officer at a crime scene cleaning up after a murder attempt.

Marcia's first message set the scene for what Ricky guessed would follow.

Tara, darling I've decided to forgive you. You failed miserably to please me before but now you deserve another chance. Tell me you still love me (I know you do), and I'll come back to Florida right away. Things haven't worked out so well in California– I'll tell you about that when we're together. Just get the sheets ironed and a bottle of champagne on ice. Marcia. (P.S. Bollinger, not that crap you bought for my birthday that time.)

The nerve of the woman! Ricky had to gasp at her bare-faced effrontery. This was probably the way she had always talked to Tara. But was she normally so broken and controlled that Marcia could assume it might work to woo her back, if Ricky wasn't around? She opened the second text.

Why haven't you replied immediately? You know the rules. Spend an hour on your hands and knees as punishment. Then call me. I want to hear you say how sorry you are. When we're together again, I'll have to teach you some phone manners, darling Tara. Don't worry, I'm planning to fly over to Tampa on the weekend. We'll be able to sort it out then. Rod and I are divorcing now the kids are grown, and I am coming back to you. Forever. We can live together now. Nothing can keep us apart.

"Wait until you meet me again," muttered Ricky, keeping her voice low in deference to the other people around her. This Marcia woman was seriously delusional.

Okay, so maybe I was a little harsh. It doesn't have to be as long as an hour. Just meet me at the airport off the seven p.m. flight from Houston next Saturday evening and all will be forgiven.

Ricky sighed deeply and opened the fourth text.

You know I was only kidding, babe, don't you? I'm a changed woman, no, really, and I can't wait until I'm back in your arms. I promise I'll be as gentle as a lamb, and don't worry, when I get my divorce settlement, we can both live in comfort for the rest of our lives. I can take care of you and Thunder. Please call me, darling. I love you, Picklepuss."

"Picklepuss?" Ricky didn't know whether to laugh or throw up. But the fourth message was obviously the most dangerous. She could imagine Tara reading it and have all her resolve go down the drain. If Marcia was being genuine and not just bullshitting about her decision to return to Florida, then they had something major to worry about.

Ricky turned to the missed calls and called Tara's voicemail. It was weird to hear Marcia's voice after all these years. It was still husky, Southern wealthy, and now that she was older, Ricky could tell it was dripping with sexual innuendo. The messages were all in the same vein as before, basically saying that Marcia was growing increasingly desperate to hear back from Tara and how they were so right for each other.

FOR LOVE OF THUNDER

Ricky could also hear the anger in Marcia's voice, even though it was being carefully controlled. The final message took them into a whole new area of risk.

I can't wait anymore. I'm coming to Tampa. Be there! You're being ridiculous. You know we belong together. I've just seen that your ranch is up for sale. Well, I'll buy it off you and solve all your money worries, darling. Now you won't have to sell Thunder or close your little riding school. See you in a few hours. Call me back, any hour. Just call, okay?

Ricky played the message again to check when it had been left; it had been earlier that morning. Marcia might even be in the air by now. Ricky saw there were also several messages from Tara's realtor. Please let the ranch already be under offer from someone else. She decided Tara should be free to read her own non-Marcia messages, so she gathered up the cinnamon rolls, picked up the phone, and gulped down the last of her coffee. Then she paid up and hotfooted it back to their site.

Tara was squatting down on the grass behind the horse truck, busily oiling Thunder's hooves. His coat gleamed like gold, and he was nuzzling Tara's hair with his muzzle, clearly playing with her as she bent over below his head. He looked as polished and plaited up as though he was going to a county show. Wow, Thunder and Tara loved each other, and they looked so good together.

Ricky's heart sank as she saw the risks in letting Tara hear exactly what Marcia had said. She'd probably want to risk everything if it meant she could keep her horse. Ricky could see herself being left standing alone in Moab while Tara and Thunder disappeared in a cloud of dust back to Tampa. But it would be totally dishonorable not to tell the truth. "Hey!"

"Hey, yourself. You didn't take long. Tell me the worst. Are our lives in mortal danger?"

Tara had clearly been processing a range of scenarios and sounded quite prepped to hear whatever Ricky had to tell her. "No, but after a lot of threats and then promises, your ex is planning a comeback. She says she's flying to Tampa today."

"Holy cow!"

"Yep. She's also gotten wind that you're selling Meadowlands, and she wants to buy it and live there with you. She wants you back, and she wants to have Thunder there too. In her mind, it's a done deal."

Tara straightened up, patted Thunder's shoulder, put the lid back on the container of hoof oil, and carefully wiped the brush on the grass. Ricky hopped with impatience to see how she was really going to react after this displacement activity. "So?" she asked impatiently when Tara still said nothing.

"So what?"

"What are you going to do? How do you want to respond?"

Tara ran her fingers through her hair and gave her sideways smile. "Ignore her, of course. She's horrible. Why would I want to spend one more second wasting time worrying about what to say to her? She's ridiculous."

Tara looked remarkably cheerful and firm about this, neither petrified nor tempted. Ricky was mightily relieved but surprised. She couldn't resist flinging her arms around her and giving her a great big hug, even if it was just a temporary brave face she was putting on. "I'm so happy to hear you say that! I thought, maybe, if Thunder was in the deal, you might want to go back to her, despite everything…"

"Ric, darling, you've read those messages for me. Thank you for sparing me. I'm sure it's given you a good taste of what Marcia is like. I wasn't totally surprised to hear what was in them. That sort of crap is so typical of her."

"You don't sound too upset."

"While you were gone, I've decided to face my problems and start doing something about them. You've been a wonderful encouragement to me. So, I've been brushing Marcia Cunningham out of my life, while I've been brushing the dust out of Thunder's coat. I gave his coat fifty brushes, and it was most therapeutic. Marcia is just so much dust as well now.

"So, there's no chance you'd consider—"

"Consider having anything to do with that poisonous bully ever again? No."

"Not even if it means you get to keep Thunder?"

"Ric! What do you take me for? I know I'm pathetic, but I'm not that weak or stupid. Marcia always kept making promises to reform, promising to give me the moon. I was taken in and believed her, but now I know I should've caught on years ago. Her promises are like piecrusts. When I compare her to you, my God, it's like apples and oranges."

"Huh, so I'm like an apple now, am I?" Ricky still had Tara in her arms and was happy to see her feeling jaunty enough for some gentle teasing. She could feel Tara's smooth biceps under her fingers and the physical power in her arms.

Tara cocked her head and whispered, "You are my wonderful woman. You are. Like a crispy, delicious, apple I can't wait to get my teeth into."

That sounded positively frisky. Tara was in recovery. Ricky had to concentrate to get them both back on track. "For now, don't eat me. Take this cinnamon roll instead. There are other voice messages and texts you should read from your realtor. Maybe someone else is interested in your ranch."

Ricky wanted Tara to stay the course and read all the messages. Then they could dump the broken phone just as soon as she'd written down a few key numbers, like the one for the guy who was buying Thunder, for starters. But Tara shook her head and even gave a little jump back. So maybe not completely in recovery after all.

"Nope, you read them, please. Finish the job. I don't want to touch that thing again."

Ricky released her, opened the phone, and flipped through. She read the messages from Tara's realtor. "Oh."

"What is it?"

"There's two from your realtor. He says there's been a lot of local interest in the ranch. A syndicate is interested in developing some of the site. They're going to investigate planning regulations and do a feasibility study or something. Nothing definite yet, he reckons, but promising. He wants you to comment."

"When did the second one come in?"

"Yesterday. How do you want me to reply?"

"Say I'm definitely interested and to keep me posted. Then

give him your phone number and ask him to use only that in the future. Say I'm traveling right now and also not to give our number or any information about my whereabouts to anyone, whoever they are."

"Sure. Hang on." Ricky leaned back against the side of the truck and quickly texted the message. "Right, that's done."

Tara looked impressed, as though Ricky had done something out of the ordinary.

She finished a bite of her cinnamon roll. "It's like when we came out of the swamps."

Ricky frowned. "What are you talking about?"

"The way humans have evolved and learned to walk on dry land. You're amazing, all you under-thirties! The way you text. Flying along, using only your thumbs."

"You could learn if you practiced more."

"Who do I have to send texts to, apart from you know who? And that will never happen again."

"What about me?" Ricky felt daring, even saying it. They still had this impasse between their different views of the future. "Will you not ever text me?"

Tara licked the icing from her fingers. "You don't need to text someone who's always right there beside you, do you?"

Tara kissed Ricky's cheek and picked up a towel and her washbag. "But now I need a quick shower. Tack Thunder up, will you? And then let's go and spend the day together doing something nice. I need a good long break from the truck."

"How's your headache?" Ricky asked. This new Tara, embracing the potential of their future together, was so exciting. She didn't want to entertain the thought that it might end along with the road trip.

"Better. Much better. You were right. It was probably dehydration. As long as we take plenty of water, I'll be fine."

"We need to do laundry, don't forget. But yes, you ride, and I'll run and let's explore the famous Moab valley trails."

And that is what they did for the rest of the day. They had a glorious day out in the hills looking at the fantastical rock formations and arches, but by the time they returned to camp, they reckoned they had enough red sand under their belts, down their boots, and under their fingernails to last the rest of the trip. Everything was as dry as dust, and the Colorado River was running at an all-time low.

In the early evening, Ricky gathered up a bundle of all their dirty, sandy clothes, the pillowcases, and the bed sheet, and whisked them off to the laundromat. As she watched their clothes whirl around together in the soapy water, she had a small moment of excited revelation. Never before had she shared a laundry load with a girlfriend. It was what couples did. She and Tara were creating a new norm by this simple little act of domesticity. Their journey toward a joint future was looking more positive by the day.

Chapter Twenty-Six

When Tara dressed the following morning, she enjoyed having clean clothes to wear from head to foot. She folded her Levi's and put them away. She felt like a new person, not just a rough, tough horsewoman, and she wanted to make a special effort for Ric, who deserved better than being seen out with a shabby cowgirl.

Today they were heading straight for Boise so there was no time for riding, but Frank Waite, an old show-jumping buddy who lived close to the city had said they could stay at his place, and Thunder could roam free in his pastures for the night. She asked Ricky to call the number, and then Tara took the phone and confirmed they were on their way. She handed the phone back to Ricky to take down instructions on how to find the place.

Thunder pulled such a disgusted-looking face when they bandaged his legs and put him in his stall that Tara had to laugh. "It won't be so long now, boy," she said. "You've got this nice comfy box, and you still have two bales of sweet hay to munch on. I promise we'll be there before you know it." She turned on the radio again to amuse him. The first thing she found was a religious channel, but there'd probably be plenty of gospel tunes, so he'd enjoy it even if he didn't find Jesus.

"I have a strong theory that horses can recognize different tunes," she said to Ricky, who had stripped down to a strappy top in the heat and was tying up Thunder's hay net. She clearly wasn't wearing a bra and looked edible.

"That would be cool."

"How else do they perform so well when they do displays, musical rides, and parades? They know just when to change the sequences, depending on the music."

"You've got a point. Maybe we should teach him one of your

favorite songs. What would you pick?"

"Easy. 'Constant Craving' by k.d. lang," she said, not missing a beat. "It's how I'm feeling right now." She turned Ric around and pressed her lips to Ric's warm, honey-colored cheek. It was as soft as a down pillow and smelled wonderful.

Ricky shifted her face to meet her lips with her own, and they locked together like magnets. Ricky wrapped her arms around Tara, and their breasts were crushed together. Ricky released a quiet moan.

"My love," Tara said and hoped Ricky understood. The horrible curse which Marcia had put on her had been lifted, and she was grabbing her freedom to love and be loved again. Today was a new beginning, and maybe tonight… Tonight she would give everything to Ricky and let her in. Whether she climaxed or not seemed far less important than simply letting go and trusting Ricky.

Ricky kissed her like there was no tomorrow. They were hidden behind the horse truck so Mr. or Mrs. Mainstream America couldn't see them, and if they weren't on such a tight schedule, Tara would have dragged Ricky down to the ground and pulled her shorts off there and then.

But they had to get back on the road.

Ricky knew that as well, but she was clearly pulsing with arousal, and her previous gentle patience and talk of therapists seemed to have evaporated. "Tonight, Tara, tonight. Promise me?"

Tara nodded. Her smile was so wide, it hurt her cheeks. She felt like a kid who'd just learned to whistle.

They eventually peeled themselves apart and prepared to hit the route back up to the I-70 and onto the I-15 all the way north to Salt Lake City, two hundred and thirty miles away. They should be there around one, just in time for lunch.

Tara drove with all the windows down, as the AC had given up the ghost, and Ricky sat on her right, researching Utah. They were making good progress. Tara felt joyful. What Ricky had finally done with her old phone, she didn't want to know. She was finally free and dare she think it, totally happy.

"Folks on Tripadvisor say Park City is a cool place to visit," said Ricky. "It's just a few miles off our route, and we could stop there for lunch. It's a ski resort in the winter snow but this time of year, it's known as a mecca for foodies."

"Let's go there then. See if you can find somewhere suitable to let Thunder out."

"Sure."

Ricky set to work and didn't complain when Tara stroked her thigh as she drove. The road wound northward, through valleys and the high mountainous hills, then down again to the level of the valley bottoms. Apart from the inevitable roadworks and light traffic hold-ups, they made good progress and reached Park City on schedule.

It was a pretty town, a gentrified ski resort with evidence everywhere of folk having high disposable incomes. There was even a horseback-riding establishment nearby, and for a modest fee, they left Thunder, chilling out in a small side pasture where he could roll and stretch his legs for an hour or so.

Tara and Ricky went into town, and Tara treated them to a meal in a decent restaurant, starting with a salad buffet full of lovely choices. The room was cool, the water jugs full of ice, and there was quiet, tasteful music playing. It was quite an oasis.

Tara chose sea bass in a fennel and lemon sauce, and Ricky ordered a plate of grilled shrimp for entrees. After they'd eaten and had ordered some iced tea, Ricky called her parents. It seemed her mom was out, and her father answered. Ricky seemed captivated by whatever he was saying. Tara began to fidget and wish her loved one's attention wasn't so fixed on the phone.

"That was rude of me, I'm so sorry," Ricky said after more than ten minutes. "But Dad seemed much brighter than usual and wanted to talk."

"What about?"

Ricky hesitated for a moment. "He talked about you actually, or rather, your place. Some of his old mates from the golf club came around to visit with him the other evening and wanted to pick his brains about an idea they have to develop part of the ranch as a housing project."

"Are they the same people my realtor was talking about?" Tara knew she should be happy, but a big lump of granite started to form in her stomach.

"Yes, but the main point Dad was making, and what he wanted me to ask you about, was whether you'd be prepared to sell them just the back three acres. They can't afford and don't even need the main house and stables as well. If you sold them just that much land, would that be enough to clear your taxes and debts? Land prices in Florida are shooting up. They're probably talking about a hundred thousand dollars an acre."

"A hundred thousand an acre?" Tara asked, her cogs already turning.

"Yes. More than that for prime locations, for residential building plots."

Tara began to think outside the box, well, outside the whole yard in fact. "You know, I think it would. Why on earth didn't I think of that before? If this worked out, I might not need to lose my home. I could even still keep a horse or two on the two acres remaining. That could be wonderful. There's just one problem."

"What?"

"I'd only want to do it if you came back with me and lived with me there as well."

"Wow, Mrs. Morris." Ricky looked stunned. "I thought you told me what happened on the road trip would stay on the road trip, that you wouldn't be good for me long term. That we had no future. This is a bit of a turnaround. Are we finally on the same wavelength at last?"

Ricky waggled her teaspoon at her, and Tara dared hope she was only pretending to be as stern as she looked. "I know. I've been such a fool to fight against my own heart. It may have only been ten days, but you've grown on me something shocking, Ricky Gates. Just think about it, okay? But if you don't want to return south, I could change my plans and move up north to New Jersey with you. I can find a job cleaning offices or something. I'll be happy doing anything as long as I don't lose you. I want us to be together. Your father's friends' idea sounds great, but they may not be able to raise the money, or even get permits. I want to be with you whatever happens."

Ricky's mouth dropped open, but she looked like a kid on Christmas morning. "You sure do know how to surprise a gal, Tara. I think this calls for ice cream."

Ricky beckoned to the server for a dessert menu. Tara waited for a reply she knew she didn't deserve but which she hoped might be in the cards.

"I've been working up to suggest much the same thing to you," Ricky said. "I don't need to ask you to leave Florida. As soon as I get home, I'll send in my resignation to my high school principal and start applying for teaching positions in the Tampa Bay area. I'll have to serve out my notice, but I should get back by Christmas. So, yes, the answer is yes. Yes, please, darling woman of my heart. Yes, please."

The server came back to ask about their choices for dessert. "Double chocolate mocha ice cream sundae for me," said Tara.

"And I'll have the same," said Ricky, her eyes shining. "I want whatever she's having."

They were in perfect accord, and Tara's chest tightened with the love coursing through her whole body. They picked up Thunder from his mid-day time-out session, and yet again reloaded him into the truck. Then they hit the road, with another three hundred miles to go before Boise. Ricky took the wheel, and Tara tried to behave, sitting now on her right, and lightly caressing her thigh.

They drove past the great Salt Lake, and Tara was troubled by how low it was getting. Was it possible such an iconic stretch of water could ever dry up? But if the drought didn't end soon, it looked rather likely, which would be an ecological disaster.

As they drove north, Tara began to work out the full implications of Ricky's phone call with her father. They had been so focused on completing their long trip, but maybe it wasn't even needed, anymore. Perhaps she wouldn't even have to sell Thunder? It would be completely wonderful, as Ricky would say, if true.

But then she thought it all through again. Selling her land and transferring the title would take months, judging by the speed at which real-estate lawyers moved, and the deadline for her tax payments loomed. The non-negotiable first installment was due at the end of the month: five hundred dollars which she simply didn't have in the bank.

Then there was the thousand dollars deposit the guys in Tacoma had already paid. That had been swallowed up by her final feed bill at the corn merchants, so she had no means of repaying it if she decided against selling Thunder. She turned back to Ric, her earlier joy tempered by the realization that they had to keep to the original plan, keep on the road trip right to the end.

As they travelled on north through Utah, Ricky quizzed Tara about what she knew of the local native American tribes in the state.

"Utah is named after the ancient Ute people, a whole group of tribes with different groups all speaking different languages. They had a rich oral culture, but much of it is lost now. Most of them were killed or pushed into reservations as the settlers arrived, even in this most inhospitable and hard to farm area. The children were forcibly removed into boarding schools where more than a third died of tuberculosis."

"It's been bad news all the way, hasn't it?" said Ricky. "A similar story to the genocide inflicted on the tribes north of the border in Canada. I heard that the Pope is in Canada currently, using that term to describe what the Roman Catholic Church did to the indigenous peoples in the name of love."

Tara needed no encouragement to get fired up. "For thousands of years the Northwest was always the land of nomadic hunter gatherers. Over to the east, from the sixteenth century onwards, the Spanish imported their horses. On the plains they were brilliant horsemen, who lived by hunting the vast herds of buffalo which were destroyed as a means of removing their livelihoods. In the eighteen fifties, it was a deliberate policy of the US cavalry to slaughter their horses as well. Tribes like the Sioux and the other Plains Indians used horses as currency. In one shocking incident, around a thousand horses belonging to the Shoshone people were shot and killed in just one day's military operation. It must have been a blood bath, completely soul-destroying and heart-breaking. There's a legend that only one pregnant mare escaped. She survived by galloping all across the mountains to Wyoming and giving birth there."

"That makes me want to cry," said Ric, giving an audible sniff.

Tara said hastily, "It is only a legend, honey. Different sources give different accounts. Maybe I should just shut my mouth and focus on one truth we can both celebrate. I love you, Ric Gates. You fill my heart with joy."

"Well…" Ricky sighed. "That's good to know. Where will we stop tonight? Will we make it as far as your friend in Boise?"

"I think so. But when we do, let's leave Thunder with Frank at his spread and find ourselves a nice little inn somewhere, with a proper airconditioned bedroom and at least a queen-sized bed. The cash will stretch to it for one night." Her insides clenched together with excitement.

Ricky said, "You mean?"

"Yes. I've strung you along for long enough. Tonight, let me make it up to you, open up to you properly and let you in."

For a while, Ricky said nothing, but Tara saw her eyes were shining. Ricky pressed her foot to the floor and the truck jumped forward on the road, as if Boise, Idaho, couldn't come fast enough.

Then she said quietly, "That would be nice," and reached across. They held each other's hand for the next five minutes until Ricky said, "I can hear Dad's voice in my head, from when I first learned to drive. "Ten to two, honey. Keep both hands on the wheel at all times. You never know what might be around the next corner."

Tara released her hand and nodded. "Fathers know best. I'll behave better from now on." But she saw with relief that Ricky didn't believe her.

The afternoon slipped by, and Boise grew closer. They had switched drivers, and Ricky had just driven up and over a long incline, and now let the old truck accelerate, taking advantage of the downward gradient on the hill. The I-15 was steep here and narrower than in many other places.

Tara felt the wind as a huge truck suddenly came down behind them on their left, blaring its horn. Ricky had no time to brake as the truck swerved erratically in front of them. Tara saw that one of its giant front tires had blown. The truck's back end swayed and crashed into their offside front wheel, and the impact sent them hurtling straight off the road.

Tara shook with the blow from the left and saw Ricky violently thrown forward onto the dashboard, despite her seatbelt. Tara grabbed the steering wheel to try and steady them, but Ricky's foot hit the accelerator pedal as she was thrust forward, and it sent them swerving down the bank. Tara felt herself turning, crashing, and banging as her head hit the side of the truck. *Thunder, what will happen to Thunder?* That was her last desperate thought just before she screamed and lost consciousness.

chapter twenty-seven

Minutes? Hours? Ricky had no way of telling. She'd just regained consciousness but almost wished she hadn't. Everything, everywhere hurt, but there were two distinct points of agony: her ankle, which had to be broken, and her neck, caused by the sudden braking and the impact. Her head ached like it had been cracked open with a can opener.

Ricky felt the movement of wheels under her and tried to gauge how long it was since their accident, the sickening horror of it still clear in her mind. She tried to move but realized her neck was pinioned in a brace to keep her spine straight. She was totally immobilized, and a spasm of panic swept through her.

What about Tara and Thunder? She tried to speak but nothing came out apart from an inarticulate moan.

"Don't worry, honey," a male voice, presumably from the person pushing the stretcher, came from somewhere above her head. "We're just taking you for an MRI scan, just to be on the safe side."

"What, where?" she managed to ask but forming a complete sentence was quite beyond her. She remembered being violently thrown forward, and Tara's attempt to grab the steering wheel. But after that, nothing except pain and oblivion.

The movement stopped. Maybe they were in an elevator. Yep, they were going down, judging by the way she sensed the pull of gravity. Her memories collided together in an ungainly heap, and nothing made sense anymore. There was no light beckoning her forward, no kindly angel waving to her with a clipboard ushering her onto a heavenly bus as she passed out once again. Ricky was convinced she'd died, and that Tara was lost to her forever.

"Ricky, honey, wake up darling. Try and wake up, baby. Your dad and I are here."

The light behind her eyelids told her something. She could hear her mom's voice, but it was as though from a great distance. What was going on? Ricky tried hard to open her eyes, to join the world again, to speak to her mom, but the waves of medication paralyzed her. She vaguely heard the words "induced coma" and "Be patient. It won't take long." Then unconsciousness engulfed her again, and she drifted away from her mom's voice as if she was floating on a large billowy cloud.

When she came to for the third time, she realized the cloud was a waterbed. Her eyes opened to stare straight at the ceiling, and her neck was still in some sort of brace, but it felt much less constricting than before. She could turn her head three inches to the left and right. The room was light, though the blinds were drawn, and a warm hand was holding hers tightly. It seemed a long time later, but maybe it was only minutes. How could she tell? "Mom?"

"Oh, thank God! Jim, she's awake!"

Ricky looked up into her mom's kind, so familiar blue eyes. She focused on her dad's dark brown ones, hovering and concerned behind her mom. "Mom? Are you and Dad… Where am I? Are we back in Florida? What happened?"

"No, honey. You're in a hospital in Boise, Idaho. Your Dad and I flew straight up from Tampa last week as soon as we were told."

Ricky's first thought was concern for her dad and his bad back. "Last week? That must have been so difficult for you. I'm sorry."

"Hush, it's nothing. Nothing compared to…"

Ricky's brain began to function as it should. Now that she was awake and looking up at them both, the cogs turned twenty to the dozen. "Why? How bad is it? What happened to us all, to Tara and Thunder? Where are they? How long have I been in here like this? Tell me!"

Her mom looked as though she was searching for something positive to say. "Shh, don't fret, honey. It wasn't as bad as it might have been. You're all alive, that's the main thing. The county sheriff contacted us the night of your accident. The horse has been taken in by someone local to Boise who is Tara's friend.

A few cuts and bruises, but his bandages, the padding on the walls, and the amount of haybales in the truck all eased his fall, and they think he'll be fine. The truck was a write-off. They gave us what possessions were retrievable."

"But what about Tara?"

"Tara broke her arm and a couple of ribs. They say she'll recover. It's just her eyesight they're worried about, something about the optic nerves being bruised."

Ricky gasped. "Where is she? I need to see her. I want to see her so badly."

"I know, love, but it can't happen anytime soon. A friend of hers came to the hospital, and she arranged for Tara to be taken away to an excellent medical facility in LA, specializing in eye problems. I'm sure she's being well looked after."

Ricky struggled to make sense of it. "No! Not Marcia. She can't have gone with Marcia. The woman's pure poison."

"Really? The doctors said it would be for the best, and when we met her, she seemed extremely caring and helpful. She even arranged for a private jet to fly Tara away immediately."

"When did all this happen?" Panic constricted Ricky's heart.

"Last Monday, three days after the accident. We arrived about the same time. She might have been named Marcia; she was an older woman with silver hair. She was certainly most pleasant to us, said she wished you a speedy recovery but not to worry about Tara anymore. She said she would be taking care of all her medical expenses. I really did think she was a family member or a close friend. She was listed on the records as Tara's only next of kin."

"What day is it now?" asked Ricky.

"It's Friday, love. You've been in here a week."

Ricky groaned. "Marcia's kidnapped Tara, and I was just lying uselessly in bed here, not able to do anything to prevent it."

Her dad took a seat by the bed. "Aren't you going to ask how you are? You haven't exactly just been in bed for fun, you know."

"Okay, tell me the worst. I presume it's bad if I've been in this neck thing and in a coma."

He said, "You fractured three ribs and smashed your ankle,

darling, and the doctors are concerned about spinal injuries. Can you feel anything below the waist?"

Ricky grimaced and wriggled her toes. Her ankle was still definitely painful. "Ouch, yes. I can feel my feet. They hurt like hell. I suppose that's a relief. But my left thigh feels numb. What does that mean?" She glanced sideways and saw the number of drips, tubing, and monitors attached to her. The sound of machines other than her own kept beeping away and made her think she might be in the ICU. Then the fresh worry of what this must be costing her parents kicked in. "How are you both coping? Where are you staying? What about the medical bills?"

"Don't worry about us," her dad said. "We'll manage. And your medical insurance covers accidental injury claims. We found your card in your purse and called them. It's all figured out."

Her dad seemed more confident than she'd seen him for years. Ricky wondered if her accident had paradoxically given him something to focus on other than his own pain and boredom. That would be one good thing, but otherwise, this whole situation was hellish. Their truck had been smashed to pieces, Thunder was probably traumatized, and goodness knew where he was being taken care of. Above all, she couldn't believe Tara would willingly go off with Marcia, leaving her in the hospital like this without a word.

"Did Tara leave me any message, write down a phone number, or give you any way I can contact her?"

"She was heavily sedated when her friend took her away, so she couldn't do anything like that. But her friend did seem like a nice woman. She even offered to pay our hotel—"

"I hope you didn't accept. She made Tara's life hell for ten years. She's a paid-up member of sadists anonymous."

Her mom patted her hand. "Not that bad, surely, honey? But of course we didn't accept. Your dad wouldn't dream of it. I expect you'll hear from Tara when she's feeling better. She knows where we live, though it'll be a while before you'll be fit to fly home. Your dad and I have rented a little apartment temporarily, so we can look after you here in Boise."

A nurse came into the room to do the usual basic tests and was all smiles when she saw Ricky alert and responsive. In fact, everyone seemed all smiles. Whoop-de-do. Ricky made no effort to join this happiness fest. She almost wished she hadn't come out of the coma. Tara had gone and maybe couldn't see. Worst of all, she was back under monstrous Marcia's control, and Ricky was helpless to rescue her. Tears began to fall down her cheeks, and great sobs racked her painful chest.

"There, there, honey, don't cry, darling. You'll only hurt your ribs."

"It's the shock and the effects of the painkillers," said the nurse. "Let her cry if she wants to. It'll do no harm. I would just leave and let her sleep now."

Her parents kissed her, her mom patted her hand again, and they left Ricky alone, giving her space to be let the heartbreak sink in. What the heck was she supposed to do now? How was she going to find Tara now she was hidden somewhere in Southern California?

CHAPTER TWENTY-EIGHT

Tara, when she realized what was happening, railed against the darkness clouding her vision and swore like a pirate. She was so angry that the hospital authorities had found her medical insurance card and acted on some computer records from five years before, when Marcia must have put herself down in the system as Tara's next of kin. It was a nightmare come true when the woman turned up in Boise.

They'd been in the hospital together in Tampa once before when Marcia had broken Tara's ulna, one of the bones in her forearm, an injury she'd pretended was due to a fall from a horse. It was one of Marcia's worst attacks, and the pain had frightened her into silent terror. But no longer. Where she'd previously been a lamb, she was now a roaring lioness…not that it did any good right now.

Marcia maintained she had flown in from her new home on the West Coast. Hearing her voice down the corridor was enough to send Tara's blood pressure shooting through the roof.

"Oh, picklepuss. What have you done to yourself?"

Tara's eyes were bandaged shut, but she'd recognize that voice anywhere. "What the fuck do you want? Get out! Get the hell out!"

"My love, don't be ungrateful. Why haven't you answered any of my messages? I've been frantic about you. But now that I've found you, I've come to look after you and take you home with me."

"You're not my love, and you're not wanted. Please leave at once." Tara's right arm was in plaster, just as it had been when Marcia had twisted it until the bone fractured. Her broken ribs were strapped. She felt physically fragile but psychologically, she was firing on all cylinders.

"She's often like this with me, she doesn't deal with pain well," Marcia said, obviously to some nurse or doctor with her. "I'm sure she's been a difficult patient, but don't worry, I'll take her off your hands and look after her from now on."

"No, you fucking won't!"

The nurse touched Tara's good arm. "Shush, honey, I'm just taking your blood pressure, and we want to keep it nice and low, don't we? Your friend's come a long way to look after you. Isn't that kind of her?"

"Fiancée," said Marcia.

"Not my friend, and certainly not my fiancée!" Tara couldn't believe this was happening. "I want Ric. I want her, not this woman! Get her away from me!"

The nurse tussled with her to hold her left arm still and said soothing nonsense, as though she was a sick child.

"I'll fetch the doctor, and maybe we can increase the pain relief and sedation. She's been noisy all night. I think it's the shock and you know, losing her sight."

"Stop discussing me as though I'm not here!" shouted Tara. "And get that woman out!"

But Marcia gripped her other arm and kissed her sweetly on the cheek. "I'm not going anywhere, honey. But if you want to get a message to your young companion, I'd happily deliver it. Only, it's such a shame, I met her parents downstairs and learned that the poor girl is in a coma. See what you've done? Your stupid idea of driving across the country in that beat-up old truck of yours has probably killed her. At best, she'll likely be in a vegetative state for the rest of her life. Just a vegetable, so sad," she whispered so the nurse couldn't hear.

The information shot like a dagger straight into Tara's heart. She tried to get out of bed. She had to make the nurse understand. "I have to go to Ric. I have to be there. She needs me."

"You're in no state to do anything, honey," said Marcia. "A friend has lent me his private jet, and I'm taking you back down to LA with me. I'll give you the best of care, and we'll never be parted again."

"No!" Tara really would have leaped out of bed if she could

and punched Marcia full in the face.

"Just a little prick now," a new male voice said and injected her.

He was the little prick, to be taken in by this monster. The last thing she heard as she slipped under was Marcia making nicey-nice with all the medical personnel.

"My poor love, she does tend toward hysteria and fantasizing. Don't worry, I'll move her back to California just as soon as I can arrange it."

When Tara came to her senses again, the nightmare had gotten even worse. She was now strapped to a gurney, fully immobilized and still blindfolded, like a shackled Guantanamo Bay prisoner, and she was being wheeled on a stretcher out in the fresh air somewhere. The sounds of planes taking off and landing were deafening. So Marcia had followed through on her threat and had actually kidnapped her. She was being taken on board a plane!

Shouting and trying to scream didn't work. Everyone must think she was out of her mind. Then before she could struggle free or do anything, they were airborne, and she knew she'd temporarily lost the battle. She couldn't move, she couldn't see. All she could do was think, and she decided a complete change from her previous behavior was the only way to convince Marcia she'd made the biggest mistake of her life.

In the past, Tara had always submitted, always succumbed to the potent mix of bullying and charm which Marcia had perfected over the years. She'd been brainwashed into thinking maybe she even enjoyed being hurt and humiliated. She'd done everything she could to keep Marcia happy.

But not anymore. Not since Ricky. She was going to resist Marcia with every fiber of her being until the woman gave up or one of them was dead. There was no going back.

The flight took an hour or two, she wasn't sure how long, and then they seemed to be descending. Her ears popped. "Where are we?" she growled.

"Coming into Burbank airport, darling," said Marcia. "You'll love my spread. It's a horse ranch, way up in the hills and completely isolated, a perfect place to recuperate."

Not a state-of-the-art medical center then. As usual, Marcia had lied.

When she felt the breeze from the plane door opening, Tara started to shout and scream again that she was being abducted, but the weight of medical equipment around her and her obvious blindness made the pilot and ground crew who met them completely trust the charming woman accompanying her, and even offered her assistance with her difficult patient.

Tara was hauled aboard a new vehicle of some sort, and they drove off. When they finally stopped, presumably at Marcia's ranch, she was moved upstairs and rolled onto a bed.

"Thanks, guys. I'll take good care of her from here on," said Marcia and Tara's last link with the outside world disappeared. "Welcome to California," said Marcia, "your new home."

Marcia released her from her strapping and removed the blindfold once they were alone. "Now don't start, picklepuss, or I'll tie you up again and gag you. I'm serious about wanting to look after you. They told me your eyesight might be permanently impaired, so you mustn't go anywhere near bright sunlight or do anything strenuous for at least six weeks. Here, you should put these dark glasses on, and I'll get the maid to bring us both a nice supper."

Tara blinked with relief, but there was no doubt. Marcia told the truth about her sight. She could barely see. Everything was fuzzy, but at least the horrible blackness had gone.

"Go fuck yourself," she said. "If you think I'm eating or drinking anything you give me, you're wrong. Get me a phone so I can call the police. I can't believe you think you're going to get away with this. You're unreal."

The house was isolated, and the road up here from the airport had been long and winding. There were no sounds of traffic. How close were they to Los Angeles? Tara wouldn't put anything past Marcia. They might be in Flagstaff, Arizona, as far as she could tell.

"No, honey, it's exactly as it's meant to be," she said quietly. "Who else is going to look after you? Who else loves you like I do? That foolish girl in a coma? She's history. You're all mine, and we both know it."

Tara screamed at her and looked around for something to throw.

"Now be a good pussy and try to behave. Don't frighten the housekeeper. She's from El Salvador and doesn't understand English, so there's no point complaining to her. I've already told her you've got severe mental health problems and can be dangerous."

Tara held out for the next three days and nights, refusing all food and drink, and just swallowing a few handfuls of water from her bathroom faucet. There was no drinking glass, removed she supposed in case she tried to slit her wrists. But she finally decided, if she was to keep her strength up, she would eventually have to break her fast and eat something. She needed to be well to escape.

But she didn't speak to Marcia except to curse her, and when her captor tried to help her wash or get dressed, she struggled so violently that Marcia left her to it. Tara surprised them both with how much strength she could muster from her damaged body.

She was confined to the top floor of the two-story house in a locked room. It was a pleasant ensuite bedroom with a TV on the wall and some *Sierra* magazines on the coffee table. There were clean pajamas and a dressing gown on the bed. Tara ignored everything. She'd looked for any implement she could use as a weapon, but there was nothing. Even the toothbrush was soft and bendy.

"Why am I a prisoner, if we're meant to be lovers?" she asked in the early evening of her fourth day of captivity.

"For your own safety, sweetheart," said Marcia.

She entered with yet another tempting meal, which Tara noticed was now on a plastic plate. The previous three dinners she'd thrown against the wall, and Marcia obviously wasn't risking any more of her fine china. Her eyesight had worried her a lot to begin with. One eye was completely hazy, but the other one had just enough sight to get by, and she hoped she wasn't imagining it when the better eye seemed to be improving slightly each day.

Marcia waved the food—steak, mashed potatoes, and green beans—in front of her, and Tara finally nodded and stuck in the little plastic fork. Maybe Marcia sensibly thought she'd try and attack her with proper silverware. If she could have, she would.

There was so much she wanted to ask Marcia, like where they were, where was the nearest city, what the hell did she think she was playing at? But it was difficult when she had vowed not to even look at her, let alone engage in conversation. Tara was way beyond making a sensible decision to play along with her tormentor, like you were supposed to do with hostage takers. She didn't want to pretend to be friends with Marcia. They were long past that stage.

Apart from heartache and acute anxiety about Ric, Tara's other worry was for Thunder. After they'd dragged her out from under the upturned truck, she'd managed to tell the first responders the name of her old friend, Frank Waite, in the Boise district.

In the hospital on the first day, before monstrous Marcia had turned up, a doctor had told her Frank had called to ask how she was and to say not to worry; he had taken Thunder and would look after him until she was well enough to sort out other arrangements. A vet had checked him over and reckoned he'd soon make a full recovery. It was the one thing in this mess that she could be thankful for.

Tara had been stripped of virtually all other hope. She'd lost Ric, most of her eyesight, and had a fractured right arm and cracked ribs. As far as she knew, she had no means of identification, cards, or cash, and ruefully realized that a cell phone might have been quite useful right now. She could remember no one's number though, not even Ric's. She was still wearing the green cotton hospital gown taken from St Luke's, so she reluctantly changed into the pajamas Marcia had put out. She'd already searched through the room for normal clothes, but the closets were empty.

So, what resources did she have? She had her wits, just about, she had the use of one arm and two legs, and she had her ability to ride any horse, anytime, anywhere. She looked out of the bedroom window across to a distant pasture where, if she shut her bad eye, she could vaguely just about make out the shapes of what might be horses grazing, and the beginnings of an escape plan began to form in her head.

CHAPTER TWENTY-NINE

Once she'd eaten the food, Tara knew that Marcia thought she'd softened her resistance, but she was simply biding her time. She still refused to speak to her tormenter.

"Have it your way," said Marcia. "I'll leave you alone until tomorrow afternoon to think about your stupidity. Then we'll do things differently."

Tara shuddered. She knew exactly what "differently" meant. Polite and rational Marcia wouldn't be on show for much longer. But for now, she left the room, and Tara heard the firm click of a key turning in the lock in the door. She had to act tonight.

As a child, she'd been raised on the Nancy Drew mysteries and decided to channel Nancy, who had always been great at getting out of tight spots. She crossed to the window and quietly drew back the drapes. The room looked out over the back of the property, and she hoped security lights wouldn't flash on as she attempted to leave.

Tara reached up with her good arm and felt along the window for the lock. When she pressed it back and forth, it clicked open, and she realized she might be able to lift the casement. To begin with, it wouldn't budge an inch. She needed two strong arms and right now, she only had one. She rested for a moment and thought of Ricky, alone and in a coma on a hard hospital bed. She *had* to get to her. She pushed at the window again, and it began to ease upward slowly.

It took her an hour, with several rests and short bursts of pushing, to raise the stiff window a couple of feet, high enough to squeeze through. It had been a full week since the crash and while she still ached all over, she was in far less pain despite the throbbing of her broken arm. She looked out into the night and tried to focus. Her right eye was still pretty useless, but her left seemed to be clearing. She could see things close quite well but anything more than two feet away was blurred.

She stared down at what she presumed must be the ground, about fifteen feet below. That would be far enough to break a few more bones if she jumped straight from the window. There were no handy drainpipes, or sturdy trellises either, or even an apple tree by the window as there would've been in a children's novel. What would Nancy Drew do? Of course, knotted bedsheets!

She pulled back the queen-sized bed covers and extracted the top and bottom large sheets. They were best quality with a high thread count and hard as she tried to tear them by standing on them and pulling with her good arm, she couldn't, so she was sure they'd hold her weight. She struggled one-handed to tie the two sheets together, corner to corner in a tight reef knot, and reckoned they would stretch to at least ten or eleven feet. Long enough. She could drop the rest of the way to the ground.

Then, what to secure them to in the room? The only thing heavy enough was the bed itself, an antique iron bedstead with metal railings. It was identical to the one Marcia had ordered Tara install in her own house. Like an idiot, she'd complied and only later realized it was perfectly designed for Marcia to secure her to it. Now, though, it would be just right for the bedsheet.

Inch by careful inch, she shoved the bed toward the window, ignoring the pain screaming through her body. Carpeting muffled the noise, but she still stopped after every push and listened for someone moving below. She was terrified of waking Marcia and had no idea where in the house she was sleeping.

Finally the bed frame was positioned as close to the window as possible. Tara fell back onto it, exhausted, her ribs throbbing. She had no watch with her to tell the time, so she turned on the television to find it was approaching midnight. She decided to wait another couple of hours before trying to leave, so she rolled over on the luxurious pillows and took a short nap.

Around two a.m., Tara woke as if on cue, feeling a surge of adrenaline and some much-needed courage. She had another Nancy Drew inspiration and picked up a chair and wedged it tightly under the room's door handle. If Marcia or anyone else came to unlock the door, they'd find it barricaded from the inside, and that might give her a few vital seconds.

Then she realized she had another problem. She had no footwear. She had no idea of the terrain she'd need to cross, but there was no way around it. She'd be quieter running barefoot, anyway.

Thirty minutes later, dressed in annoyingly easy to spot white silk pajamas, Tara clung to the sheet tied tightly around the bedpost and eased herself, feet first, out of the bedroom window. Despite wanting to scream from the pain in her ribs and arm, she slid down her makeshift escape ladder to the ground. The house was built in traditional California mission-style with overhanging porches and a low shingled roof, so even though she swung precariously for a second or two, it wasn't too far to make it without injury, and with a final jump she landed safely. There was no choice but to leave the large white sheets hanging like a banner for all to see, then she fled across the garden, cursing her poor eyesight.

She'd discarded the dark glasses, useless in the middle of the night, and struggled to make out the shape of the property. She couldn't see a gate into the back pastures, so she hauled herself over a wooden fence. Her pajama trousers caught on a nail and ripped a little, scratching her leg, but she ran on regardless until she was close to the area where she thought she'd seen horses grazing.

She pulled out the makeshift halter she'd fashioned from the silk dressing-gown belt and with this unusual little piece of harness, she padded across the fields to find a horse. The local drought was so severe that even in the dead of night, there was no dew on the ground. Once or twice, she stood on a sharp stone or some rough weeds which made her flinch, but she finally saw what she thought were three horses standing together in a corner under a tree, large gray shapes in the night, and quietly approached them.

They must be Marcia's, so were quite likely to be well-bred and nervous. The last thing Tara needed was for them to start whinnying or to begin to gallop about. She moved slowly and made a low clucking sound with her tongue against the roof of her mouth, a trick she often used to quieten horses. Her innate empathy and skill with anything equine kicked in, and as she circled the small herd, she could tell they were interested more than frightened. She slipped between them, hiding from anyone looking out from the house, and as gently as a Sioux warrior stealing a horse from the US Cavalry lines, she quickly chose the biggest and strongest-looking horse, a fine black mare, and slipped the dressing-gown halter over her head. She'd have to ride bareback and without a bridle, but these weren't wild mustangs. Marcia would only have bought the best, well-schooled animals, and they would hopefully follow standard voice and leg commands.

It took all her strength to climb on from ground level, and the painful weight of her broken arm and cracked ribs didn't help, but Tara eventually managed to mount the tall mare by leading her over to a boulder which she used for a mounting block. She scrambled up onto her back and then quietly urged her away up the sloping grassland.

The horse was well-trained enough to leave her companions without argument, so as soon as Tara settled onto her broad back, they started to listen to each other. Tara was experienced at riding without even a bridle or a bit in the horse's mouth, so within thirty seconds she'd swallowed her fear and pushed forward into a gallop, taking off as fast as she could. The property boundary fence loomed suddenly ahead of her in the darkness, but she could feel her new friend gather her legs together, preparing to jump, and then they soared over the fence. Perhaps the horse wanted to escape Marcia as much as she did.

"You'll have to lead the way, my friend," Tara said. "Take us out of here." She could do little to guide the mare from then on. She had no idea where they were, although the glow stretching behind her across the night sky indicated it might be somewhere above the Los Angeles basin. Her aim was to put as many miles as she could between her and Marcia. She guided the horse mainly with her legs, gripping its mane and keeping her seat despite the slippery nature of her nightwear, and she rode off into the wilderness.

CHAPTER THIRTY

It was the toughest ride of her life, but having a strong horse to carry her, who was also a comforting companion, meant escaping from Marcia was at least a possibility, something Tara could never have achieved on foot. The night sky was illuminated from below by a dull orange haze caused by city lights, so she guessed they might well be north of the Los Angeles basin. It was not an area she knew at all, but if LA lay to the south, then she decided to head southeast toward the northern suburbs around the San Fernando valley, where she might be able to find some help and report her abduction to the police. Riding half-blind in the dark across unknown terrain was perhaps the most stupid thing she'd ever attempted. No, that would be falling for Marcia in the first place.

Tara's heart beat faster at the thought of the woman chasing after her, and she urged her new friend forward into the night. But the horse was more sensible than she was and rather than gallop, picked her feet carefully over the stones and seemed to find tracks through the undergrowth. The hills were covered with sharp thorny bushes and cacti, as well as small trees and low-level scrub, and Tara's legs and feet were soon scratched and bleeding. She was only saved from worse injury by the height of her mount.

They moved on under the starlight, and then after what seemed hours, a faint light began to creep up the sky to the east. Pitch blackness slowly turned to a gray mist, and finally a pre-dawn lightening allowed her to see something of where she was. There were thick woods below her, and the shapes of isolated rooftops set among the trees emerged from the mist. She was nearing civilization at last. As she descended down the canyon, a huge weariness came over her, and when the ground fell away from her suddenly, and the black horse stumbled, Tara slid forward over its shoulder and couldn't stop herself falling. The days of starvation and the adrenaline expenditure of her escape combined to make her lightheaded and she fainted.

Tara heard voices as she came around. Oh God, she must have fallen and, judging from the pain on her forehead, whacked her head on a stone. She could feel a trickle of blood running down her right temple, which was already being gently tended to by some burly guy. As his paramedic's uniform passed before her better eye, it gave her a temporary nightmare flashback to the truck accident. Disoriented for a few seconds she thought she was still being pulled in agony from the shattered vehicle. But then, as she came back to the real world, she remembered how she had successfully escaped Marcia's clutches.

How far had she ridden the black horse standing beside her? They seemed to have traveled for hours over the foothills, until both were exhausted. She guessed she'd finally come to the end of her strength and fallen off. That wouldn't have done much for her ribs or her broken arm. Not eating more than one meal in the past three days maybe hadn't been such a good idea either.

Now she felt both bewildered and ridiculous. The two paramedics by her side seemed enthusiastic about the idea of lifting her onto their gurney and carting her off down the mountainside. She must look terrible, a mass of bruises and abrasions still from the accident, now with a new cut on the temple, battered feet, and skinny as hell from self-imposed starvation. She tried to sound upbeat and chirpy, and pushed away their hands. "No, no, I'm fine, thanks all the same." She sat up and immediately felt sick.

"Are you sure? You appear to have really been through something."

This voice came not from the men but from a tall woman with striking blue eyes and a stylish haircut standing just beside them. Tara looked up but the low sunlight blinded her, and she couldn't make out the woman's face. "Sorry, where am I?" She struggled to stand but regretted it and stayed seated, as the movement made her head throb even more.

"Just on the Montpellier Media back lot. We own the whole

hillside; we sometimes use it when we're filming Western dramas. But your appearance was pretty dramatic by itself. I saw you and your horse moving down the canyon and came to investigate. Then I lost you for a few moments when you fell. I called the paramedics, and they were in the area, so came at once."

The woman's voice was vaguely familiar; was she someone from the TV? Tara shivered. She could see there would be a hell of a lot of explaining to do, and she was still clueless as to where she was. "No, I mean, where am I? Which city? Are we anywhere near LA?"

"Yes, ma'am," said one of the paramedics, looking just as puzzled as she was. "You're concussed, or have you dropped in from another planet where they go horseback riding bareback at dawn in silk pajamas?"

Tara wondered how to start. "Not quite that far. But I need to talk to the police. I've escaped from being kidnapped from a hospital in Idaho and imprisoned for four days in a house somewhere in this area, around twenty miles or more from here. I had to borrow the horse to get away. Can you help me, please? I need to get back to Idaho at once."

She knew she sounded like Dorothy from the Wizard of Oz and felt equally disoriented. The tall woman bent down and helped her to her feet, as she saw her determinedly try to stand.

"What's your name?"

"Tara Morris. I'm from Tampa, Florida. It's a long story. Who are you? I recognize you from somewhere."

"This lady is Katherine Konrad," said the older of the guys proudly, as if he was in some way connected to her. "If you don't know that, you must surely have come from a long ways away! Been kidnapped you say? Really? There's a women's penitentiary not far from here, and several secure rehab facilities. Sure you haven't slipped out the back door from one of them?"

Both the paramedics looked extremely skeptical about her story. "No one in their right mind would ride a bareback horse across these steep hills in total darkness," said the other one.

"Hush now," said the woman impatiently. "Whoever she is, she needs help. You guys can get going. I'll deal with it. And don't go talking about our visitor to all and sundry. I want this kept confidential, understand?"

They nodded. It was obvious to Tara that her new friend's words carried some weight. Agreeable to being dismissed and free to respond to their next call, the two men packed up their gear and their gurney and retreated back down the stony hillside.

"Just watch her for a concussion," was their parting shot. They obviously thought Tara was some real crazy lady.

She gingerly stood up, wobbling a little, but at least staying upright. The black horse still stood faithfully on guard by her side so she patted her, trying to reassure her that things from now on would definitely look up.

"Tara, come on," Katherine said. "Hold onto me with your good arm for support. I'll lead your horse, and we'll get you somewhere more comfortable. I want to hear everything that's happened to you, and I have a good friend in the LAPD who'll be interested as well. We can call her from my office."

Tara reached out and took Katherine's arm. *Surely not* the *Katherine Konrad?* The name had finally registered with her now. How was she going to explain everything? Her story was so bizarre, why would anyone believe it? And technically, she had stolen the mare. In the old days, she would probably have been shot for doing that. She trusted California had rescinded that law by now.

Barefoot and disheveled, she clung to her rescuer, and together with the horse, they made it slowly to the bottom of the hill and then across the manicured lawns to the huge television station complex, which lay along an entire block above the leafy northeastern suburbs of Pasadena. Katherine handed the black horse over to one of the security guards standing in front of the building. He looked a little nervous of his new responsibility, especially given the flimsy nature of the harness.

"Get hold of Marshalls and ask them to pick up the horse and care for it until further notice," said Katherine, and the man nodded.

Tara wanted to stay with the horse and check she was going to be well cared for, but by the time they were through the main revolving doors, she was completely exhausted. The night's adventures were really catching up with her, and she swayed again as Katherine guided her into an elevator and up to the top floor into an enormous office.

"Don't worry," said Katherine. "You're quite safe here. You rode down the right canyon, and I'm sure we're going to be good friends. I'm completely intrigued by what's happened to you and want to hear your story."

CHAPTER THIRTY-ONE

Katherine sat Tara down on a billowy cream leather couch and started to make the first of several phone calls. Coffee, muffins, a fresh set of clothes, and shoes were all mentioned. She must be instructing various employees. It was still so early, Tara wondered who else would be at work, but she supposed television companies were staffed around the clock.

"We have a huge costume department here," said Katherine. "Every taste in every size. What are you, a six? And shoe size eight or thereabouts? Let me guess, comfortable casual clothes maybe? I forgot to tell them to bring up something loose on top to wear over your cast." She was immediately back on her phone again.

Tara was more concerned about the black mare. "I need to tell the police. I should be looking after the horse. I only borrowed her. She'll be thirsty and will need water. She'll also have sore hooves from all the rocks we scrambled over."

"You must be some horsewoman to have made it here," Katherine said. "Don't worry. The horse will be well taken care of. Marshalls is nearby, a corporation of equine experts who provide all the horses for our TV shows and films. My gateman will call them to pick her up and give her the best of care. Now, lie back on the cushions, put your feet up, and tell me everything."

Tara looked down at her poor battered and bleeding feet. They could tell a tale in themselves. But relaxing under the stunning intensity of Katherine Konrad's focused but friendly stare, she decided to trust that if she told her the whole weird story, she wouldn't be thrown out or immediately put into handcuffs. "Well, the first thing to say is that for a long time, I was in a toxic relationship…"

She hadn't been progressing for long with her mortifying

account before Katherine said, "Sorry, Tara, just wait there a moment," and made another phone call. "Sue, yes, it's me. I need you up to come over to Montpellier Media right now. Yes, as soon as you can, please, and come yourself. I want you to hear this. That's my detective friend," she said, turning to Tara. "She's going to join us shortly, so why don't we wait until she gets here?"

Two young women came into the office bearing clothes, shoes, and towels, which they placed on the table in front of Tara.

Katherine smiled. "Now, we have some fresh things for you, so if you feel up to it, why don't you take a little time out to shower and change? Please, use my private bathroom."

"That sounds like a great idea." Telling her story was more stressful than Tara had expected, and she was longing for a hot shower. She gathered up the bundle of towels and clothes and headed in the direction Katherine indicated.

"Don't lock the door," said Katherine, "just in case you feel faint again. I can be right in to rescue if you shout for me."

Tara wondered if this was how all world-famous divas treated waifs and strays who trespassed on their land. Katherine Konrad was certainly unusual. She threw away the torn and dirty white pajamas into a wastebin and reveled in her shower. Washing her hair and letting the water pour over her head eased her aches and pains, even though it was hard keeping her broken arm out of the cascade.

She emerged, dressed in fancier clothes than she'd ever worn before, to the smell of hot, freshly brewed coffee and cinnamon buns, which immediately took her thoughts back to Ricky, who had loved them and had brought her a bagful on their last morning together. The emotion caused by that simple memory nearly overcame her. "How could I have forgotten?" she said. "I must call the hospital in Boise immediately. I need to get back there. My lover's there in a coma. I want to be with her—"

"Sshh, drink this, and eat some food first. We'll support you in everything you want and need to do. It's still early morning. We'll set up a call for you a little later."

Katherine passed her a large white coffee and settled her

down in a comfortable chair opposite the couch. "Thanks, I'm famished," Tara said. "I've been on a hunger strike all week and only ate last night to get up sufficient strength to escape."

Before she finished the breakfast, a large, confident woman joined them, complete with an LAPD name tag.

She flipped open her wallet as well and showed Tara her ID. "Detective Sue McCauley. Kat tells me you've been through a really bad abduction and made a brave escape. Care to talk about it? Do you mind if I take notes?"

Tara started at the beginning again. After years of secrecy and shame, it felt good to be telling the truth about her relationship with monstrous Marcia, and it was certainly a story worth telling, if only as a cautionary tale. She finally got to the point in the saga about how they had split up three years earlier at Marcia's doing, how Marcia had come storming back into her life, the accident in the truck, and the way she'd been abducted from the hospital and spent four days since in captivity.

By the end, both women, who had been attentively listening, looked completely shocked. Tara ate the last cinnamon roll and wondered what they'd do next. She realized she'd eaten the whole plateful but hoped no one would mind. She was still famished.

Detective McCauley was already on the phone, and Tara listened to her side of the conversation.

"The suspect's name is Marcia Cunningham. Run it through the computer for the address and get a car over there at once. Yes, of course. Get a warrant to search the place, take her in, and get the SOCO team into her house. She may not have had a chance to remove the evidence yet. I'll meet you and question her as soon as she's in custody."

Tara was cautiously relieved. "So you do believe me? I was worried no one would because her name was down as my next-of-kin. But that was without my knowledge."

"Yes, I do. Your account can easily be verified."

"I believe you too," said Katherine. "I know all about abusive relationships. But how did you manage to ride here overnight across all the hills? That was quite a feat."

Sal looked at her phone where a new message had just arrived.

"The Cunningham address is way over toward Santa Barbara. You've ridden for more than twenty miles, probably further, traversing up and down all those canyons."

"Will I be charged for taking the horse away?"

Sal smiled and shook her head. "No, I'm sure you won't. It was an unusual but valid means of escape. You've turned the mare in, and she's unharmed."

"Didn't you think about taking a vehicle instead?" asked Katherine.

Tara shook her head. "Not easy with a broken arm. I've got several cracked ribs, and I'm also more or less still blind from the road accident in Idaho. I couldn't drive even if I found an open car with the keys in the ignition. I can barely make out your faces. Most things further away are just a blur." She allowed herself a smile as both women looked even more astonished. "Now, I can't wait any longer. I have to call St Luke's in Boise. Can you find me the number, please, and maybe dial it for me, Katherine? I need to find out what's happened to Ric."

CHAPTER THIRTY-TWO

Ricky rolled her neck and sighed. Her spine had been badly bruised and while it hadn't been severed or damaged enough to paralyze her, the messages between her head and her legs still weren't getting through very reliably. She could feel her toes, and her broken ankle was throbbing inside its plaster cast, but her right thigh kept twitching and tingling. When she'd tried to stand, she'd fallen. The doctors had insisted on another week of bedrest and said after that they'd check to see if light exercise would help restore the nerves.

A week may as well have been a year. What horrors would Marcia inflict on Tara in that time? "I'm a PE teacher and an athletics coach," Ricky said to the physical therapist who came to her bedside. "How soon will I be able to run again?"

The woman tried to look positive, but doubt crossed her face before she could hide it. "You've clearly been fit, so let's hope for the best. It may take a while before you're back on your feet. My job is to keep your muscle tone as strong as I can while you're under bedrest. I have a program of breathing and arm and leg exercises which should resonate with you if you're a phys. ed. teacher. Look on me as your personal trainer."

Ricky groaned, but despite herself, she liked the woman. She learned her name was Andy, and she'd moved to Boise from north Idaho. The exercise session lifted her mood and by the time her parents came to spend the afternoon by her bedside, she felt well enough to enjoy their company. She couldn't get over how much better her dad looked. He still walked supported by two sticks, but his whole mood was cheerful. He looked like a new man.

"We've been getting to know Boise," her mom said. "It's so different from Tampa, but there are some nice bits to it. Downtown isn't bad."

"We were only going to spend one night here," Ricky said, "and now it must be at least a week since the accident. Can you find out where Thunder is? I think Tara's friend was named Frank. I don't know his last name, but he's a retired professional show jumper, and he might know about Thunder. He must be known in the area, if you ask the right people. I'm desperate to know if Thunder is recovering okay, and Frank might also have heard from Tara."

"We'll do our best," said her mom. "I know how much the horse meant to you."

"*And* his owner." Ricky squeezed her mom's hand gently. "Mom, on the trip, Tara and I, we realized we truly love each other. We're going to be together always. I have to find her and rescue her. She would never have gone with Marcia willingly." Ricky gave them some more details and did her best to make them understand what Tara meant to her.

"Shouldn't be too difficult," her dad said. "All we need to do is search through a few local sites online. Horse training, horse ranches, even country feed stores. Someone will know who your man is. I'll get onto it right away."

Ricky watched her dad type words into his phone with considerably more skill than Tara ever showed.

He scrolled through a few pages. "I think this might be him. I'll go outside where I can get a better signal." He tucked his phone into his shirt pocket and swung himself out on his two sticks.

"Dad's perked up a lot," Ricky said when they were alone. "I'm happy to see my accident has had at least one positive spin-off."

"Your dad's been depressed for years, mainly because he's felt useless. But his buddies coming around and wanting him to be part of their team to develop Tara's ranch has really bucked him up. I hope it isn't all off now that she's incapacitated. It must be terrible to go blind."

Ricky shook her head as if she could shake away the reality. "No, don't talk like there's no hope. I asked the nurses who said she won't necessarily stay blind. If her optic nerves are just bruised, she should recover. If only I was with her, I could help her heal. I know we'd both be okay. A far worse threat is the woman you saw here, Marcia Cunningham. I'm not kidding. She's truly dangerous, life-threatening."

Ricky told her mom a little of what she knew about Tara's ten-year relationship with Marcia.

"I think we should go to the police," her mom replied, clearly shocked. "This is serious."

"But will they listen to us?"

"We can always try. You're right. We owe it to Tara to make every effort to find her and rescue her."

"My lovely mom, I knew I could depend on you." For the first time since the accident, Ricky saw real hope ahead.

Her dad returned, waving his phone triumphantly. "I've found out where Thunder is probably being stabled. He's most likely with Tara's friend, who is quite a celebrity in these parts. He was once on the Olympics equestrian team. I've got a name and a number. Do you want to call him?"

Ricky trembled with relief and nerves combined. "Yes, yes, of course."

"Here you are. His name is Frank Waite, and the number's on the screen waiting for you."

Ricky pressed to call and held her breath.

"Brookstone Stables," a female voice answered.

"Hi, I just wondered, I was the groom…" Ricky realized she was talking garbage. "Sorry, I'll start again. Do you have Tara Morris's horse, Tacoma Thundercloud with you? We were in an accident on the I-15 last week, and I'm concerned for him. I was the groom. I'm Tara's friend."

"Wait on the line," she said. "I'll just get my husband. He'll be able to give you all the information you need."

When Frank Waite came to the phone, Ricky poured out probably too much information, about why she hadn't called before, about being stuck in the hospital, about Tara being taken away probably against her will, and of course, asking him all about Thunder.

"Your horse is recovering well," Frank said. "I've had him

stalled for a week or so to settle him down and help his bruises heal. We called in the vet though at the beginning, who made sure there was no serious damage. I've let him out for the first time this morning into the house corral, and physically he seems fine. Would you like me to send you a video?"

"Oh, yes, please. That would be wonderful."

"This is a coincidence. Tara called me ten minutes ago."

"She did?" Ricky gripped the phone tighter. "But I thought… Where is she? How did she get out? Do you have a number?"

Frank sounded puzzled. "Hasn't she called? She said she'd been trying to get through and was going to call the hospital again, right after our conversation. But essentially she's okay, somewhere in California with friends. She's hoping to travel back up here as soon as she can."

"What?" Ricky gasped and handed the phone back to her dad. "Please, you talk to him. Get Tara's number. I can't…" She burst into tears.

Her dad carried on a far more sensible conversation and explained Ricky's current, fragile emotional state. But as Ricky listened and clung to her mom's arm as she tried to control her tears, she was overcome with relief. Tara and Thunder were both safe. That was all that mattered.

The minutes ticked by as she waited in an agony of anticipation, until finally a junior member of the ward staff came to her bedside.

"Pick up your phone. We have a call waiting from someone named Tara who says it's essential that she speaks to you."

"Why didn't the hospital switchboard put her straight through?" Ricky reached across to her nightstand and grabbed the phone handset.

"No idea, but they're having problems."

Ricky put the phone to her ear and whispered, "Tara? Tara? Is it really you? How did you escape? I can't believe it!" She couldn't control her sobs and broke down.

"Hush, my love," Tara said. "Don't cry. I'm sorry it took so long to be able to call you. But you mustn't worry. I'm quite safe and healing fast."

"What about your eyes? What about Marcia? Are you still with her?"

"No, she's toast," Tara said firmly. "My eyesight's going to be okay. I'm seeing an eye specialist this afternoon, then I'm making a formal statement to the police and flying back to Boise tomorrow. I'll be with you in twenty-four hours max, honey."

Ricky tried to steady her own voice. "We've just called the man who's boarding Thunder. He said you called him earlier."

"Not before I called this hospital. Did they not give you my message?"

Ricky shook her head. "They're always busy. Maybe I'll get it later. Tara, it's so good to know you're safe. But what happened? Where have you been? How did you escape?"

"That's quite a tale," Tara said. "You know the old saying, 'If wishes were horses, beggars would ride?' Well, I wished for a horse, and one was given to me so I could escape. I'll tell you about it after you tell me how you are and how you're feeling. I need to know everything. The last thing I heard, from a most unreliable witness, was that you were in a permanent coma."

"Slight exaggeration, as you can tell," said Ricky. "I was so scared you were blind. Just come here as soon as you can. I need to touch you, hold you in my arms."

"Of course," said Tara. "But for now, we can only talk, so let's do that."

Ricky's parents exchanged a look.

"Look, we've not eaten lunch yet," her mom said. "Your dad and I will go down to the cafeteria and find something. We'll come back in an hour or so. You two catch up. In the meantime, let me have a word with Tara."

Ricky reluctantly handed it over.

"Hi, Tara," her mom said. "Ricky's told me about the two of you, and I just want to say, she couldn't have chosen a better woman. Welcome to our family."

Ricky couldn't hear Tara's response, but it was somewhat lengthy, and her mother looked close to tears herself when she handed the phone back.

"She sure loves you, honey. You're a lucky woman."

"Thank you," Ricky said. "No one knows that more than me. See you both later."

When she was alone to talk to Tara, Ricky asked, "So how is your sight, truly? No BS. Be honest."

"Left eye is creeping back to normal. Right eye is still blurred and pretty useless, but Katherine has arranged up for me to have a consultation with an ophthalmologist this afternoon."

"Katherine? Who's she? I'm so full of questions, I don't know where to start."

Tara chuckled. "It was surreal actually, like a Hollywood movie. Have you ever heard of Katherine Konrad, the media queen?"

"Yes, who hasn't?" Ricky asked, already intrigued as to where this story was going. "She runs Montpellier Media Corporation. My dad watches her channel's news hour most evenings. He has a huge crush on her."

"Well, it was Katherine Konrad who found me and rescued me out on the hillside above her company headquarters."

"No! That's amazing. What were you doing out there? You need to tell me the whole story. And what about Marcia?"

"Marcia's right where she should be, in the custody of the LAPD. Katherine has a good friend in the police department, and she sent people up to her place with a warrant to check out my story. They found the room where I was imprisoned and from where I escaped last night. The door was still locked from the outside, and the sheets were hanging from the window where I left them. Marcia wasn't even aware I'd gone. I don't think she'll ever trouble us again. Even if they let her out on bail, I'm told they'll apply to put a restraining order on her so she can't stalk me or come near me."

"I still can't believe you're safe."

"I wish I could get into bed with you right now, but I'm still eight hundred miles away, sadly."

"How will you get here? Do you have enough money for the flight?" asked Ricky.

"Katherine has offered to bring me from here in one of the Montpellier news helicopters. She is coming along too because she doesn't seem to think I'm fit to travel alone. She's already become a good friend."

Ricky wondered just how friendly Katherine Konrad was getting with Tara. After all, she was one of the most famous gay women in the States. Not another Marcia situation, surely? "You? Good friends with Katherine Konrad, gay icon, international media boss, and one of the world's ten best-dressed women?"

"Yep. Don't be horrible. It's weird but I think she likes me. Don't worry, she's happily married to a much younger redhead named Catriona. There are pictures of them together all over her office walls. I told her about you, and she wants to meet you."

"Sorry, Tara. I'm being horrible. Why wouldn't she like you? You're completely wonderful. I'm just so madly in love with you, and so frustrated I can't come to you instead of you having to come back to me, it's driving me insane."

"Ric, I'd cross the Gobi Desert barefoot if it took me back to you," Tara said. "But don't forget, we also have Thunder. It's for love of him that we started on this journey, so even if you weren't there, I'd hotfoot it back to Boise. I promise I'll be there tomorrow."

Ricky was content then to let Tara go and prepare for her visit to the opthalmologist. "Call me this evening to tell me what the doctors say about your eyesight," she said.

"Of course, my love. I'll call at eight."

One more day and they'd be reunited, and despite her earlier sarcasm, she was excited at the prospect of meeting the famous Kat Konrad. She reckoned lying in a hospital bed covered in bruises wouldn't make the best impression though.

Then she remembered her parents, still downstairs in the hospital cafeteria. How to warn and prep her dad, so he didn't behave too much like an over-enthusiastic puppy in front of their celebrity visitor?

CHAPTER THIRTY-THREE

Despite normally being unfazed by celebrities and famous people, Tara was a little overwhelmed by the glamor of Katherine's world and even more by the attention she paid to her. She'd said, "Call me Kat," and then insisted on dropping her entire schedule for the day to drive Tara to the hospital for a consultation with one of the top optical surgeons in California.

To Tara's relief, the man pretty much agreed with what the emergency room doctors had told her in Boise; there was no structural damage to her eyes beyond inflammation and swelling. Even better, her foolhardy ride over the mountains hadn't caused further damage or caused her sight to deteriorate. She came away with eyedrops, prescription dark glasses, which she was told to wear in daylight at all times, and advised to stay off alcohol, avoid any stressful activity, and get as much sleep as she could.

"That's easy to arrange. After we visit the police, I'm taking you home with me to Pasadena," said Katherine. "The house is quiet. My three daughters are away at camp, and my wife's visiting her folks in Oregon. She'll be back later tonight, and you can meet her then."

Tara was too tired to argue. They spent more than an hour with Sue McCauley again, and Tara made a formal, signed statement about her kidnapping. It exhausted her but recounting the saga all over again reinforced her awareness that it was by her own strength and determination that she had escaped. Ricky had been right. She had no reason to blame herself. She wasn't a complicit victim. She was a strong survivor, and her self-respect soared accordingly.

Kat lived in a beautiful heritage house in the most exclusive section of Pasadena. She escorted Tara to a guestroom where someone had already put out a tray of snacks and fruit. The AC quietly hummed in the background, and the queen-sized bed looked irresistible.

"If you need anything more, our housekeeper, Maria, will look after you," Kat said. "Just pick up the bedside phone and press nine. Take a nap for as long as you like. I should be home from the studios by eight, and then we can eat supper and I'll introduce you to my wife."

Tara nodded her thanks and sat down on the bed. She undressed and pulled off her shoes. She barely heard a car pull away outside before she felt herself falling asleep. It had been a stressful day, and tomorrow would only bring fresh challenges. But the main— the only—goal she had was to be reunited with Ricky. And, of course, with Thunder, her shining chestnut horse and best friend.

Sunlight spilled through the blinds when she was next awakened by Kat bringing in a large mug of coffee, and for a moment Tara thought she had slept for only a couple of hours. "Sorry. Marcia took away my watch. What's the time?"

"You've slept around the clock. It's almost seven in the morning, and I think we should be getting on our way if you want to fly back to Boise today."

Tara was astonished and ashamed for sleeping so long.

Kat waved away her apology. "Don't worry about it. You needed the rest, and you look better for it this morning. Come down to breakfast when you're ready. Cat came home late last night, and I'd love you to meet her before we leave. I've arranged an eight thirty take-off from the Montpelier helipad."

Tara pushed herself out of bed and accepted the coffee mug with her free hand. "I'll be there in ten minutes."

"Do you need help dressing?"

"No. I'll manage."

Katherine grinned. "I'm sure you will. I've left a few more things to choose from on the chair by the door."

Tara looked across the room at a small pile of pleasant designer wear. Her clothes from yesterday had vanished. She did seem to have landed in fairy land. Katherine retreated, and she was left to shower and change into the fresh clothes. When she found her way downstairs a few minutes later, there were voices coming from the kitchen and she followed the sound.

An intense red-headed young woman wearing a turquoise kaftan hurried forward to greet her. "Tara! Kat's been telling me as much as she knows about you, which isn't enough. How are you feeling now? Let me help you to the table. You're some wonder woman!"

Tara hated to be the center of attention at the best of times and felt embarrassed by the compliment. "No, not at all. All I did was cling on. The horse did all the work."

But Catriona's enthusiastic welcome and guiding hand beguiled her into sitting down and being quizzed about what had happened, while she was plied with waffles, French toast, maple syrup, and strawberries. It was all rather overwhelming, but she couldn't resist the food, having slept through dinnertime the previous evening. Between mouthfuls, she tried to answer Cat's questions.

"It would make a great film," said Cat, pausing from her interrogation.

"Oh no!" Tara almost shouted in protest. "No one needs to have their prejudices about gay women reinforced by hearing about Marcia's awful behavior. Please don't even think of it. I couldn't bear the publicity."

"No, I completely understand." Katherine was quick to reassure her. "Cat just gets carried away sometimes. She sees all of life in cinematic terms."

Tara saw her shake her head at Cat who bit her lip and looked a little ashamed. "Sorry, I didn't mean to snap. My nerves are just a little jittery still," she said quickly to show there was nothing to forgive.

"No, my bad," said Cat. "I was being totally insensitive. Here, let me give you another waffle. Kat says she's excited to be flying with you up to Boise. If you haven't traveled by helicopter before, it's a great experience. They fly much lower than a conventional airplane. You'll be able to see Northern California and Nevada in detail as you take the route to Idaho. Oh, it's such a shame you won't see it clearly with your damaged eyes. Oh, whoops, I shouldn't have said that, should I? You must be constantly worrying about it. I'm so sorry!"

Tara was amused by her rambling efforts to change the subject and couldn't take offense at Cat's comment about her eyesight. There was no malice intended in her tumbling words, which she'd meant kindly, unlike Marcia, who had repeatedly exulted in her misfortune. "Ric and I drove all the way from Florida, heading for Tacoma, and we spent seven days on the road. We also had an extra night in Moab to give our horse a rest. You do get to see America that way, well its highways, at least. Now I truly don't want Kat to sacrifice a whole day acting as my escort. It's a privilege enough to be given a ride in a helicopter."

Katherine shook her head. "Don't give it another thought. I have an ulterior motive for visiting Boise. Idaho is one of the few states not to accept funding for my young musicians' scheme, and I want to ambush some officials in the education department there and lobby them as to why their children are being deprived unnecessarily. Neighboring states Utah and Oregon have accepted, and they have children's orchestras flourishing now in several cities."

Tara was intrigued. "Please, tell me more about your music scheme."

"I will once we're in the sky, but for now, we need to run."

The Filipina housekeeper, Maria, appeared with a small carry-on, which she handed to Tara.

"Your clothes from yesterday, laundered and packed up as a little present, along with some more treats," said Kat.

"Maria, thank you. You shouldn't have." Tara went hot with embarrassment.

"Nonsense," said Kat. "You've had a horrific experience, and it's our pleasure to show you that not everyone in the world is a psychotic bully. A bit of spoiling never hurt anybody."

As she saw them off from the front of the house, Catriona pulled Tara in for a gentle but warm embrace, which she received as gracefully as she could. The kindness of strangers was still overwhelming, but she tried not to be taciturn and churlish.

Katherine drove her back to her Montpellier headquarters where the helicopter pilot was already seated, conducting his pre-flight checks. Tara tried to control her excitement, but she had been waiting for this ever since she and Ricky had been torn apart by the accident. Then she remembered. Her lovely companion was still trapped in her hospital bed. She'd promised to call her the night before. How could she have forgotten?

CHAPTER THIRTY-FOUR

I'm sorry, but can I call Ric before we take off, just to reassure her I'm on my way?" asked Tara as they slid into Kat's reserved parking bay. She pulled out of her pocket the scrap of paper she'd used to write down the hospital number and the extension code.

"Of course, but no need to be sorry."

Katherine immediately handed her phone over, and Tara was reminded of how Ricky had told her not to start every sentence with "I'm sorry." She wondered how many famous names and numbers must be stored inside Kat's phone. This time, when she gave the right extension number to the hospital reception, her call went through without any problem.

Ricky answered immediately, sounding breathless with anxiety. "Oh my God, I've been worried about you all night. Are you okay?"

Tara felt so guilty for not calling the moment she'd woken up. "Yes, my love, I'm fine. I just slept straight through for twelve hours. We're about to take off, so I'll see you this afternoon."

"And is Katherine Konrad really coming with you?"

"She is indeed."

"Well, we're excited to see you both. My dad is out right now getting a haircut."

Tara laughed. "I look forward to meeting your parents again. We're about to take off, so I have to go. Bye for now." She handed the phone back to its owner. "Modern tech. It was like she was right here. I still wonder at it all sometimes."

Katherine smiled and handed her a pair of ear protectors to wear. "Come on, my friend. Let's get ourselves aboard, and I'll tell you what to expect on the flight. It's different from riding in an airplane, more immediate and certainly noisier."

Tara flew so infrequently, in fact she couldn't remember when she'd last taken to the skies, that she felt as excited as a child, even though she privately did curse her poor eyesight, which meant she could barely make out details of the landscape below. But some things were impossible to miss, including the far-reaching wildfires burning throughout Northern California, and the columns of smoke rising up to meet them at five thousand feet and then forming great clouds higher in the atmosphere.

"Cat and I were caught in a terrible fire in Oregon the first time I visited her family three years ago," Katherine said. "It scared me half to death. Her grandparents' farm was completely destroyed. We're still working with their community to rebuild and reconstruct homes there."

"Who do you mean by 'we?'" Tara asked. "Do you finance all that charitable work?" She had already seen enough of Katherine's kindness to guess her wallet was often open.

"Not at all. I just have a knack for making money, and while I'm not at all religious, I think it's a good rule of thumb to invest long-term in good causes. Pay it forward, if you like, for the greater good. Montpellier makes a great deal of money, and someone very wise once said to me that too much wealth is like congealed life. It needs to be spread over the land and shared, then it will bear more fruit. Left in one person's possession, hidden in a vault and hoarded, it does nothing good. So I have a whole department working with me to fund different not-for-profit initiatives."

"Is that how you fund your music program? Tell me more about it."

"Montpellier Media runs a number of special projects, one of which is a foundation I set up a few years ago to organize music lessons and instrument hire for marginalized kids all across America. It now works in twenty-five of the more enlightened states, although Idaho has yet to opt into the program. Where local communities have accepted the money, it has transformed young people's experience of music, and great things have happened to them and their communities."

"That sounds wonderful. I wish I could start a similar program to offer horseback riding and animal care classes to the marginalized kids in Florida. I think all young Americans would benefit enormously from being able to work with horses and understand them more. The joy of riding transformed my life as a child and got me through the death of my father, whom I lost very young. He was a park ranger, patrolling the Everglades and they often used horses. They didn't scare the wildlife and could get the patrols through to places where no vehicle could have penetrated."

"Yes," said Kat, looking thoughtful. "I too longed for a chance to ride when I was young but due to personal circumstances, it wasn't possible, especially where we lived."

"Where was that?"

Kat seemed to pause momentarily. "Trenton, New Jersey."

What a great coincidence. "That's where Ricky teaches. What a surprise. I wonder if you know any of the same people."

Kat frowned for the first time since Tara had met her and shook her head. "I doubt it. It was a long time ago. I left the state very young, and I've never been back." Then she lightened up. "But your idea of horseback riding classes for inner-city children, that really excites me. We should talk some more about it later." She pulled some paperwork out of her attaché case. "Sorry, I have an hour or so's work which I must finish. Do you mind if I concentrate on it for a while?"

"No, of course not," said Tara, very happy to sit back in her window seat and look at the clouds and patches of deep blue sky as they continued northeast. Before long, the throb of the blades whirring overhead lulled her back into sleep.

Their pilot broke the journey once to refuel in a regional airport in southern Nevada, but the weather was calm and all went well. The helipad next to St. Luke's Medical Center finally came into view beneath them, and they slowly descended toward the ground.

"Here we are," said Katherine, pushing her papers back into her case. "Prepare for the inevitable gang of people waiting for us, local reporters, etc. We had to inform the hospital authorities I was coming, so word will have gotten out. They were anxious to assist after I informed them that there would probably be a police investigation into how they allowed an injured victim to be abducted from the hospital quite against her will. There always seems to be a three-ring circus whenever I arrive anywhere these days. Just duck your head and let me take your hand to help you down the steps."

Tara's first instinct was to panic and hide, and her shades barely provided sufficient protection against press cameras flashing. But Kat stood up and stretched out her hand, and Tara took it gratefully. Still broken, bruised, and battered, inside she felt like a million dollars. She was back in Boise, and in a matter of a few minutes, she'd at last be in Ricky's arms. That was the only thing that mattered.

Kat strode briskly through the waiting throng, a business-like smile fixed on her face. In answer to several questions as to why she was favoring conservative Boise with her radical presence, she said, "I'm on personal business right now, but I can give you a press conference before I leave, if you'd all like to return here at six p.m."

That seemed to satisfy the journalists enough for them to let them move forward into the hospital, and Tara sheltered in Kat's shadow as they entered the building together and were met by one of the chief administrators. It was very different from the way Tara had been forcibly removed six days before, and her energy and anger grew as they were escorted upstairs to Ric's room.

Kat had the sort of personal confidence and charisma which opened doors and achieved results, and Tara guessed she'd never let herself be abducted and assaulted. She needed to borrow some of that self-belief and power and learn from it. Her assertiveness grew accordingly, and by the time they had reached the fifth floor, she was positively swaggering.

They were led through a final set of swing doors, and she could see Ricky lying in a bed in a side room. Tara broke from Kat, ran forward and, careless of all their injuries and restrictive dressings, flung herself into Ricky's open arms.

CHAPTER THIRTY-FIVE

At last!"

"We're a matching pair, aren't we?" Ricky didn't care how many people were watching. She kissed Tara over and over again, clinging to her, and trying not to cry with relief. Then she noticed the woman behind her and felt somewhat embarrassed. Her face grew warm.

"Hi. You must be Katherine Konrad. Thank you for bringing Tara back to me."

"It's Kat, and how could I have done anything else?" Kat came forward and squeezed Ricky's hand as though they were old friends. "Tara here has told me so much about you, Ricky, that I just had to come myself and meet you. I'm so sorry to see you're still in recovery from your terrible accident. When do the doctors say you'll be discharged?"

Ricky's normal color begin to return, and she managed a shy smile. "The end of the week probably, although I feel fine, and want to get up right now." She struggled to sit up, still wrapped in Tara's arms.

"Are these your parents? Hi!"

Her dad and mom stopped hovering and came forward.

"Yes, Jenny Gates, and this is my husband, Jim," her mom said. "We're so grateful. Ricky has been distraught. She'll be able to recover much faster now she has Tara back safely."

"My pleasure. Now, I've managed to squirrel some of your daughter's story out of Tara. But I gather there's more to tell. Where exactly is the famous Thunder, whose sale has brought you all the way up here to the Pacific Northwest? Is he going to be okay after the accident?"

"We've located him," said Ric's dad. "He's safe in an equestrian center a few miles out of town. We were hoping to take Tara straight over there this afternoon once she and Ricky have had some time together."

"I'd like to see him myself. Do you have a vehicle?"

"Yes, a rental car."

Kat seemed to be doing some speedy mental calculations. "Look, my friends. I have to scoot off now to talk to some local music educationalists but give me the address of the horse place, and I'll meet you there in a couple of hours. Does that sound feasible?"

"Totally, if you're sure you have time to come. Can we give you a ride?"

Ricky's Dad was holding it together very well, all things considered. He hadn't asked for a selfie yet.

"Thanks, but no trouble on that score. I have a car waiting downstairs."

Kat reached over, took her father's phone, copied its number into hers, and pinged him a message. He looked stunned with joy.

"Just text me across the location, Jim, please. Sorry, Tara, for barging in like this, but I think we should talk some more about your brilliant idea for a horse-riding foundation, and I want to meet the other love of your life."

Ricky, still with her arms around Tara, turned to her. "Is this all okay with you, love?" She wondered how enthusiastic Tara would be at including Kat in what was bound to be an emotional reunion with Thunder. But Tara seemed unfazed by the idea.

"Sure. We'll wait there for you, Kat. And thanks. Thanks again for everything."

"De nada. Not another word of thanks. It's been an honor meeting you all. Goodbye, Ric, and take good care of Tara. She's quite a special person."

"No need to tell me," said Ricky. Her parents went with Kat to escort her back downstairs, and she and Tara were finally alone. They spent several minutes gazing into each other's faces. Ricky made Tara remove her shades. Her eyes were still bloodshot, with huge bruises around them, but she seemed to be focusing okay. She just looked exhausted. "You must be totally beat by now," said Ricky. "I wish you could stay here with me all day, but I know you need to go and see Thunder.”

"I do, and then I suppose I have to call his buyers and explain the delay in delivering him to Tacoma. I'm hoping, given the circumstances, they'll send transport down here to take him the last leg of the journey.”

"Don't even say that! I can't bear the thought of us losing him, not after all this trauma. Dad seems to think he and his friends buying some of your land will definitely happen. Can't paying your taxes wait until their investment comes through?”

"No, honey, sadly they can't. Besides, I've already been paid a thousand dollars deposit for Thunder. I can't repay that, which I'll need to if I go back on the agreement.”

"Then I have to see Thunder before he goes. I can't bear to think of him being carted away while I'm stuck here in bed.”

"I'll make sure it happens, my love, even if I have to walk him into the hospital grounds and bring him under your window.”

"Life's horribly unfair at times. It's all too bad.”

"It is, but with the bad, there's also the completely wonderful, good sometimes.” Tara leaned forward to kiss Ricky once more and lightly pinched her ear.

"Oh, yeah, like what?” Ricky's frustratingly long days in bed had made her petulant, and she was heartsick at the thought of Tara still having to sell Thunder.

"Like your return into my life and then letting me love you,” said Tara. "Nothing can take away my joy over that. It's the most wonderful thing that's ever happened to me.”

"But I feel so useless right now. I want to look after *you*. If I'd been conscious and able to stop her, Marcia would never have been able to kidnap you.”

"Let's not talk about her. You'll be able to do plenty of looking after me, as much as you want, in a few days. You need to be patient, honey, just for a little while longer.”

Then Ricky's parents returned, and in far too short a time, the three of them had left. Ricky felt bereft but knew Tara needed to be with Thunder. For something to do, she turned on her room's television and flicked through the channels until she reached Kat's station, Montpellier Media. There was a re-run of a recent

Sunday evening *Montage* program, and she was stunned to think how the person on the screen had just been chatting by her bedside.

As president of her company, Katherine wouldn't normally have appeared in front of the camera, but it was common knowledge she retained the Sunday evening edition of *Montage* for herself, which gave Ricky a whole fifty minutes of viewing in which to familiarize herself with Katherine's character and stunning on-screen persona.

Someone had once described Kat as "Rachel Maddow in Gucci," but this woman exuded even more vitality and more "Who gives a shit" bravado than anyone else on television, man or woman. Her interview technique resembled that of a knife thrower, and Ricky knew now why right-wing politicians had mostly given up venturing onto her show. One had even dubbed her the Cyanide Queen, which wasn't nice, but Ricky suspected that Katherine didn't care.

Watching her run rings around her guests on the current program, Ricky understood why she and Tara had hit it off so well. They shared a great deal of characteristics, even if Tara couldn't see it. Ricky was curious to find out more about this horseback riding foundation.

CHAPTER THIRTY-SIX

At first sight, looking at him from across his enclosure, Tara was shocked to see how Thunder had changed. Not so much in his physical state—she knew he'd been badly bruised and still walked very stiffly—but in the anxious and downhearted look in his eye and by his loss of condition. His coat was dull and his eyes sunken. His head hung low. Frank said he'd taken no interest in any of the staff or any other horses on the yard and had needed to be cajoled into eating.

But when Tara approached him and whistled, his head shot up and if a horse could look overjoyed, Thunder did. He ran over to her, whinnying, rubbed his head up and down her shoulder, and nibbled her hair. Tara put her good arm around his neck and gave him a huge hug. She felt his warmth through her body and swore he quivered with excitement.

"Damn me," Frank said. "You know, I reckon he thought you were dead, maybe both you and Ricky. That's why he's been so low in spirits. I've never understood why some fools say horses can't empathize or feel emotion. They're a quivering mass of sensitivity and feelings, more than even dogs, in my experience. And now he knows you're alive, he'll soon be a happy horse again."

Tara agreed, but then something told her Thunder wasn't a hundred percent pleased with her. He kept sniffing and snorting, and even turned his head away like a small child whose parent has been absent without its permission. He also kept banging his head into her chest. "He's being huffy with me. He knows I've been with another horse. He can smell the black mare on me, and he isn't happy," she said. "Don't worry, boy. She was a good horse, who probably saved my life, but I never had time even to learn her name. I only borrowed her for half a night."

Ricky's parents were watching.

"You're not really going to sell him still, surely?" said Jenny. "Ricky's told us about your problems. She's heartbroken. We can lend you the money to keep him. We have some savings. For God's sake, Tara, you're going to break Ricky's heart if you sell him, let alone your own."

Tara's longing to accept their generosity battled with her stubborn determination to accept no more loans or be reliant on other people. She hadn't even wanted to accept Ric's money. Then she remembered. She turned to Frank. "Do any of you know what happened to our truck? Where would it be taken after the crash? It won't still be down the canyon next to the highway, will it?"

"No, it'll probably in the scrap yard by now, if it isn't already reduced to a cube of crushed metal."

"The police gave us your two pieces of luggage, Ricky's hat, and her purse."

"But there was also a small candy tin in the top locker compartment with a thousand dollars in fifty-dollar bills inside. Ric gave them to me, and I stuffed them away in there. Jim and Jenny, if I stay here with Thunder, could you go and investigate for me? That money would cover Thunder's deposit, and then we could take him back home. You're right. Ric loves Thunder as much as I do. She'll hate me if I didn't do all I can to keep him. I've been a stubborn fool."

"Ricky could never hate you, but we'll get on it right now."

The Gates drove away to consult the police traffic department, while Tara stayed with her best friend, sitting on a hay bale next to him and telling him all that had happened to her since they'd last seen each other. At first, Thunder just stood quietly beside her, nuzzling her hair. But then he turned around a few times and dropped stiffly down on the grass before resting his head in her lap, almost as though he'd learned it as a circus trick. "How remarkable." She sat there transfixed, with his heavy head on her knees and cradled his face and neck gently. His eyes closed, and he seemed almost to fall asleep.

The sound of Kat's chauffeured Mercedes brought her out of

her reverie.

"Wow, I see what you mean. You are close to that horse!"

Tara shifted position, and Thunder opened his eyes. He pushed himself up onto his hooves right in front of Kat and shook himself from head to foot. If she hadn't known better, Tara would have thought he was self-conscious about their little tryst and preferred to pretend it had never happened.

"Hi, Thunder. I've heard a lot about you." Kat reached up and stroked him. "Has he forgiven you for disappearing?"

Tara stood up, grinning. "Hi, Kat. That's nearer to the truth than you might think. Yes, we're good again."

"Where are Ric's parents?"

Tara told Kat about the mission she'd sent them on.

"Oh, for heaven's sake," said Kat. "Are you telling me that the need of just a thousand dollars is what's causing you to sell this adorable animal? That's ridiculous."

Tara bristled. What would Kat with all her millions know about her financial problems.

"I have no choice. You can't understand what it's like to be penniless."

Kat shook her head. "But you're not, are you? Penniless, I mean. You have a property and more importantly, loving friends. Not penniless like I was when I first went alone to California as a kid of sixteen. It's nothing to brag about, but I starved for four days on a Greyhound bus to get there, and then I waited tables, eating leftovers from customers' plates until I got my first paycheck. Now that money isn't a problem, I could easily give you as much cash as you need."

"You've done enough. I'm not taking handouts."

"Tara, don't be so stubborn. Why the heck not? Don't you know that's how all the rich get richer? But I'm not handing you anything. I want you to be my partner. I've been thinking about it while I've been driven over here, and the idea you had this morning was so right on. I'm going to expand the music program, and I want you at its center."

"Sorry, but I don't see the relevance. How could it involve me?"

"I need you to follow through, run the program for me."

"But I'm not into music."

"Of course not, but what would you say to replicating the basic music education model with a new national program to teach horse care and kindness to animals, as well as horseback riding for youngsters, especially those with special physical and mental needs? People have forgotten how integral horses were to the history of our country and especially to the indigenous communities. No one needs to ride anymore, and it's meant that riding is generally considered a pastime for the very wealthy. Too few people now know much about horses, but I believe that all kids deserve a chance to ride and learn about those magnificent animals. Don't you agree, Thunder? See, he's nodding his head."

Light finally dawned in Tara's mind. "You mean, together we could set up a pilot program in Florida? That would be wonderful. I've seen children benefit enormously from the chance to ride and work with horses. I also know the immense healing power of therapy horses."

Frank was walking back toward them. "You should see Tara in action. She's a superb horsewoman and I'd bet an even better teacher."

"There you go, then. I knew Tara would be the perfect person to work with me and my people on this. But to do that, you'll need your own horse, won't you? And your stables. So don't jump down my throat if I mention money. I'm thinking of an initial injection of seed money of half a million dollars. How would that sound?"

Tara looked at her in complete amazement, shocked into dead silence. She had trouble taking it in, but as her brain gradually processed what her ears were hearing, the enormous heavy boulder lodged inside her heart began to lift and ease, and she could almost feel it start to crumble away into dust, like the red sandstone of Utah. She should stop being so stubborn and accept Kat's proposal and her generosity. Miracles did sometimes happen. Between the syndicate's offer to buy land and Kat's wish to invest in her teaching abilities, she would get to keep Thunder. They could go on together, and she would never need to sell him. "Can you kindly just run that by me again?" she asked in a choked voice.

Katherine, chuckling a little, did just that. Then Kat's phone rang.

"Hi, Jim. Yes, I'm with her now." She handed the phone over. "It's Ricky's dad. He wants a word with you."

"Great news, Tara," Jim said. "We got there in time. In fact, there was no hurry. The bashed-up truck is in a police impound lot. The crash investigators will take weeks to complete their final report on the incident, but we persuaded them to give us access, and we found your stash. We've signed for it, and we have the cash here now, along with a pile of old CDs. "We'll bring it over to Frank Waite's place now and pick you up. You'll come back to stay in our apartment of course, won't you?"

Tara nodded. "Thank you. But I have to go find Ric and tell her the news. I still can't believe the reason for our road trip no longer exists."

"I have to return to LA shortly," said Kat, "but I'll get my team onto drawing up some initial business plans, and as soon as you can give me your bank details, they'll make a transfer. Don't worry. The money is sitting there in the foundation account, just waiting to be put to good use."

When Tara arrived back at Ricky's bedside to tell her they didn't have to sell Thunder, she had expected joyous excitement but not her loved one bursting into tears of relief and happiness.

"So, in the end, you were right not to spend my thousand," Ricky said. "I'm part owner of Thunder now, I hope you realize!"

She seemed exuberant that it was her money that had solved the problem of the deposit, and Tara let her take all the credit.

It took a little time to rearrange the future course of her life, but Tara found she was becoming rather good at being joyful and acting accordingly. After a few days, Ricky was able to leave the hospital on her one good foot with the help of crutches, and Jim and Jenny booked seats on the same flight for them all back to Florida.

Thunder was coming home too. Katherine's magic wand seemed powerful enough to conjure up a horse transport company to fly him home like the celebrity he was, and the would-be buyers from Tacoma were told they would simply have to manage without him. Tara transferred the thousand dollars back into the buyer's account, and Ricky was triumphant.

As Ricky sat next to Tara on the Southwestern flight, she leaned her head on her shoulder and looked down at all the many states they had driven through only a few weeks before. "Didn't we travel a long way? We never finished our road trip though. I still want to dip my toes in the Pacific Ocean one day."

"That might happen sooner than you think," said Tara. "Kat wants us both to visit them in Pasadena next month to discuss the new business. She also seems to have found out from someone how interested I am in the horse culture of various first peoples and wants to pull me in as a consultant for a feature she's planning to produce on the subject. I wonder who told her that."

"No idea."

Tara reached out and took Ricky's hand and held it close to her heart. "Ric, darling, will you work closely with me to make all these plans come to life? Will you qualify as a riding teacher so we can run the new business together? I can't do it without your help, as my eyes may never totally mend well enough for me to use a computer properly. But together I'm sure we can transform Meadowlands into a flagship program for youngsters who would like to ride but who can't afford to pay for lessons. Would you give up your teaching job for me and make it happen?"

"Of course I will," Ricky said. "You don't even have to ask. What about Dad's housing scheme though? He's so buoyed up by the idea of working on it with you, I hate the idea of him being disappointed if you don't sell the land."

"Oh, he won't be. We talked for hours while you were in the hospital, and it's definitely going ahead. I'm selling off the old house separately, along with the two acres. It has far too many unhappy memories for me to want to take you to live there permanently. Your dad has offered to build us a new house on a corner of the remaining land. a brand-new start in a brand-new home. How does that sound?"

"It sounds totally wonderful. God, I love you, Tara."

"I love you too, Ric."

Tara pulled Ricky to her. She kissed her on the ear, and then on the neck, and then with total commitment, firmly on her mouth. She didn't care if any other passengers were affronted. They were going home to Florida to prepare the stable for Thunder's imminent return, and it felt good. In fact, it felt more than good. It felt, to use Ricky's favorite expression, totally wonderful.

EPILOGUE

D on't forget to do your back exercises."
"Hm?"

"Every morning, that's what the physical therapist said."

Ricky rolled over in their large comfortable bed and squinted sleepily at the altogether lovely sight of Tara's naked back sitting up beside her. Hadn't they exercised enough during the night already? Now, with the sun peeping through the blinds, she only wanted to sleep, wrapped in the arms of the woman of her dreams. It was a cliché, maybe, but wasn't it Tara who'd once said there was nothing wrong with a good cliché?

All Ricky's dreams were good ones these days, just as she trusted Tara's were. She'd assured Ricky that any Marcia-induced nightmares had retreated into history, even though they were still sleeping in the room where the woman had so often bullied and demoralized Tara in the past. The first thing Tara had replaced was the bed though.

Today, the last day of August, the Meadowlands sale was going through and they were about to move out of the old ranch house for good, temporarily renting an apartment down the road. They were surrounded by packing boxes, and the previous night had been their last one on site.

Ricky's dad and his team of builders had promised their new house would be completed by Christmas, and Ricky would be moving back from New Jersey to a new home and a new wife. Their wedding date was set for December twenty-first. Ricky had submitted her notice to quit to her high school principal back in July, and the next season of games would be her last.

"Don't get up. Come back to bed, just for me, baby." Ricky fluttered her eyelashes and ran her fingers lightly all the way down Tara's spine.

Even though she heard Tara sigh and complain, she knew she'd agree. Tara never needed much persuasion to linger in bed.

One of the most beguiling things about her was the way her stern exterior melted into caramel as soon as Ricky asked her for sex, anytime, anyplace, but especially in the early mornings. Tara's old "One-two-one-two" regime of being up with the birdies had dissolved since they'd returned from Idaho. It needed to. Ricky had spent the last eight weeks re-educating her beloved in the art of being happy and silly in bed, and her coaching had paid off. Tara had discovered there was nothing wrong with her libido after all, and Ricky could bring her to orgasm within minutes. She also learned that sex could be gentle, loving, unselfish, and at times, hilarious. Theirs seemed to involve a lot of tickling, which Tara was fiendishly good at.

"Maybe just for another thirty minutes then, if you insist."

Ricky opened her arms and drew Tara's slim body back to her own. It was the way they had slept on the narrow bed in the truck but even here, with all the space in the world, she loved the intimacy of spooning her, holding her gently, and caressing all those secret curves and folds, the perfect shape of her pert and balanced breasts, the feel of her ribs.

She liked to read Tara's body like a book, study her like a three-dimensional poem, hum sweet nothings into her ear, and treasure her sex like a precious jewel.

Tara snuggled in, and their bodies melded together. Tara had put on some weight, and while she was never going to be plump, there was at least something to hold onto these days.

"You spoil me something rotten. I should really go deal with the horses."

"Shush. Why do we have help? Jo and Mary will take care of the early feeds. You can stay with me, my queen. I'll have to abandon you soon enough and then you'll be totally free to get up at six and clean out water buckets to your heart's content."

"Don't remind me. How will I ever cope without you?" asked Tara.

"Haven't we figured it out? We'll manage through the Fall, living weekend to weekend. All the flights are booked. One weekend you come to me, then the next I come back here to you. Then we stick it out for the third weekend. Four times. Then I'll be home for Christmas and the wedding. We'll get through it. With all your new horses and new pupils, you'll be too busy to worry about anything."

"You always make me impatient to go to bed with you. I can't help it."

"We can do phone sex, you know."

Tara turned in the bed and faced her, looking deep into her eyes. Then she pulled a funny face. "I know. Kat said that's how she and Catriona cope when they're apart, but I've never been any good with words. Just looking at you makes it impossible for me to say anything at times. You're so beautiful, so lithe, and strong, and merry."

"There you go. Who says you're no good with words?"

"I can hear Thunder making a noise over in the yard. He's kicking at his stable door."

"He's trying to attract the attention of that darling Appaloosian mare you bought me. Coming home has put so much new life into him and seeing the yard fill up with horses again has made him positively frisky. Now, let me make love to you, my darling, darling, Tara. I'm feeling kind of frisky as well." Ricky gently drew Tara in toward her and began to match actions to words.

"Ric, it's eight o'clock! We've been asleep for more than two hours!"

"How can you tell?"

"I can see the time on the clock over on the wall."

"Hey! For real? You couldn't have told me what the clock said last week."

Ricky kissed her shoulder and hugged her with excitement. Tara closed one eye, and then the other, and looked again at the wall clock. "You're right. My eyesight's coming back to normal. And they used to say that too much sex makes you short-sighted."

"You don't want to listen to what people say. There are a lot of fools out there who say dreams don't come true. I used to be one of them. But I know much better now."

"Let's go out for a ride before the removers get here."

"Sounds like a great plan."

"Are you going to wear your new fancy britches?"

"Of course. I suppose you'll still be in those worn-out Levi's, even at our wedding."

"What else?"

"I love you, Tara, you old hobo."

"I'm somewhat fond of you as well, Miss Priss."

Ricky left it there. She didn't push her luck by asking whether she ranked higher than Thunder in Tara's affections. Where she sat was good enough. And while they might have to endure a temporary separation, she felt their hearts were already fastened together with cords tighter than wet baling twine.

They went out into the Florida sunshine and saddled up their horses. "What do you think about babies?" asked Tara out of the blue as they rode into the quiet Florida scrubland bordering the stables.

"Which babies?"

"Ours, of course. When we start a family."

"I thought you didn't like children."

"I never said that, especially not if they were our own."

"I'll put a baby on the list of to-dos then, okay? For after the wedding?" Ricky tossed Tara's remark off lightly, amused to see her suddenly appearing broody, though she guessed she'd be the one to give birth if they ever did want to start a family. But as she thought about it, her heart warmed. She'd said before she wouldn't consider having children until she had a stable home with her life partner, and now, of course, she had that. The prospect of becoming a mother delighted her. "We'd better wait until well after the wedding, I suppose. No need to frighten the horses, after all."

"No. No need to frighten the horses."

"Is Thunder going to be your best man?" She decided they'd been serious enough.

"Ric! Horses can't do that. He couldn't make a speech, for starters."

"Or organize a stag party."

"And he's bound to lose the rings."

"Shame though. He'd look so good in the photos. He'd have to be there in some capacity." Tara looked adamant.

"The obvious thing is for you to ride him into the ceremony." They turned a corner of the field. "Why have I always been Ric to you, never Ricky?"

"Everybody else calls you Ricky. You're extra special to me, so you're Ric."

"I was always Ric to you, though, even when I was young."

"You were always extra special."

Tara turned and looked her straight in the eye. She blew her a little kiss, which made Ricky's heart flutter. "Monstrous Marcia was right then, after all?"

"Only about that one thing. She could see you were my favorite pupil, and no doubt suspected that one day it might turn to something much deeper than simple affection."

"Poor Marcia. At least they've let her out on bail."

"She has to wear an ankle bracelet though. She'll hate that."

"Was it true she tried to smash the windows in at Montpellier Media when she discovered it was Kat who helped you?"

"So Kat told me. They're adding it to the list of charges."

"She won't be trying to come on honeymoon with us then?"

"No, darling, only you and me. No fear of Marcia."

"You, me, and a horse, maybe?"

"Two horses. Then we can both ride."

Tara pushed Thunder into a lope, and Ricky's mare quickened to catch him up. They cantered together to the end of the trail.

Ricky watched Tara riding in front of her. "I wish you weren't so beautiful, Tara. It hurts me to look at you from behind sometimes; your ass is so lovely."

Tara scoffed and turned Thunder around. "I wonder about you sometimes, if you're quite all there, Gates. Never mind my ass, let's go home and finish packing."

"Do you think Thunder understands what we say?"

"I'm sure he does, but he won't comment, don't worry."

They turned back to return to the stables, riding along the same route where Ricky had followed Tara's lead so many times as a novice rider. It was along this trail where she had first learned to master the rising trot and where she had first fallen in love with her beautiful, enigmatic riding teacher.

Now they rode side by side, and when Tara reached out to grasp Ricky's hand and drew their horses even closer together, Ricky bent her head and gently kissed her fingers. Their love of Thunder might have brought them back together, but however far apart they might have to be for the next few months, she knew their hearts would always be joined.

"I'm so glad I came to see you back on that Sunday evening in June," she said softly, looking ahead to the freshly painted sign welcoming all visitors to Meadowlands.

"I'm glad you did, too," Tara said. "By coming just when you did, you saved me, and you saved Thunder. I can never, ever repay you for giving me your love and helping me through what would otherwise have been a terrible road trip."

"Sshh, you repaid me the first time you kissed me. I adored you then, and I worship you now. I will never stop loving you, Tara, as long as I live."

Ricky released Tara's hand and jumped off her horse's back to go forward to open the gates, so Thunder and Tara could re-enter. When both horses and riders were safely in the yard, Tara dismounted, dropped her reins, and pulled Ricky into her arms.

"Let me add some dividend payment then," she said, drawing Ricky's mouth close to her own and kissing her tenderly, something they both knew marked an investment for life.

"We have to get going," said Ricky finally. "I'll unsaddle the horses, if you clear the kitchen." And she watched as her lover, still dressed in faded blue jeans and scuffed jodhpur boots, walked back toward the house with a definite sashay of her hips. Tara was one class act, that was for sure.

"Make us one last coffee," she called. "I'll be in in a minute." Then she led the horses into their stalls, the smell of leather, hay, and warm horse filling her heart with joy.

If you enjoyed this book, please leave a review and rate it on Amazon. This will help future readers decide if they would like to read it.

About the author

Under the pen name Maggie McIntyre, Susanne Garnett started to write women's fiction in 2018 after three decades working in international development, campaigning, and supporting struggling communities worldwide.

An account of her years travelling round the world working for a number of different agencies, and as a freelance consultant, can be found in her autobiographic memoire, **The Back of the Bus: Forty Years of Learning from the Poor** by Susanne Garnett, available through Amazon or the author.
ISBN 978-1-64871-025-4

In 2021, Susanne also published a volume of poetry, **Waiting for Trains** available through Amazon or the author
ISBN 979-8-7559004-99-8

Maggie McIntyre's novels are set in both the UK and in the USA. The smell of new books, spring flowers, warm animals, and rain clouds are among her favorite things, and she loves to laugh. One day she hopes to write something decent, but as she often says, the longer you try, the harder it gets!

The following books are all available through

Amazon Kindle Unlimited and from the author through her website,
www.maggiemcintyrewriter.com

Maggie McIntyre has a Facebook page, Maggie McIntyre Author, which has news of upcoming projects, special offers, and promotions. You can also follow her on Twitter @maggiem_author

Other books by Maggie McIntyre

SERIES ONE: ISABEL AND FRIENDS

Isabel's Healing

A devastating road accident leaves climate-change campaigner Bel Bridgford broken and bitter, but when a young assistant steps into her life, can she learn to live again? Lesfic Bard Award winner for Best New Writer category 2020
ISBN 979-8-650898-73-3

A Girl on the Plane

Isabel's project manager, Steph Miller, fears the worst when a terrified young girl approaches her on a plane from Kinshasa, as she flies home for Christmas. In this passionate and emotional sequel to Isabel's Healing, Steph and her partner Alana struggle to save both the girl, and their own future together.
ISBN 979-8-573921-82-2

Into the Rough

Restless Canadian nun, Jenni Argent, finds new friendships working for Isabel's development

agency, but meets open hostility from Isabel's best friend, sportswoman and golf fanatic Jane Walkley, who fears and distrusts all religions, and especially nuns. Will they ever make friends? A warm and humorous look at a most unlikely love affair, on and off the golf-course.
ISBN 979-8-705709-31-1

Love Under Lockdown
Isabel, Bryony, their friends, Jane, Jenni, Steph and Alana are locked down in England as COVID rages across the country. The three couples each take different pathways through the pandemic, but sustain their love, friendship and hope for the future. An uplifting and novel about the power of friendship.
Finalist in the 2022 Lesfic Bard award for romantic fiction.
ISBN 979-8-790844-63-8

SERIES TWO: BEHIND THE CAMERA

Heatwave
Katherine Konrad, self-made millionaire and head of Montpellier Media, is a force to be reckoned with in television, but she meets her match in Catriona Sinclair, straight out of the Oregon backwoods and fiercely ambitious for a career in filmmaking. It's hot in the city, and the heat also runs through the pages of this fast-moving and passionate story set in present-day California.
ISBN 979-8-677313-92-9

Wildfire
Cat Sinclair takes her lover Kat Konrad home to meet her eccentric family. But this turns out to be

the least of their worries, as they are swept up in devastating wildfires which ravage the rural Oregon community. Will they and their loved ones even escape alive?
Runner up in 2021 Lesfic Bard Award Category Action and Adventure.
ISBN 979-8-550424-98-8

Love and Money
More adventures and another challenge face Kat and Cat as they face a hostile takeover of Montpellier Media, and discover something rather strange is going on in a suburban elder-care home in Orange County.
ISBN 979-8-529933-53-4

(For Love of Thunder is fourth in the BEHIND THE CAMERA series.)

Standalone novel

Up the Garden Path
When international celebrity Cait mistakes Maisie for an insolent waitress, their relationship sours before it even begins. But Maisie and Cait soon find themselves drawn closer together. This is a delicious romantic comedy set in an English summer garden as both women discover love can be found in the most unexpected places.
ISBN 978-1-739637-00-2

www.ingramcontent.com/pod-product-compliance
Lightning Source LLC
Chambersburg PA
CBHW071430200726

48294CB00002B/580